Olath's Bride

A NOVEL BY
FRED TERLING

vestige
press

Library of Congress Control Number: 2022922982
Terling, Fred, author,
Olath's Bride / Fred Terling.

ISBN: 979-8-9874914-0-9

Printed in the United States of America

Cover Image by: Ellerslie Art, Italy

Cover design and book layout by Banished Rascals Design
www.banishedrascals.com

FIRST PAPERBACK EDITION: NOVEMBER 2022

Visit the author on the web at www.fredterling.com

For my brother, Sean.
Thanks for always supporting my flights of fancy…

"You can blast my other passions,
but revenge remains—revenge, henceforth dearer
than light or food! I may die, but first you,
my tyrant and tormentor, shall curse the sun
that gazes on your misery."

– Mary Wollstonecraft Shelley,
Frankenstein

Prologue

It was the summer of 1975. The hospital hill gang gathered for their daily afternoon wiffle ball game atop Dunning's hill on the backside of Daiseytown hospital. Made up of five boys, aged twelve to fifteen, this activity is what they lived for in the dog days of summer following the conclusion of the school year. The boys all shared a commonality. They were all outcasts who formed a bond through their love for America's greatest pastime. The previous spring, the hospital hill gang attended their first live professional ballgame, even meeting a few of the players during batting practice. That only served as fuel for their ever-growing fire. Passion sparked wasn't something easily extinguished, particularly at their ages.

Quickly they unpacked the gear from paper route satchels that doubled up to serve this purpose.

"Hey, let's get it going, grandma! Sun's gonna set before we even get the first batter up," said Mickey Tolliver, the smartass of the group.

He was the youngest at twelve, which made his comments that much more comical. It wasn't like he had the stature to make them comply, standing at a mere five-foot nothing, weighing a buck o' five.

"Yeah, yeah. Don't get your panties in a bunch, shortstop." That was his elder brother by two years, Paul. He was the patient one of the gang. Having to corral Mickey, can you blame him?

The remaining boys scurried onto the field, taking positions as pitcher, outfielder, catcher, batter and general infielder. With only five team members, there weren't enough players to cover all bases, but that was okay. This was a fun, bonding exercise, not competitive.

The outfielder, Lukas Wright, stood waiting patiently for the first pitch. His mind wandered. It always did. He was the dreamer and artist of the group. After their trip to the live game in the previous spring, he discovered paint pens. They were sloppy, but he put in the time to master the ability to make straight lines, write names, and draw team logos. Each of them presently wore T-shirts of their favorite players that Lukas created. For their purposes, not only were they for fandom, but reflective of what they wanted to be. Character identifiers represented by the various professional team players. This was a special time as the matters that typically accompany race, color, ethnic origins hadn't tainted the hospital hill gang. They like who they liked. That was simply that.

———— ◆ ————

The afternoon went on, as did the breaks, which included trips to nearby Dunning's kitchen for chocolate yoo-hoos and tomato sandwiches. It was their fuel. They returned to the field, greeted by the setting sun.

Mickey Tolliver again took the lead as he stuffed three pieces of Bazooka Joe in his mouth, storing the comics in his front jeans pocket to add to his collection when he got home.

"Okay, knuckleheads, we got maybe a half hour left. Let's make this count," he said.

It was Paul's turn at bat. As the white plastic ball whistled towards him, he took a mighty swing, sending it over Lukas' head. The ball landed in the thick brush that surrounded the hill, just short of the tree line. Lukas gave chase. Behind him, the cheers and jeers rang out, blending in a wave of white noise as he searched the brush for the ball. Looking left, then right, it eluded him. He was sure he zeroed in on the precise location, but it simply wasn't there. Cautiously, he stepped forward. Because the field on Dunning's hill was just that. A misstep could cause one to stumble, rolling uncontrollably into the tree line. It happened before. Not that it wasn't fun. It was the stopping that hurt.

Suddenly, the object of his search appeared. Not in the brush, but rolling towards his feet. It startled Lukas at first.

"What the hell?"

As he reached to pick it up, something caught his attention. It was a set of eyes looking back at him in the brush. Startled, Lukas fell backward, landing on his backside. The eyes weren't threatening nor menacing. They possessed a warmth, a depth that made him feel comfortable, but far from safe. The figure stood up slowly. He followed her emersion into the light, inch by inch.

Silhouetted by the sun, she appeared fully. She was beautiful, yet flawed. Long locks of dark hair framed her face. A horizontal scar reached around the base of her neck as if it were strangling her beauty. The neckline of her dress plunged downward to her midsection with a single silver ornament dangling from a chain, drawing a direct path to her cleavage. If that was the item's intention, it wasn't necessary. Lukas never saw a woman like this up close in the flesh, outside of the ones that filled the centerfolds of the magazines he would smuggle from his uncle's house. He noticed the scars circling her wrists as well.

The skin doesn't match, he thought.

His heart beat increased, his mouth dried. The sounds of the game behind him had suddenly silenced, unnaturally, as if the players simply vanished. She moved towards him, appearing to glide. This made Lukas dizzy. All his senses were overloading, all out of his control. What was happening?

She stopped directly in front of him, smiling. The urge to fall back overcame him. It was a ten-ton hammer weighing his arms down. He looked up at her again. The woman's legs were curved, shapely. Urges were clouding his perceptions. More scars above her ankles, knees, peeking out from the slit in the lower half of her dress. No, not a dress. More of a gown, but sexier. At fifteen years old, this awakening was a year or two before the natural course of development should occur. Making eye contact, he felt the weight shift to the middle of his chest. It drove him back onto the ground.

Light was disappearing quickly. Glancing up from his now supine position, the woman's face hovered. Slowly, another face joined hers. Then another. The other two appeared to be twins wearing baseball hats. The hats were paneled with alternating yellow and burgundy colors. If it weren't rude to think so, Lukas would have characterized them as very chubby. Name calling wasn't his thing, however, nor was it practiced by any of the rest of the hospital hill gang. They heard enough that sort of labeling being slung their way almost daily by the bullies at the junior high school.

The two ball-capped figures looked at each other, chuckling as they reached down to help Lukas to his feet. With his bearing re-established, he looked around the baseball diamond of the hospital hill only to witness the area abandoned, except for an unnatural shadow that fell over the infield. Lukas blinked, refocusing his vision on the darkness. It wasn't right as he still felt the sun on his neck, meaning the shadows should fall forward towards the Dunning's porch, not towards where he stood. Where had everyone gone?

Lukas Wright turned slowly around to face the woman. "How'd you get up that hill and where'd my friends go?"

She said nothing, only raised a finger to her lips, instructing him to silence. Leaning in, she gave him a gentle kiss. It startled the young man more than anything that happened in the past several minutes. This brought a roar of laughter from the twins in the baseball caps who each, in one stroke, severed Lukas' arms from his shoulders with something he didn't quite see. It happened so fast, so unexpectedly. All he saw was the flash. There wasn't any pain as he slumped down on his knees, following with a face forward dive into the dirt.

His eyes flickered as dust had gotten into them. Instinctively, he reached up, but he now only possessed phantom limbs. They had been removed quickly, expediently by people who were quite experienced with killing. Was it shock or something else that kept him from feeling the sensation of what happened? He didn't know. All he could feel was a rush of cold closing in from both sides of his body, collapsing inward.

Breathing became a chore. Lukas attempted to move, pushing his body with his feet. That's when he saw two more flashes.

The woman kneeled in front of him, looking puzzled. Beyond her, the twins were placing two arms and two legs in the paper route satchel that the hospital hill gang took turns carrying up to the field before each game. Today was Mickey Tolliver's day. Lukas cleared enough of the dirt from his eyes by blinking tears to make eye contact with the woman for the last time. There wasn't any fear in his eyes, nor pain. She rose to her feet, stepping back. It was as if she were afraid of him. The movement was enough to clear his view of the horizon and the setting sun.

As his life bled out into the sunset, his focus withdrew slowly to a clump of grass inches from his nose. The tendrils fluttered gently in the summer breeze. The wind. Air. Intangibles that couldn't be captured, particularly by his lungs at the moment. By observing the blades of grass, it blew from left to right, or was it east to west? He wasn't sure. Gasping deeply, the only thing Lukas Wright knew for sure was there was no air left for him. His eyes fluttered and closed to clear more of the dirt. They would never open again.

A wind gust swept up the hill carrying a parachute of late blooming dandelion pappus high above the ball field. The view from above presented a morbid scene framed within the tree line of Dunning's hill. Three figures looked down at the torso of a young boy haloed in a circle of crimson-soaked earth. The woman reached up for the item that hung on the chain around her neck, blew once, then dropped the pendulous whistle back to its resting place.

The infield shadow trembled like a great black balloon struggling with slightly more air pressure than exceeded capacity. On the whistle's cue, the shadow mass broke into a torrent of small, humanoid creatures rushing towards its source. Reaching the woman and twins, the creatures fell into a school circle around their apparent masters. Behind them, four other figures laid in similar halos of that encircling Lukas Wright, two of them unidentifiable as they had been stripped to the

5

bones. These two members of the hospital hill gang weren't marked for harvest, but consumption. The woman turned, leading her minions back over the hill, through the brush. Following close behind were the twins with their blood-soaked paper route satchels.

The pappus drifted slowly to the ground as the wind died down, scattering seeds randomly across the untainted side of Dunning's hill. Rain would inevitably cleanse the field, supplying nourishment for the following spring upstart dandelions, only to fall under a spinning mower blade. Life cycles have an unusual way of replicating. On some occasions, even by unnatural means.

OLATH'S BRIDE

Three years later. One hundred seventy-six miles northeast...

FRED TERLING

Chapter One

The streets of downtown Kinston were buzzing for a Friday morning. The circus was coming to town! More precisely, the Kinston Volunteer Fire Department's annual fair. It certainly wasn't Ringling Brothers and Barnum & Bailey, but it gave enough of a good time for this small hamlet of two thousand, two hundred and forty-four, according to the last census, to create a wave of excitement. The big attraction, of course, was the Independence Day parade, which was the second largest in the state. With an average attendance of thirty thousand plus in town for the day's festivities, the locals became quite the news item by putting out their chairs a week before the parade. They certainly didn't want to yield any curbside real estate to outsiders.

In the bustle of activity, an older bicycle navigated the back streets and traffic of Kinston. The bike was handed down to the second generation of Allen boys. Judson "Jud" Allen was the current custodian. The day he received it a year ago, it was in disrepair. He had a bit of work to do on it, which he gladly accepted. Following a rear fender replacement, new chain, two tires and a seat, Jud guided it into the work shed out behind his house with the final touches of a candy apple red paint job. It was far from the newest Huffy ten-speed, but it was his. There was a lot of him reflected in the spirit of refinishing that old bicycle. Besides, there wasn't another one on the planet like the Jud Allen special. He liked that.

Most boys his age already graduated to automobiles, but Jud's interest lay elsewhere: motorcycles. He'd been socking money away in his savings account at the Kinston Savings and Trust in a Christmas savings account his aunt opened for him when he turned six years old. Budgeting his income from the paper route, summer lawn mowing and winter snow removal, he was getting closer to owing his first dream machine, with an allotment for creature comforts like comics and records, of course. For now, the bicycle would have to do.

The special pulled up in front of the town's bookstore, aptly named "The Bookstore." Jud just got paid by his aunt and uncle for painting the porch, an annual summer job, and the extra money was burning a hole in his pocket, although he deposited most of it in the savings account. Leaning the special against a telephone pole, he secured the front tire with a padlock. The key to the lock was on his keyring with the spare to the back porch door to his house, not that the Allen family ever locked their house doors. Kinston was a safe place to live.

He was at least two months behind on the latest comic books. Wandering in through the front door, he made his way to the wall of comics, one section over from the Hollywood magazines. The adult magazines were on the top shelf above those, but even a glance in that direction embarrassed him. In the back of the store, the greeting card section. He had never been back there. Those he got closer to home from Devlin's Pharmacy.

Reaching the comic section, he left faced to peruse the titles. There wasn't a ton of room to navigate in the bookstore, just a measly eight feet of space between the magazine shelves and the counter. Quickly, Jud scooped up his regular titles with a glance to see if anything else came out that may interest him. A king-size Spiderman caught his eye. Spiderman wasn't something that he typically read. Super teams were more his taste over individual heroes.

After making his selection, he rushed to the counter. There were three more items he had to purchase with his hard-earned money. His father loved a particular type of cigar. They came encased in glass tubes. Anytime Jud and his father were in town together, the two wandered into The Bookstore, each with a different purpose. Jud never even asked for them. The storekeeper simply took three out and rang them up when he saw him approach the counter. Although he was only seventeen, everyone knew everyone in the small town. It was never an issue.

Jud paid for the merchandise, then headed back out to his bike. One of the most useful additions to the special he made was the gear bag that he attached above the back fender. It was a World War II rucksack that he had gotten on his first trip out to Top Arnie's Army surplus store, about twenty miles out of town. He was struck with sensory overload the first time he entered the place. There was so much to see, yet alone purchase. The rucksack was the perfect thing for him to carry anything while navigating the streets, alleys, or off road on the way to his favorite fishing holes along the bank of Rogers' Mill Creek.

He affixed the upper loop on the seat post of the bike, securing the shoulder straps with a triple loop of fly line. It was not only a piece of engineering ingenuity, but field expedience at its finest. He hoped whatever soldier parted with it would be proud that it was still in service.

Jud placed the comics and cigars in the sack, leaving the special chained to the pole. A poster for the fair was stapled just above his head on the same pole. Was it there before? There were also hundreds if not thousands of old rusty staples where other posters were affixed from years past.

Pretty cool, he thought. *Bet some of those staples are way older than me!*

His next destination was only two storefronts up, so he left the special where it was. Jud approached Goodman's Music Mart. As always, there was an index card taped on the front glass door that read: "Back in 15 minutes." It was always there. Always. Peering through the door, Jud saw Mr. Goodman sitting behind the counter on the other end of the store eating a sandwich, reading the newspaper through his half glasses. He tugged on the door. It opened with the bell on the top, signaling his arrival. Goodman looked up from his paper.

"Hey, Jud. C'mon in. Just grabbing some lunch. Got a bunch of new 45s in for you to rummage through."

Jud bounced forward to the counter, where the 45s were stored in a wooden case on top. He browsed through the selection, dropping them forward to rest on the front of the case. There was one in particular that he was looking for but didn't dare ask for it. It was far more fun to do it this way. He pulled one title, then another. Getting near to the end of the second row, his hopes dwindled. It wasn't there.

Goodman looked up at him over his bifocals.

"I suppose you're looking for, what are they called again, Kiss? I don't know what you see in them, Jud, with all that makeup and long hair. Back in my day, it was Glenn Miller and Tommy Dorsey. Why don't you try some Sinatra once in a while? Your dad loves him, ya' know? Used to play him all the time when he spun records."

That caught Jud by surprise. "Dad spun records?"

"Yup. Used to go by the name of Tony Braille. Many people still call him that."

Jud knew little about his father's early years. He didn't talk about any of that. Mr. Allen was private when it came to his personal life with his family. There were chores, dishes, and the cardinal rule: be home for dinner every night. No exceptions. Fred Allen was a strict disciplinarian. There was a brick wall between parental guidance and personal outreach. He made sure that line was never blurred. Regardless, Jud reached the age where he needed that personal connection to his dad. He craved it with most of his being. Whether that would ever happen was an entirely different issue. That didn't mean he would not try.

Jud finished with the last tab of the third row of records. What he sought wasn't there. He placed the two that he found in front of Mr. Goodman, ready to check out.

"Three dollars and fourteen cents, with tax."

Jud was a little confused, as he only had two records of ninety-nine cents each. He looked at him, only with confusion. Goodman returned a smile, then sighed, throwing his hands in the air.

"Oh, almost forgot. I held this one for you when it came in. I know it's a couple of years old, but you were looking for the single. He handed Jud the 45 in the familiar brown Casablanca sleeve with the tan camel. The front label read, "Calling Doctor Love" on the flip side, "Take Me."

"Yes!" Jud was beside himself. He'd been hunting for this for at least a year. "Thank you so much, sir!"

"Thank you, Jud. Even though those boys creep me out, happy to see young people appreciate music. Even if I don't quite get." Goodman winked at him while placing the records in a bag.

Jud ran out onto the sidewalk again, carefully placing his purchases in the rucksack. After unlocking the special, he pushed the bike forward, leaping on the seat side-saddle like cowboys in the westerns he watched most Saturday mornings. His last stop laid just ahead.

He rode down East Main Street, crossing over North Central Avenue onto West Main, around the bank and up the alley to the parking lot across from the borough building. On approach, he saw the fair workers already set up most of the rides and games of chance on the amusement row. Screeching his breaks, Jud looked around for his father. There he was, talking with the fire chief and mayor. Jud approached with caution, not sure of the correct protocol when addressing famous people like the three of them. His dad was obviously important enough, he knew that as he was the chairperson for the Independence Day celebration. Of course, the mayor and fire chief fit the bill. The chief noticed him first.

"Good afternoon, Jud. Ready for tonight?"

Positioning the special out of the way, he deployed the kickstand. "Yes, sir. Really excited to see what dad has in store for me to do."

He walked over to Fred Allen after retrieving the cigars from his rucksack. Reaching out, he handed them to his father. Fred Allen took the three tubes, sliding them into the front pocket of his short-sleeved dress shirt. He always wore short sleeves, even with ties. Jud waited for a response, but none came. His heart sank a little, as it had a few scant moments ago in the music store. Not that he expected a response. It was a fifty-fifty proposition with his dad. The senior Allen just returned his focus to the conversation he was having with the chief and mayor.

It wasn't intentional. Maybe that was part of the problem. His father wasn't a warm man. Well, on the home front anyway. Out and about with the citizens of Kinston, during his parade meeting and at work, Fred Allen was the center of attention, always dropping the well-placed joke. His sarcasm was quick and never, ever aimed to harm. It was a bonding thing he was told by his Uncle Robert, assuring his nephew that his dad always dealt with a self-confidence problem, even going back to his youth. Perhaps that was something they should bond over?

Jud stood to the right back of his dad while the last details for the fair were hammered out between the three men. He felt like a fish out of water. Awkwardness was feeding his anxiety like a raw steak to a pack of hungry wolves. Disappearing wasn't an option. That would just spawn more awkwardness when the time did finally come for Fred Allen to focus on his son. He was about to be tossed a much-needed lifeline.

"Hey, Jud!" The female voice caught him off guard.

He turned to see who called out his name, loud enough to defeat the sounds of the fair worker's tools assembling the Ferris wheel.

It was Rhonda Coulter, the woman of his dreams, the jam in his jelly roll, the reason for his very existence. Beyond the comics, vinyl records, fishing trips and the special, she trumped all those things combined every given day. There she stood, five feet away from him, bookbag in hand. Next to her, one of Jud's best friends, Emma Adams. He and Emma were in homeroom together since kindergarten. Emma was also Rhonda's best friend. It was a bit of a mystery why Emma and Jud never got together as a couple, but Emma was firmly in Jud's friend column, although their Sunday morning conversations lasted for hours discussing the previous night's episode of Chiller Theater. After church, of course.

He stood there out of his element, still reeling from the anxiety of being the fourth man out in his father's conversation. Emma felt his uncomfortable surprise.

"You going to say something or just gawk?' She knew how and when to tease her lifelong chum. This was one of those situations.

"Oh, yeah. Hey you two. What's up?" he said.

"We were over at the library and swung by to see what was happening," said Rhonda.

Jud heard her words, but his mind was lagging a little. He was too lost in her big, brown doe eyes to hear properly. The two girls sense it and giggled to one another. Certainly not his intention, but they found his lack of response cute. Rhonda reached into her bookbag, pulling out a book titled, "The Shark: Savage of the Sea" by Jacques-Yves Cousteau and Philippe Cousteau. He knew it well. Nearly had it memorized.

Rhonda held it out, offering it to him. "Anyway, the library was having a used book sale and Emma said you love this one. I can tell by how many times your name is on the checkout card. The cover is a little worn, but I'm sure you can fix that."

The girls laughed again.

Jud reached up to retrieve the gift. His hand was trembling as he took it. He didn't know what to say. This was pretty much turning into the best day ever, and it was still morning.

Emma broke in again. "I believe, Mister Allen, that a 'thank you' is in order?"

He was still fixated on the book cover, more so now knowing who it came from. Jud broke away from the spell put on him by the mere appearance of Rhonda Coulter. His mind finally caught up.

"Oh, Rhonda. This is amazing! Seriously. I really don't know what to say!"

"A 'thank you' will do."

"Yes, of course. Thank you. Big time!" He looked around in a panic, patting down his pockets, spinning around toward his bike. "I wish I had something to give you back."

She smiled, pointing at his tee-shirt. "Cheap Trick, huh?"

"Yeah, went to see them last week. You want my shirt?"

This really ignited the laughter. "No, silly. Next time take me. I love them!"

"Tell them who opened," said Emma.

Jud was as uneasy with the question as he knew the opening band, but little about their discography. What if Rhonda tossed out a follow-up question? He prided himself on his knowledge of music. Current music anyway. There was some dabbling in pre-seventies stuff, but only a few deep tracks.

"The Crimson Dolls," he answered.

"What? Get outta town!" Rhonda punched him lightly on the shoulder. "I'd die to see the Dolls!"

Emma and Rhonda broke into an impromptu sing-along. "They say it's not proper for a girl to make a move. I'm not waiting anymore, 'cause I really like your groove. What's holding you back boy, holding you back, boy. I got your back, boy. Ready or not, I'm takin' your love... Uh, go get it!"

Emma spun around, falling into Rhonda's arms. Both girls laughed hysterically. Jud admired such a show of confidence. Although he knew lyrics from every record in his own collection, he would never imagine singing beyond the confines of his bedroom. Jud was speechless.

Wait, did Rhonda Coulter just ask me to ask her out? His brain lag caught up again. His heart was double-timing, head spinning. First the book, now this. Wow!

Rhonda slung her bookbag over her shoulder and Emma returned to normal, whatever that was.

"You going to be around here later?" asked Rhonda.

"Yeah. My dad has me working at a booth. Not sure doing what yet, but I'll be here early. Like around five-thirty?" Jud answered.

"Cool, we'll see you then. Maybe I can help with whatever you got going on?"

His excitement was barely containable. "I would love that. Could be epic fun. If you wanna, I mean, if there isn't —"

"See you at five-thirty."

As the two girls walked away from him, Emma swung around, mouthing the words to him. "You owe me big time."

Smiling from ear to ear, he mouthed back the word, "anything."

As they faded from his sight off in the distance, he completely forgot about his father. Now, something else garnered the spotlight. Rhonda freaking Coulter was going to help him work at his booth.

So, this is what cloud nine feels like? I dig it! he thought.

In his mind, he started his own Cheap Trick sing along with his own contextual spin. "Would you like to go to heaven tonight?"

"Jud!"

That voice breaking his daydream. He knew well. It was his dad.

"Let's go, Ace. Let me show you what I have in mind for tonight."

His dad used his nickname, "Ace." He was the firstborn of his two other siblings. When he heard that term, it was a step in the right direction towards that bonding he struggled to achieve. Not that he wanted to feel favored over the other two. Well, maybe just a little, but it certainly was a rebound from his initial welcome to the parking lot. Not that he expected a public show of affection, but he was his son. The first born. His ace.

Fred Allen led him over to a lot next to the amusement row. There sat an old car, the make and model, he didn't know. Jud wasn't into cars. The car was in decent condition, just missing tires at first glance. It was roped off, and the two stepped down off the sidewalk of the parking lot to get to it. Leaning against the curb were three sledgeham-mers. His father picked one up, then began the instructions.

"Here's what's going to happen here, Ace. Fifty cents a swing, three for a dollar. They can hit the car anywhere they want. If they break something off, just toss it in the back seat. All the glass has been removed, so it's safe. Once in a while, you have someone come up that will ask you if they can keep the piece they knock off. That's fine, but that's ten bucks flat. Don't argue with them. Hold your ground. If they give you any shit, find a cop. Don't get into it with anyone, especially the drunks. They're usually the best customers. This may seem silly, but when we did this with the Jaycees, turned over five hundred dollars a night. The only setback, we went through three cars and too many sledgehammers to count."

Jud stared at the car in awe. This was going to be one cool job to have. Expecting to be on some sort of clean-up crew or ticket sales, he never imagined this was going to be his task for the weekend. Rhonda is going to freak out.

"This something you can handle?"

"Yes, sir. Seems pretty straightforward and fun."

"It is. Especially the people you're gonna meet. I'll have a change apron with a hundred dollars starter cash for you when you get here tonight. Just go to the fair trailer over by the borough building, I'll give it to you. At the end of the evening, bring everything you have, and we'll count it. See how you did."

"Thanks, dad."

Jud hugged him. His father hugged him back. What a morning.

"Go do what you gotta do until then. I still have some people to talk to. See you at five-thirty, Ace. Be careful heading home," he paused, "oh, and thanks for the cigars."

Fred Allen squeezed his son's shoulder, then set off across the parking lot. Judson Allen just stood there momentarily, wondering what act in a former life he performed to get such a treasure trove of riches this day. And it was only the beginning.

He jumped on the special, saddled up, and headed back in the direction he came. Jud hoped this dream would last forever. Unfortunately for him and the residents of Kinston, the nightmare was about to begin.

Chapter Two

The tapping on the steel door was maddening. Two portly figures with burgundy and gold alternating paneled ball caps took turns with the disturbance. They exchanged glances, giggling as they struggled to balance themselves on the concrete floor outside of the door. They were currently intent on breeching it.

"Stand up straight!" said one.

"No, you sloucher!" said the other.

"I wish you would just —"

"—shut up and mind your own business."

"Real mature, you —"

There was a pause in their volley back and forth. One started a sentence, the other finished it. Everything about the two denoted twin brothers, in a very macabre way. Size, appearance, clothing, hats. The conjoined speaking of the two was just plain odd.

"— nerd!"

The first brother roared with uncontrollable laughter. "Nerd? That's the best —"

"—you got? Porky!"

That comment ignited the first brother, who immediately took a swing at the second. Both slipped on the slimy floor, crashing under the weight of gravity. The harder they tried getting up, the more they slid around. If it weren't a massive pool of blood they were sloshing around in, it may have even been comical. All that was missing was calliope music.

A panel on the steel door finally slid to one side to address the commotion in the hallway. A pair of deadpan eyes peered out from black, encircled eyelids or sockets. It was difficult to see in the dim light.

"Frick! Frack! What type of shenanigans are the two of you engaged in? Are the preparations complete?"

They both got to one knee, as if they rehearsed the act prior to their blood feud. Frick spoke first, as was customary.

"I told him that —"

"—we should have finished before knocking."

The eyes behind the door responded, lacking the enjoyment of their buffoonery. "Know that I am not amused by your hijinks. Return when your tasks have been executed. We only have seven hours until we begin our work. Begone!"

"Yes, Professor —"

"—Olath, sir!"

Frick and Frack finally got back to their feet, trampling down the hall with caution so not to fall again. Professor Olath slid the panel shut on the steel door, returning to the work he was doing before the disturbance.

Olath wandered over to the control terminal of the herringbone parlor. He walked as if he were trying out new legs for the first time. Perhaps he was. His form was long and spindly, flesh tone cold and white. The black rings around his eyes did indeed look more like sockets than eyelids. His slick bald head didn't shine, nor reflect the ceiling lights, rather looked powdered down to resist any sort of glow. Because of his appearance, his body and shadow trail projected a lithe spider gliding across the floor. Decked out from neck to toe in black leather with large buckles fastening his tunic, it only added to the specter of an oversized arachnid.

This facility served as a multilactor milking station for goats. Currently, it was quiet and abandoned. Frick and Frack moved the stock over to the slaughterhouse. That was their portion of the program. With a little luck, they corralled them into the stockyard, through lairage, up the ramp to their first stop in the bleeding chamber. By the looks of the hallway outside, that much had been done. The professor needed the blood to create more help. It was a complicated process he refined over the centuries. Through time, trial and error, Olath and his team became good at their grim operation. They were precise, quick, and efficient.

The herringbone parlor was reserved for a more important purpose than milking. To them anyway. The multilactor system was quickly converted to a dispensing system, as opposed to one of extraction. Milk was not their goal. Olath tended to the connectors, augmenting them with small vials of a dark, viscous fluid. He needed more. Much more. That was the purpose of tonight's mission. Only he knew the contents of the vials. More importantly, only he possessed the knowledge of how to create the serum.

He learned the art of alchemy from his master, Johann Konrad Dippel, on December 8, 1733. Olath was the alchemist's apprentice who had taken a particular interest in an aspect of his work, the elixir vitae, or elixir of life. Dippel, a chemist among other claims, created what he labeled Dippel's Oil as a by-product of his work on the elixir of life. It served its purpose as an agent for tanning hides. Locally, women used it as a salve to calm distemper from pregnancy. Ingesting the foul-smelling concoction was unwise and certainly would have led to death, as the base composition included potash, a component of potassium chloride.

Whether Dippel ever discovered the secrets of the elixir vitae was always a point of conjecture, as many believed it was simply a con on Dippel's part to swindle the Castle Franckenstein from the Landgrave of Hesse. Either way, Olath made a discovery of his own concerning the concoction. As the base of the Dippel's Oil was composed of potash and animal ingredients, what if he swapped out animal for a more desired component? It was then that he combined his passion for the dark arts, borrowing from Dippel's discovery and augmenting with human remains, instead of animal. On a singular night in 1733, after multiple failed experiments, independent of his master's efforts, one took shape yielding success. At 02:41 in the morning, Darmstadt, Germany time, Olath the apprentice supplanted the master. He reanimated a human hand with his own elixir vitae. Four months later, on April 25, 1734, Johann Conrad Dippel died unexpectedly. Coincidentally, Olath also discovered potassium cyanide in his independent experiments as well. Unfortunate for Dippel.

Over the following decades, Olath worked tirelessly experimenting, finding new applications for and enhancements for his discovery. Eventually, using the elixir on himself as his body began surrendering to old age. He was reborn. Regrettably, his fountain of youth was fleeting. An unanticipated side-effect was rapid aging following a two-year suspension from death, although certain parts of the body were prone to quicker decay than others. That called for replacements. Luckily for him, major organs were exempt from the aging process, which was a blessing for Olath, as he was no surgeon. Olath hadn't perfected his elixir to the point of immortality. That's when his ghoulish trek began.

Across Germany, down through Italy, up to France, eventually stopping in England before setting sail with a crew bound for North America. Never staying too long in any one location, he learned to stick to the smaller villages. Not only did this help to keep the authorities out of his nefarious activities, but also, he could use up a village's human resources, repair whatever parts he needed to replace and plunder any valuables he would need to keep moving. Inevitably, he became quite wealthy.

When arriving in America, it was a time of opportunity with westward expansion. It was this period where he recruited help in the way of introducing the elixir into living tissue. Expecting the same results that he experienced, once again he ran into merely temporary success. His living minions quickly developed a taste for the dead, particularly the smoke from burning corpses. Olath concealed his crimes somehow. The minions developed in hours, instead of years, transforming into creatures that no longer resembled men, but scurrying monsters from the darkest dread nightmares. Controllable? Yes, but only as long as the home fires remained burning.

For a moment, he considered returning to his homeland of German in the late 1930s. There was a young visionary named Adolph Hitler that he felt would be an asset to his work, and he could contribute to his. The centuries of being the sole proprietor of his little body salvage and looting enterprise also pushed him over the edge of anything resembling sanity. Not that his initial enterprise was that of sound mind. His apprehension in turning his talents for the potential exploitation of the painter turned dictator from Braunau am Inn, Austria turned out to be a wise choice, as his reign was fleeting.

Professor Olath's field experiments would have to continue on United States soil. Occasionally, his dispensing of the elixir yielded favorable results. Those experiments accompanied him on his travels and put to work.

Twenty-four years ago, Frick and Frack were two of these abnormalities. The boys were retrieved from an early grave in 1954, hours after their burial. Not only were they responsive to the reanimation process, but have also consistently aged at a normal biological level. Neither of them ever needed to receive replacement parts. The key to everything Olath dreamed remained hidden in their genetics. It was part of the reasons he put up with their childish antics. Their bodies may have aged, but their minds did not. They remained children. Even when they insisted that the functional recruits were to be dressed and made up like clowns, he acquiesced. It was just a matter of time before he unlocked their secret. Presently, there was more work to do.

Olath spun around in his chair, hearing the semi-trucks pull up outside of the stockyard. He leased them for the night's festivities. The drivers did not know what kind of payment they were about to receive. He rose to his feet, heading down the walkway between the rows of multilactors, when a voice summoned him from the shadows. It was a female voice. She spoke more with a command in her tone than a query.

"Are we ready?" she asked.

Olath turned in her direction, bowing his head as though he were addressing royalty.

"Yes, Elizabeth. All preparations are in motion."

"That wasn't the question."

He was reticent in a response. There was fear in him. Deep fear. What did this woman Elizabeth hold over him? He was the alchemist who cheated death itself, traveled half of the world for nearly a quarter century.

"Frick and Frack have cleared the parlor. The hoard is enjoying the comforts of the condemned room, secured, of course. With much trepidation, I was moved slowly to consecrate by flame, by one of the older ones, in order that a flow of fresh exhaust would soothe them. The storage vehicles have arrived, which I was presently in route to tending."

He awaited validation that he was doing a good job, but nothing but dead air. "We were most fortunate in this instance to secure an agricultural locale that boasts the multiple facilities that are so apropos for our requirements. I trust you found your current accommodations to your liking?"

"They are adequate. The hardwood and velvet were nice finds, particularly in this town."

Olath clapped his hands together. A positive. That was enough.

"Nothing but the finest accoutrements for you, dearest."

She moved back into the darkness, stopping before she departed.

"You know never to address me with even the slightest term of endearment. Let's keep it that way if I must stay on this ride. You may also want to check the usage of that word, my dear professor. I'm not fluent in French, but I know it has nothing to do with my 'current accommodations.'"

Olath bowed in acknowledgement before resuming his original path towards the trucks as she faded from sight. Reaching the loading dock of the facility, he was greeted by a caravan of tractor trailers, twelve in all. A group of drivers exited their rig, forming a conversation circle, most sipping hot coffee from thermos cups with over half of them smoking cigarettes.

Nasty habit, Olath thought, seeing the billows of nicotine smoke twining in the late morning air.

The drivers pulled an all-night to get to Chooch's Farm, which was twenty-three miles off the interstate, mostly on service roads. Not exactly opportune for a convoy.

Olath retrieved an umbrella from a container that Frick and Frack placed outside the loading dock. They appreciated their master's aversion to light. More of his temper if they didn't hold that appreciation as a priority. Opening the umbrella, taking refuge under its canopy, he strode toward the group in long strides fit for a spider. On approach, the men reacted with a mixture of surprise and, what was the word, repulsion? The professor was definitely not built for the light of day.

"Gentlemen, it is with great enthusiasm that I greet you. I hope your journey was met without incident?"

The men looked around the group at each other. Who would be the appointed spokesperson? A larger gentleman in a flannel shirt, thermal vest and Peterbilt trucker hat stepped to the forefront, swallowing down the last gulp of coffee, screwing the cup back onto the thermos lid.

"That we did. Except for all these goddamned back roads. Nothing to see out here but cow shit and cornstalks. You Olath?" The man asked, spitting tobacco juice to the ground as he offered his hand for a shake.

Olath recoiled at the gesture, gripping both of his gloved leather hands on the handle of his umbrella.

"You are correct in that assumption, sir."

The group of truckers chuckled at the response. The lead man looked over his shoulder at the men. Just because they were getting paid didn't mean they couldn't have a little fun at their strange benefactor's expense.

"Good to know, there. But you know what they say when you assume?"

The group continued their murmured laughter.

"I believe you have me at a disadvantage, sir. I do not comprehend what one may enunciate in that given situation," said Olath.

All the men burst into raucous laughter. One man taunted the spokesperson of the group.

"He got you there, Berty!"

Berty, the spokesperson, was not amused. He felt as if Olath got the better of him, particularly since he only understood a handful of the words the strange, pale, lanky man with the umbrella just said. His demeanor changed as quickly as the spit he cast out on the ground.

"Well, then. You got our money?"

Olath tugged on one buckle of his shirt, revealing a whistle affixed to a chain. He blew it. The group of truckers winced at the high pitch ringing in their ears. From the far-right rear of the slaughterhouse, Frick and Frack emerged, running as fast as their legs could carry them. Between the boiler and rendering plant, past the effluent treatment plant, the two sped. Frack's forward momentum gave way to gravity as his feet couldn't keep up. He fell to the ground. As if on cue and previously rehearsed, Frick fell also for no reason at all. Both rose simultaneously after retrieving a briefcase they were both holding. They gave chase once more to the sound of the whistle.

Arriving at Olath's side, the twins had changed from their blood-soaked clothing into dark suits with oversized bow ties. The suits were too small; the bow ties were too large. Still wearing their paneled ball caps, Olath rolled his eyes at their appearance. At least they bathed and made an attempt. Extending their arms together, Frick and Frack handed the briefcase to him. Tucking the whistle away, he waved his hand at them. They saluted, spun around, bumped into each other, and ran off back towards the slaughterhouse.

"Cute kids. They yours?" asked Berty to the delight of the other truckers.

"Not originally," Olath answered with an ominous grin.

He handed the case over to Berty. This got the other men in the group to move forward. Opening the case, Berty dispensed the envelopes. Each man tore into them, fanning through the hundred-dollar bills inside. There was six-thousand dollars for each man for a job that would have usually only garnered a fraction of that amount. This was a great run. So far. Berty closed the empty case after each driver received his pay, handing it back to Olath.

"This recompense is adequate as agreed upon?" he asked.

"Damn, straight!" answered Berty. "By the way, where we headin'?"

Olath produced the razor-like grin once more. "A small hamlet, fifty-six miles, northeast of here. It goes by the name of Kinston."

Chapter Three

Rosie's was a small tavern on the outskirts of Shermer. Servicing mostly coal miners on shift work, there was always a steady flow of patrons all day. Cold beer and hot sandwiches were the draw, particularly the Friday fish fry, boasted by many to be the best in the state. Not limited to Lenten season, Rosie's served the famous four pieces of hand battered cod on fresh rolls, hand cut fries and coleslaw made fresh every morning. There was a savory tint to everything Rosie cooked. It was the special magic of the place, proprietor and cook, Rosie Babin would say with a twinkle in her eye. Her husband, Michael J., as everyone who ever met the lawman referred to him, would just laugh and say it was the community grease in the deep fryers. Referring to the fact that she fried everything in the same grease, it became his running joke as he regarded his wife as the straight man to his punchlines.

The couple purchased the old corner grocery store after the previous owners, Marge and Speedy Florencik, decided on retiring to sunny Florida. Dumping their retirement savings into fixing the place up, Rosie and Michael J., converted it into a tavern. She spent thirty-five years in the public school system as an elementary school cook. He was a career cop, serving as a military police officer in World War II, then twenty years on the force in Kinston, retiring as the then Chief of Police. Not being able to give up the life of protecting and serving, he became a constable following forced retirement. Still, the two ran the small tavern with the mom-and-pop cozy feeling that locals relied on.

The place was unusually quiet for a Friday night. Rosie attributed the empty tavern to the opening night of the volunteer fire department's fair in nearby Kinston. Most of the fish dinners were takeout during the day.

Katlyn "Kat" Ellis swayed in the corner to the jukebox. C-29, Smokestack Lightning by Howlin' Wolf, was her favorite to play. Rosie didn't get it. Kat was only twenty-four years old, years past the blues man's heyday. She just shook her head, lighting up her eighth Kool cigarette of the day.

"Those are gonna kill you one day, ya know?" Kat said while she moved to the rhythm and gravel voice coming from the speakers.

Rosie just exhaled a smoke ring in her direction as she started on the dishes after pouring herself a rock and rye. Kat was a stray that the older couple took in. She and her brother Johnny were the neighbor's children when the Babins lived back on Coal Run Road in Kinston. An unfortunate accident at the transformer plant that employed half of the town's citizens took the life of their father. Kat and her brother Johnny's mother, Sarah Ellis, took the death hard. Too hard. Sarah surrendered to a life that wasn't conducive to child rearing, eventually leaving the two one afternoon while at school. Mrs. Ellis hadn't been seen since. That was ten years ago.

The Babins' generosity was a blessing for both. Kat excelled with all things financial, keeping the books. Johnny was a hard worker that never complained and possessed the strength of five men. Although he was developmentally challenged, he never viewed it as an obstacle in getting done whatever task he committed to. Emotionally, he simply hadn't grown. His early psychological profile set him stunted at nine, the precise year Kat and Johnny's mother abandoned them. Coincidence?

Continuing her appreciation for the blues music playing on the jukebox, Johnny made an appearance. In his hand, he held an old cigar box filled with game tokens. Rosie's had one pinball machine, Gorgar. The demon themed machine spoke seven phrases with a heartbeat sound effect that increased in speed as the game went on. It wouldn't be available to the public for another year yet, but a few test machines were dropped across the country. When Rosie was offered the game with all proceeds being kept by the bar for a monthly evaluation form, she simply needed to complete the form, which Kat did for her. It was a simple decision. Rosie's enjoyed the good fortune of having a nephew in the business of amusements, including restocking of cigarette machines. An added benefit for her Kool consumption.

Johnny Ellis loved the game as it talked. Taunting the player as their skill level increased, Gorgar enticed Johnny to try even that much harder in mastering the spinning ball and flippers. The game tokens were infinite. If he worked his way through the box on any session against his red horned nemesis, Aunt Rosie, what both Kat and he called her, simply opened the side panel to retrieve the spent tokens. He dropped his first token of the night into the slot, being greeted with the challenge. "Gorgar, beat me!" Pulling back on the plunger, he let the pinball fly.

Rosie continued the dish washing, occasionally tapping the cigarette ash into a long-neglected cup of coffee serving as an ashtray. Kat joined her from the other side of the bar with a deck of Rider Waite Smith tarot cards, her own amusement. Removing them from the box, she began shuffling the deck.

"You know, if I looked a little older, I could have probably gotten a job reading at the fair this year," Kat said.

Rosie just grinned at her as she kept her focus on the dishes.

"I'm the best reader I know. You would think by now in this area, everyone would know I'm twenty-four. We've only lived here our whole lives." She continued shuffling, pondering what spread she may drop on the bar. "I mean, everyone here likes when I read for them."

Stuffing out her cigarette in the mug, it was the last item Rosie needed to wash. "I think you scare the hell out of people with those things, Kat. They rather play euchre."

She was probably right, as Michael J. insisted on a set of playing cards, scoreboard, and pegs on most of the tables in the tavern.

"Maybe Pastor Don and Father Riley, but they don't understand divination any more than most of the people go to church around here just to buy their way into heaven with how much money they put in the collection plate."

Rosie made a sign of the cross. "Don't talk like that. Jesus is going to strike you down one day with the blasphemy."

"It's true Aunt Rosie. You think Clyde Parker, with all his girlfriends and a wife, cares anything about Jesus striking him down?"

"Bite your tongue, Kat. You know I hate gossip. What he does in his own time is their business."

"Maybe, but Mathew 7:1-3, 'Judge not, that ye be not judged. For with what judgment ye judge, ye shall be judged: and with what measure ye mete, it shall be measured to you again. And why beholdest thou the mote that is in thy brother's eye, but considerest not the beam that is in thine own eye?'"

Aunt Rosie crossed her arms. "Sounds like some twenty-four-year-old is doing a bit of judging herself. What do your cards say about that?"

"Just because I know that stuff doesn't mean I believe in it. I passed the Hierophant stage years ago. Just making a point."

"You smart ass kids and your points."

"See, even you still call me a kid."

Rosie moved to the end of the bar, lifted the bar flap and walked to Kat. Throwing her arms around her, she kissed the top of her head.

"You'll always be my baby girl. Hierophant, bible verses or whatever. Your Uncle Mike and I love you like our own."

This brought a huge smile to Kat's face. Aunt Rosie knew exactly what to say. Her timing was impeccable. There were never any arguments, as most things were said in jest. What she said to the young woman bearing the frustration of missing the fire department fair was true. Rosie and Michael J. never had children of their own. The couple raised these two, officially adopting them after the mandatory time passed for the abandonment statute. Out of respect for their father, Kat and Johnny requested that their last names remained Ellis. It was a small price for pay for the memories the two provided by their much older adoptive parents. Besides, love was love, whatever you called it.

"What time is Uncle Mike going to be home?" Kat asked.

"I don't know. He's working the fair and has to escort of the money to the bank like he does for bingo games. I'm guessing eleven, eleven thirty?"

"Fuck you, Gorgar. Asshole, bastard, son of a bitch!" Johnny's voice shouted across the tavern as he kicked the leg of the pinball machine. The demon was getting the best of him.

"Johnny Ellis, watch your language! Another outburst like that and I'll take your tokens for the night."

"Sorry, Aunt Rosie. He cheats," Johnny said, slumped in shame, wearing disgrace for both words and actions.

Kat shook her head. "Kids..."

Jud Allen stood in front of the old car, change apron around his waist with a sledgehammer in hand. He enthusiastically awaited the opening of the fair, more importantly, he awaited Rhonda Coulter. Rehearsing his stance, he repeated various greeting in his head, occasionally out loud to see which one sounded best. His self-evaluation ran the gamut of cool to sweet. Holding the sledgehammer, he felt powerful, but it simply wasn't him. Dropping it to the curb with the others, he wandered over to the car, leaned up against it.

"Wassup?" he asked no one there.

Shifting positions, Jud Allen continued to experiment, searching for the best opening presentation.

Unknown to him, Rhonda and Emma arrived and watched him from behind the rope separating the old car from the potential participants. Instead of interrupting, they continued to observe his rehearsal ritual. It was sweet to the two girls. Flattering even to see a boy work so diligently in selecting the right opening words. Feeling as if he were being watched, Jud spun around, expecting to see his father standing there. The girl's unexpected appearance threw him for a loop. All that practice, all the preparation. He uttered a single word.

"Hey."

Closing his distance back to the rope, Rhonda lifted it, joining him by his side. He ran to do the gentlemanly thing, taking her hand to steady her stepping down from the curb. Jud never held a girl's hand before. Drawing it back, Rhonda squeezed it, interlocking their fingers. His heart went into overdrive. Emma smiled, clasping her own hands together. Her work here was done. Besides, her interest lay elsewhere. Billy Ford was working the high striker on the amusement row. The two girls teased each other earlier in the day after discovering what Jud was doing as the objects of both of their affections were working fair stations involving sledgehammers, although Billy's was more of an oversized mallet.

Emma waved to Jud and Rhonda as she took her leave. "Ta-ta for now, you two lovebirds. Maybe we can all go out to the Castle for apple pie and cinnamon ice cream after?"

"Yes!" Rhonda yelled back.

As Emma wandered off, a man in a cowboy hat, long duster, with saddlebags slung over the rear of his motorcycle, rode slowly past on West Main Street. This caught the attention of Jud. He may not have known much about cars, but motorcycles were a different story.

"Damn..." he said, conveying a dreamy astonishment previously reserved for the beautiful young woman who presently kept him company, which of course sparked her curiosity.

"What?" she asked.

"That's a 1973 Harley-Davidson FL Electra-Glide. Four-stroke, 45-degree V-Twin, OHV, 2 valves per cylinder engine. Tillotson 1-5/8-inch dual venturi diaphragm with accelerator pump induction. Electric ignition made the kick-start pedal useless as the shifting is done by boot now. First Harley with front and rear disc brakes for better axle breaking. Check out that standard chrome trim. It even has the original AMF badge still on it. See, in 1969 AMF purchased Harley Davidson and put that badge next to the Harley logo. This pissed off a lot of owners, who removed it and repainted their bikes. Sweet seeing one in original condition, although it's only a few years old."

He never took the eyes off the bike. For the first time, Jud Allen wasn't at a loss for words. They spilled out of him as naturally as breathing. Rhonda was impressed.

"Wow, you got all that from one glance?" she asked.

The bike sped off, but Jud's gaze followed it.

"Yeah. It's really something else to see one in the wild. I've only read about them in Motorcyclist Magazine. The Bookstore carries them. I stray from comics once in a while," he answered confidently.

"Impressive, Mr. Allen."

Her admiration snapped his focus back to her. If only he had such confidence with women, it would make things easier. Although Rhonda was doing a great job, setting him at ease. She took the lead in their budding relationship, establishing a comfort zone that he welcomed. In time, he thought, maybe he would develop the confidence with the fairer sex that he had with his knowledge of motorcycles. It was a matter of interest; he supposed. Rhonda Coulter certainly supplied that interest in spades.

Tapping into his growing confidence, he picked up a sledgehammer. "You ready to do this?"

She retrieved one, picking it up, slinging it over her shoulder. "Hell yeah!"

It was going to be a good night.

———————

Three hours passed. The sun set, and the fair was bustling with life. Laughter rang out from the various rides as the bells, horns, and whistles from the games lining the amusement row rang out. It was, without a doubt, a carnival atmosphere. A good time was being shared by all.

Jud and Rhonda went through the three sledgehammers, with Fred Allen having to run off to Western Auto and Hardware to purchase three more. Luckily, they were open until 10:00 pm. Even their initial vehicle was towed and a replacement brought in because of the utter destruction of the first one. Some man name Tom spent a hundred and fifty dollars knocking off parts for the taking, which bolstered Jud's happiness knowing the night's receipts would be favorable as this was only night one of three. Emma was making substantial progress with Billy, which made them happy. Rhonda kept checking in with her hourly since the fair opened.

While awaiting the replacement junker car for the sledgehammer station, Jud and Rhonda shared their first kiss behind the bank. Then another and another. He had long forgotten the motorcycle. Everything else, for that matter. Moments after the second junker dropped, the two resumed their positions with the fresh sledgehammers. Before the anxious line of would-be demolition experts could start taking the swings, the fair goers were collectively drawn to blasts of air horns from tractor trailers that started arriving, lining the sides of West Main Street, next to the fair. Twelve in all.

The mayor, police and fire chief, along with Fred Allen, left the borough building to investigate the disturbance. Jud and Rhonda looked on with curiosity. Across the street, Constable Michael J. Babin was the first to approach the convoy. That's when all hell broke loose.

Chapter Four

Outside of Rosie's tavern, a stranger on a 1973 Harley-Davidson FL Electra-Glide pulled up, cutting off the engine, engaging the kickstand. Rosie was moving towards the door to lock up, as there was no reason to stay open for regular business hours if the place was empty. It would be nice to have a night off for a change. That was not to be. She was six feet from the door when the stranger entered. He stood tall in a cowboy hat and a long duster jacket. His blue jeans were worn, but no worse for wear. His shirt was faded by the sun, a Native American squash blossom necklace hung from his neck. The odd thing about this stranger, he wore dark shaded sunglasses with side blinders. The same type worn by those who were vision impaired. He walked toward Rosie with an air of confidence, with no type of help, so blindness was ruled out immediately.

"I was just about to close up; can I help you stranger?" she asked.

He grunted with dissatisfaction. "Was hoping to have a quick drink. Maybe a meal. Had a long journey, but I don't want to trouble you. Is there any other place hereabouts that may offer either?"

Her heart wouldn't let her turn away from someone in need. Plus, it wouldn't take but a few minutes to make a quick sandwich and put on a pot of coffee. She talked herself into accommodating him. The makeshift snack would take less time that it would to turn the open sign around on the door to the flip-side, which read "closed."

"Well, come on in then. Take a seat at the bar. I'll whip you up a scrambled egg and pepper sandwich. Won't take over five minutes to get a pot of coffee going if that's okay?"

He winced at the coffee. "Actually, ma'am, if it's okay with you, you can hold the coffee. I was hoping for something with a little more of a stiff kick. That is, if you don't mind?"

She grinned, understanding his request. "Sure, grab a seat at the bar."

Rosie met him from the other side of the bar, picking up a bottle of whiskey. "This do it for you?"

"That will do just fine."

She poured him a drink, leaving the bottle, then disappeared into the kitchen to tend to the sandwich. Johnny retired to bed for the evening, but Kat was still awake, sweeping up the seating area of the tavern. Putting down the broom, she followed the stranger to his seat, taking the one closest to him. Kat reached for her deck of tarot cards and started shuffling them.

The stranger glanced around the bar. In front of him was a large mirror lined with bowling trophies. Above the mirror, a sign hung. It read, "I am not a slow bartender. I am not a fast bartender. I am a half-fast bartender." The saying brought a smile to his face after being on the road for the past several days, with minimal stops allowing an hour or two of sleep each night. While busy perusing the bar's décor, he didn't notice Kat sitting next to him.

"Hey. My name's Katlyn, but everyone around here calls me Kat. You got a name, stranger?"

He took the drink of whiskey down in one swallow. Glancing over his shoulder at her, he didn't respond. His demeanor didn't dissuade her attempt to talk with him. The deck would help. She stopped shuffling, drawing three cards, lining them up in a row.

"Let's see if I can figure it out by the cards," she paused with another thought. "Anyone ever tell you that you look a lot like Sam Elliot, the movie actor? A little older, rougher, more distinguished, but Sam Elliot all the same. Ever see that movie Lifeguard? Saw it two years ago. Got carded, but that happens a lot. People think I'm a lot younger that I am. Guess it has its advantages."

One-by-one she flipped the cards over. "The center card here is the King of Swords. That's you, well, where you are presently. This tells me you're in power, ruling from a place of authority and respect."

The stranger snickered. Kat continued regardless. She was used to the response by those who didn't particularly prescribe to the art of divination.

"You stand in your own truth with deep conviction, driven more by your intellect as opposed to your emotions. You look at situations with impartiality and maintain balance."

She suddenly had his attention. Kat flipped the card over on the left.

"Fun, the death card. Many people fear this one. This position represents your past. Although scary looking, it's a natural change card. One major phase of your life ended; another one began. Change can intimidate, but as the king of swords, you welcome these kinds of things, thrive on it even. This position tells me the change may not have been of your choosing, but you know you can't go back."

The last card flipped over by her hand. Judgement.

"This one is your future. If you follow the current path that you are on and nothing changes."

Before she could explain the card, Rosie reemerged from the kitchen with a plate containing the sandwich, a small cucumber salad, and a slice of apple. She put it down in front of the stranger.

"Here you go, service with a smile."

The stranger reached into his duster, handing her a Morgan silver dollar. He apologized for offering the old coin. Rosie grabbed his hand before he could return it to his pocket to pay her with more contemporary currency.

"Wait a minute there. Is that real?" she asked.

He handed her the heavy coin. She examined it closer, as did Kat, who was interested in her aunt's fascination with the coin. Rosie looked at the date stamp, 1886. Flipping the silver dollar over, she noticed the "CC" on the bottom of the coin, under the eagle.

"Carson City, huh? This is pretty rare, cowboy. You wanna make sure you keep hold of this one."

Realizing she held more than a casual interest in rare coins, he placed it in her hand, closing her fingers over it.

"Consider it payment for your kind hospitality," he said.

Aunt Rosie looked closer at the man's face. His eyes were obscured by the glasses, which was a major obstacle. As a barkeep and purveyor of a place of hospitality, she was required to listen to more stories than she cared to hear. It came with the job. This man was different, though. From the moment he walked in, she could tell he had a story. The kind of story she wanted to hear. One she would remember for however many years she had left on earth.

"You got a name, stranger?" she asked.

"The name is Sturgess, ma'am. Colt Sturgess."

Back in Kinston, the convoy of tractor trailers sat still on the street. Most of the fair attendees returned to their amusements following the blast of the air horns. Whatever was happening, it was none of their concern. They were mistaken. The police chief was the second on the scene. He approached the lead truck. Their windows were all tinted dark. How peculiar. Constable Michael J. Babin, husband of Rosie and co-owner of the tavern that sat empty other than the one wayward stranger presently, converged with the chief from around the front of the rig.

"What do you make of this, Pistol Pete?" the chief asked. Pistol Pete was Michael J.'s nickname from years on the force.

"I don't know, chief. Seems odd to me. No doubt caution is in order here. I'll cover you."

The chief tapped on the door of the lead truck. "Hey you in there. What's your business here? Road has limited access because of the fair. No parking unless you have business!"

The fair's manager, Earl Hollister, joined the two. "These aren't mine, chief. We're all set up for the weekend."

"Um, hm. Figured as much."

Again, the chief tapped on the door. This time, the window of the truck rolled down slowly by the crank handle. A face appeared. It was Berty, one of the contractor's that Olath hired. He peered out at the chief.

"You in charge of this convoy?" asked the chief.

"Yes, sir."

"What business you have here? You lost?"

Berty reached across the seat. This prompted both the chief and Pistol Pete to draw their weapons.

"Nice and slow there, governor!" Michael J. warned Berty, as he couldn't see what the truck driver was reaching for, the view obscured by the dark glass.

Berty threw up his hands, slowly passing a piece of paper through the window.

"Here's my bill of lading, chief. Special delivery for the town of Kinston."

With the distraction from the officials on the driver's side of the truck, fair crowd on the right, the opening of the passenger doors on each of the twelve tractor trailers went unnoticed, except for Jud and Rhonda, who watched the odd circumstances. From the cab of the lead truck, a long, spindly, pale character slithered out of the door. The second two trucks, the doors opened simultaneously as two chubby figures in matching baseball caps appeared, moving in perfect symmetry. Four through twelve, clowns deployed from the trucks like circus performers. All twelve of the passengers crept towards the back of their respective trailers.

"Huh. What do you think that's all about?" asked Jud.

"No clue. Weirdest thing I've ever seen. Some sort of performers maybe?" she answered.

Colt Sturgess finished his sandwich, along with half the bottle of whiskey. Rosie and Kat watched him intensely. He didn't speak after presenting his name. Kat broke her staring, figuring it may take the pressure off the man. That may get him talking a bit. She shuffled her cards, laying them out once more. King of swords, death, judgement. Again, she drew the same three. She ran off to grab a different deck from her satchel on the floor next to the jukebox, shuffled them, cut them, and drew from the new deck. King of swords, death, judgement. She slammed the deck down on the bar.

"I don't get it! Been reading cards for going on ten years now. Whenever I look at you, Mr. Sturgess, I draw the same three cards."

He poured another glass of whiskey, swallowing it down, handing Rosie back the bottle. "You don't say."

"There's no explaining this. The odds are unthinkable. Infinitesimal."

He said nothing, just swiveled in the bar chair before getting to his feet.

"You sure you're okay to drive out there after all you've had to drink?" asked Rosie.

"Oh, that's nothing. Just wet my whistle." He smiled, placing another Morgan silver dollar on the bar. "Don't spend that all in one place now."

"Well, you are welcome to hang around here a bit. My husband is down at the fair over in Kinston. Won't be back for at least another hour. Not a proposition, mind you, I'm far past the age for that. Just wouldn't mind the company and a little uneasy being alone with the kids here at night when he's not home."

"For the millionth time, I'm not a kid. I'm twenty-four freaking years old!" Kat reminded her.

"No thank you, but much obliged." He walked to the door, pausing, "Actually, tell me about this town, Kinston. How far is it and what direction?"

"You got business there?" Aunt Rosie asked.

"Perhaps. Haven't decided yet," he answered.

"Pull up a seat."

Rosie disappeared into the backroom, taking the phone book out of the utility drawer, ruffling through some papers. She found the map and returned to Sturgess, who took a seat at a table. He was fiddling with one of the score pegs on the euchre board. Laying out the map before him on the table, Rosie wondered if he could make out any of the details with the dark glasses. She tried to see past the blinders on the side of the rims, but no luck.

"Here we are in Shermer. If you follow the service road out to interstate nineteen, head northeast, about thirty-seven miles, exit forty-five to route nine eighty. That will get you to the western part of town. Hang a left at the first light, follow the signs for downtown. Easy to miss, just a little burb." Rosie took a seat, crossing her arms. "What exactly are you looking for, Mr. Sturgess?"

After pausing, he motioned to Kat, still shuffling and pulling the same three cards at the bar.

"Like the girl said, 'judgement.'"

Jud and Rhonda continued watching the strange characters maneuver into positions behind each of the semis. The line forming in front of the demolition car grew impatient.

"Hey buddy, stop gawking. I'm up for some smash up derby!" said the next customer. His friends roared at his mildly amusing joke as he flexed his non-existent muscles.

"Oh yeah, right?" Jud switched mindfulness to his customers, handing the jokester one of the new sledgehammers. "Fifty cents a whack, three for a dollar, ten bucks, and you get to keep whatever you knock off."

The man handed Jud ten dollars. "Here you go, sport! I'm takin' me a souvenir home!"

He rushed the junk car and began flailing mercilessly after his first blow missed the mark, sending the sledgehammer to the ground. Jud and Rhonda laughed, as did the man's friends. Although offering the appearance of a good time, slamming a hammer into a welded piece of steel took a bit of calculation, or the experience could be painful.

While the jokester continued his assault on the vehicle, Jud watched the convoy. All the passengers who took up position outside of the trailer doors were just standing there. Straight and erect as if they were in a military formation. What were they doing?

On the driver's side of the trucks, the chief took the bill of lading from Berty, handing it to the mayor, who joined the group along with Fred Allen. The mayor flipped through the papers, reading the signature at the bottom of each.

"Who's this Professor Olath character?" he asked. "Never heard of him."

None of the men gathered around him ever heard the name. Kinston was a small, close-knit community where everyone knew everyone. Strangers stood out. Just then, Jud noticed the passenger from the front cab, the lanky one, remove something from his shirt. Something shiny. He blew a whistle, which sent each of the others into motion, unlatching the trailer doors. Each swung open, pouring hell onto the streets of Kinston.

Small, dark creatures spilled from the backs of the trucks, moving across the curbs and into the unaware crowd of fair attendees like a massive shadow. From his vantage point, it looked like a swarm of... he didn't know what. They scurried along the ground on two legs but carried their momentum forward at superhuman speed, covering the parking lot across from the borough building. Screams roared out. A few at first, becoming a chorus in seconds. The first eleven trucks released their payloads. The unaffected part of the crowd turned to witness the commotion, not yet alarmed. As the hoard of dark creatures made their way towards them, they ran. By then, it was too late.

At the entrance to the fair, Emma flirted with Billy. It was looking as if it were turning into her night as well. The two never heard the whistle over the noise of the amusement row, nor saw darkness closing in faster than they could be expected to react. By the time she saw the first wave of creatures, there wasn't even enough time to process what she was seeing. There was only the pain of razor-sharp teeth, a chill, then darkness.

The creatures ripped into the legs of their quarry, preventing any peaceful escape. The clowns followed closely behind, tagging certain people who succumbed to the attack of the swarm with what appeared to be pin flags from a golf course, driven directly through the torsos of the fallen. Each was numbered. What they signified; Jud didn't know. The only thing he knew for certain was they need to run and now. He grabbed his rucksack, flicking the release lever, and slung it over his head.

He called for Rhonda, grabbing her hand. "Let's go!"

"What's happening?"

"I don't know, but it's not good. Let's find dad!"

The two sprinted across the bottom of the lot, scooting behind the shrubbery that hugged the bank. Jud last saw Fred Allen walking towards the other side of the convoy, then behind the side he couldn't see. As they cleared the front of the trucks, they barely avoided the onrush of the mob streaming down Main Street, the creatures in hot pursuit. They barely made it. Forcing their way around the bumper of the lead tractor trailer, Jud's blood froze cold. It was a nightmare.

On the ground lay the mayor, both chiefs, Earl Hollister, Constable Michael J. Babin, a man with a Peterbilt hat and his father, Fred Allen. All eviscerated, cold and lifeless. Up ahead, two overweight twins were pulling one driver from the cab of truck number eight, slicing through his midsection with the alacrity of a butcher. Jud was paralyzed. Stunned. That bond that he so longed for, the bond he felt was a work in progress with his father, was nothing more than a visage of emptiness as he looked into his father's lifeless eyes.

"Come on, Jud. We have to go. We really do. I know this is totally screwed up, but if we don't move now, we're going to end up just like them."

Rhonda was doing her best to bring him out of his unexpected spiral of grief. This is the last thing she expected from this night. She knew it was the last thing Jud expected to see in his lifetime. Again, she pleaded.

"Jud! We gotta go!"

An enormous explosion on the outskirts of town added to the whirl-wind of chaos, but snapped Jud Allen from his temporary shock. It was the Western Penn Central Phone terminal office. He knew it well; it was on his delivery route and the only building out in that direction. Pretty much a vacant lot. Construction on the new commerce park was scheduled for next spring.

Looking down, he spied one of the glass-tubed cigars in his father's torn and blood-soaked shirt. He ran forward, retrieved it, then turned back to Rhonda. There were no tears yet. There would be a time. But not here or now. The town was ablaze with chaos as the pair struggled to cross the street to the back alley.

"I know a place. If we can get there. It should be safe; nobody knows about it except a couple of us that used to pry the grating off," he said.

Jud led Rhonda to the alleyway, sliding down the hill on their backsides just below the bakery. He grabbed onto an old sideways pole that stuck out of the ground about three feet. The break was timely as another four or five feet, they would have an eight-foot drop onto the side of the railroad tracks. Pulling her up the hill with one hand, she saw the grate he was talking about.

Taking out his handy Swiss army knife, he pulled out the blade that served as a pair of mini pliers. Jud twisted the makeshift safety lock, a twisted piece of wire that someone had since used to secure the grating. It swung open once the wire was loose. The couple scooted into the pipe, re-securing the wire from the inside.

They crawled through the pipe, which ended at a boarded-up entrance. Jud kicked it. Once, twice, the third time it fell to the floor. He dropped into the room first, then helped guide Rhonda to a sure footing. Picking up the wooden obstruction, he discovered it was nothing more than a pallet with a few extra boards nailed into it.

"Wait," he said.

Placing his rucksack on the ground, he searched the content. Retrieving a flashlight, he fiddled with the lens, sliding in the red-colored dampener. This gave them vision, but not cast any unwelcome attention from white light. A nifty little thing he picked up at the surplus store. Clicking on the flashlight, he checked the pipe they just exited. There were twin hooks on both sides near the top of the hole. A nail on the bottom that he kicked out laid on the floor. Lifting the pallet up, he hung it back on the hooks, but didn't dare draw any of the creatures to their location by banging the bottom nail back in. It would have to be enough. He was curious as to why it was nailed to the wall, more specifically, who nailed it to the wall, but that would be a mystery for later pondering.

Jud guided Rhonda to the shabby steps of the room that led up into the back area of the old bakery. It shut down two years ago, so he wasn't expecting anyone there. Crossing the dusty lobby, they continued their trek up another set of stairs. These were hidden by a dummy wall next to a long-neglected glass display counter.

"Nobody knows about this. I saw it by accident when I came in to get a black and white donut before school one morning. It's where the owners lived. Figured out how to open it once I started hanging out here," he said.

"You hang out here?"

"Yeah. Well, I used to. It's kind of my sanctuary. Everybody needs their space, ya' know?"

Rhonda nodded. She did, more than he was aware.

Sliding the panel open, the steps were revealed. She started up, while he secured the door behind them with an internal deadbolt, only accessible from their side. They reached the top floor of the old bakery. The moonlight shone through the windows of the room. It was obvious someone had been there, as they were clean, bordered by semi-new curtains. Some of the furniture remained, as was evidence that Jud set up a type of headquarters here, complete with a box of comics, chips, a few packages of now and later candy chews, and a case of strawberry soda. He expected a negative response, but Rhonda looked over his set up with amazement.

"This is so fucking cool. I mean, really. Wish I was hanging out with you then. This is a dream place."

Jud was shocked by her response. He, of course, was attracted to her physically and all the cool things Emma told him about her, but he never gotten to know more about her. Tonight was supposed to be that first step. Unfortunately for them both, it hadn't quite turned out the same way the day began.

"Shit. Emma. I wonder if she got out of there?" he asked.

It was the first time he thought about his best friend since they started to run. At the moment's chaos and shock of his father, his adrenaline gave a brief pause to prioritizing his thoughts. He hadn't even yet considered his mother and siblings. Mom was at home with his older brother, and his sister was volunteering over at the church. How far did this plague of death spread in the past several minutes?

Rhonda turned to him. She completely forgot about Emma in their rush to safety. This brought about her tears. "Oh, Jud. I hope so. I feel so guilty —"

"Don't. It's okay. Like you said. If we didn't move, we would have been the next victims."

He switched off the flashlight. Slowly, carefully, he approached the window. Screams continued to fill the night, but the sound of some sort of construction operation sounded as if it was taking place. Main street was strewn with dead bodies, either by the teeth of the creatures or the stampede of fair attendees fleeing the massacre. The tractor trailer at the end of the convoy pulled onto the grass in front of the borough building. A ramp led from the back of the trailer into the street. Several construction loaders were in motion, scooping up the flagged bodies, loading them into the back of the truck at the eleventh position in the convoy. That tractor trailer moved forward, positioned next to the others. Bulldozer followed closely behind, pushing the untagged bodies into piles. The clowns worked busily, setting the makeshift burial piles into flames with an accelerant from sprayers they wore on their backs similar to Jud's rucksack. Whoever they were, they were extremely well rehearsed, organized, planned out and efficient. Whatever they were doing with the confiscated bodies was a mystery.

Rhonda joined him to watch the scene below them up the street. "What do you think they're doing?"

"Shh!" he said, pulling her to the floor.

Below them, two of the clowns wandered the alley with a flashlight of their own.

"Why do we even look for these things? Those strays could be a hundred miles away by now," said the first clown.

"You see how they spring out of the back of the trucks when we let 'em out?" asked the second.

"Like bats out of hell. Just what they are too. Let's get back up. Nothing down here," answered the first.

Jud sat, looking deeply into Rhonda's eyes. Maybe for the first time he really saw her. There was a sadness, a loneliness that transcended the situation at hand. His intuition knew it beyond knowing. Not once did she express any concern or worry about anyone other than Emma. Curious? She turned to meet his eyes. Rhonda Coulter was crying hard. It was time for Jud Allen to release his sorrow as well.

FRED TERLING

Chapter Five

"You can take the map with you, if need be," Aunt Rosie said, offering the folded paper.

He smiled back at her, tipping his hat. "That's quite alright, ma'am. Memory is like a steel trap. Much obliged, though. Thanks again."

He stood, crossing the planks on the floor, a few squeaked under his weight. During the day, with the rush, they weren't noticeable. Michael J. would have to fix that. Rosie and Kat watched the man reach the front door. He never turned back for a last goodbye, just opened the door, disappearing into the night. Rosie lit up another Kool. Exhaling, she turned to Kat.

"Well, that certainly was interesting. Wish he would have opened up a bit. Strange, don't ya think?"

Her niece, by adoption, slammed down the cards again. The same three cards. Without facing her, she aired her frustration. "'Strange' isn't the word."

Colt paused under the dome of a starry night. It was clear and quiet. Taking a step towards his Harley, he halted. Something wasn't right. He could feel it in the folds of darkness surrounding him. Sturgess spun around in time to see several compact forms skittering up the downspout of Rosie's, crossing the roof. Silence settled in once more. The bike was only two meters away from where he parked it. In less than a second, he closed the distance, grabbing the saddlebags off the pillion. Another two seconds he rushed the front door, entering to the surprise of Kat and Rosie.

"Forget something?" asked Rosie.

"Kill the lights!" he answered.

"Excuse me?"

"Turn the lights off. No time to explain. Then get to someplace safe. Someplace with no windows."

He dropped the saddlebags on one table, unbuckling the right one, retrieving two single-action, pearl handled peacemaker pistols and a bandolier of speed loaders. Slinging them around his neck and shoulders, Colt focused on the door.

"I'm sorry, Mr. Sturgess. Although my husband served in the army and we support the second amendment, no guns in the place. Firm rule!"

Colt spun around to face her. "I can appreciate that, ma'am, but in the next minute all hell is about to break loose in here and if you don't get to some place safe, you're only gonna be in my way. Not in me to be rude, but if you wanna make it through this night, you'll heed my warning. I'd be much obliged."

Aunt Rosie stood still, crossing her arms. Noone was going to tell her what to do in her own diner. Her attention was distracted by the sounds of something audibly scampering across the outside of the roof. Colt moved directly in front of her.

"For the last time, move!"

In the doorway to the stairs leading up to the living quarters next to the right side of the bar, Johnny Ellis appeared, wiping the sleep from his eyes. He caught Rosie's attention.

"John Paul, what are you doing awake?" she asked. John Paul was the name used by her when he was in trouble or required attention.

"I couldn't sleep. There's something on the roof. Can't be a sandy claus, it's not snowing," he answered.

At that moment, the windows to the right and left of the front doors smashed in from the outside. They were no longer alone. Colt took aim at the overhead lights. Three well-aimed shots took them out. He had the darkness he requested. Sturgess shouted his request one last time.

"Get to someplace safe!"

Rosie grabbed Johnny and Kat by the hand. They ducked under the bar flap just in time as the creature that awakened Johnny crashed down on top of it. A black, gangly arm reached for them unsuccessfully, scarring the underneath wood with deep scratches intended for their flesh. Colt fired again, but the creature leapt away into the safety of the shadows. Rosie continued with the group, crawling to the kitchen. Only a few more feet. Sturgess covered their movement with several more shots above the bar, shattering bottles above but behind them, calculating their progression. Seeing the door open, close, then hearing the bolt latch behind the trio, he knew they were safe. Good thing, as he was out of ammunition in his right revolver. In a singular motion, he released the cylinder on the peacemaker, spun it and seated the rounds, allowing the speed loader to drop to the floor.

Colt Sturgess stepped backwards into the shadows. Lowering his respiration, he entered their world. He didn't fear it, or them. Now it became a waiting game. They expected easy prey, but they miscalculated. By the sound of it, there were three creatures in the bar somewhere. Nothing moved. Who would blink first? The silence settled in. There was a creak from the floorboards, then another. Sturgess looked down in the darkness to see small streaks of light permeating the boards. They were packed tight, but his vision wasn't that of a normal man. The smallest flaw he could detect. This flaw wasn't the sound of the creaking floorboards. He dealt with these creatures before. They were fast, superhuman fast. By the time there was an audible sign, he knew they were feet beyond that location. No, this give-away was the tiny dust particles that trailed them through the small emanations of light. Those he could track. Another creak.

Colt spun around, firing three shots four feet to the right center of the sound. A scream cut through the air. Not quite animal, certainly not human, disturbing enough for Rosie, Johnny, and Kat to cringe behind the kitchen door. The creature dropped to the floor, trembling before bursting into flames. Fortunately, it wasn't the type of fire that would engulf the tavern. This fire had a simpler purpose, reduce the creature to ash. That is precisely what it did.

Two left, Colt thought.

The waiting game resumed as Sturgess melted back into the shadows on one knee. Watching. Waiting.

In the kitchen, Rosie looked at her two children. Adopted or not, she was their protector. This was also her bar. She and Michael J. invested their life savings in it. Whatever was happening on the other side of the door, she would not let this strange cowboy with the silver dollars defend her turf. She looked around the kitchen for something she could use. That's when it caught her eye next to the sink. It was what she used to make the stranger's scrambled eggs and peppers. Moving towards it, Kat released her. Johnny did not.

"John Paul, let go of me. You're nearly a foot bigger than I am. No need to cling to me like a little baby!"

"But I'm scared Aunt Rosie."

"I know you are, but there's no reason to be. Remember what Uncle Mike told you about fear?"

"Yup, not but fear itself." He said with an air of pride for remembering it.

Often things got a little cloudy for Johnny, causing him to wander off in his mind, creating irrational emotional spurts like he had with Gorgar. This was her way of grounding him by extinguishing any wanderings into uncontrollable emotional outbursts.

"Good. Now sit down over there and grab a beef jerky. I know you love them," she said.

He complied, popping open the top of the plastic cannister, selecting the perfect one. Johnny sat down.

"Can I have a grape soda too?" he asked.

She nodded at Kat, who retrieved one from the small refrigerator they kept in the kitchen for go-to snacks when they were busy cooking. Kat popped it open on the edge of the counter and handed it to him. Rosie shot her a glance of disapproval. Even in this emergency of high duress, she hated when Kat opened bottles on the counter's edge.

Rosie picked up an eight-inch cast-iron skillet, then walked slowly with unstoppable purpose towards the door. Kat reacted immediately with a panicked whisper to not draw any notice from what was still in progress in the tavern.

"Are you crazy? Where do you think you're going?"

Rosie looked over her shoulder as she unlatched the top lock. "Just bolt up after I leave."

Kat rushed to the door, but was a second too late as Aunt Rosie slid through the opening, disappearing behind the bar.

<hr />

"What the hell?" Colt saw the crease in the door. Someone stepped out from the other side, now crouched down behind the bar.

"Shit…" he said.

Immediately, one creature sprung at Aunt Rosie. With a blow that the mighty Casey would have appreciated, she swung with all the strength her five foot three, one hundred ten-pound frame could summon. The blow sent the ugly thing airborne across the bar, landing on the pinball machine, shattering the glass.

"Gorgar, beat me."

Lights flickered, going haywire until the machine cycled through all seven of its pre-programmed phrases to fade out with the lights and bells that accompanied. Colt followed up with two shots to the creature's head when it sat up wearily to recover from the blow. It dropped back onto the machine, catching on fire, transforming into a pile of ash. He waved at her with a mixture of desperation and anger. What the hell was this woman thinking? Rosie smiled at Colt, giving him the thumbs up before slowly sinking back behind the bar.

A dirty shame about the machine, doubt the dealer would replace a prototype. Rosie thought

Johnny loved playing the thing. Maybe she and Mike could get a different source of amusement for him. Christmas was four months away.

Silence returned. Two down, one to go. To his surprise, Sturgess heard something. It was faint at first but gotten louder. Much louder. Tuning in senses like a radio receiver, he zeroed in on the location. The thing had a heartbeat. This was new, something not previously encountered on a quest that remained hidden. As he moved closer, he heard the rhythm of it quicken. It was afraid. That, too, was something new.

Kicking over a table for cover, he locked the sight of the pistol on it. The moonlight streaming through the broken window granting perfect alignment and a sight picture. He hesitated. Something deep within him felt sadness. Pity even. Was this his genuine emotion or was this that thing people called empathy? For the first time, he was afforded the opportunity to see one of these things up close and personal. Typically, they moved so quickly, decaying even quicker. There wasn't any time to see what these creatures looked like beyond a mere glance.

There it sat. Wrapped up in dark, dry skin. Wide eyes. Human eyes. Bald, chubby like a baby, despite the elongated arms and legs, tipped with long black nails. The thing smiled up at Colt with sharp teeth. Was it asking for mercy? There was something in its eyes. A kind of desperation he saw in his dreams but couldn't place. Whatever it was he saw, it sent a ripple of emotions that overwhelmed him, causing him to lower the aim of his peacemaker. That's when the thing leaped at him.

Colt Sturgess read in a book somewhere during his travels a quote, "Opportunity is a haughty goddess who wastes no time with those who are unprepared." He liked it. Preparation was something that he hadn't done on the night he was attacked so many years prior. That quote was befitting this situation as the cherubic creature he hesitated to kill seconds earlier attempted to sink its teeth deep into his arm. Instead, a loud screech vibrated across the bar when the razor-sharp teeth encountered a metal plate, splintering them off landing on the floor.

Besides the twin pistols in his hands, Colt fashioned a set of metal bracers, greaves, and a leather chest plate after encountering these same creatures over the years. "Necessity is the mother of invention," was another quote that Sturgess may or may not have been familiar with. What was empathy transformed into purpose as he held the struggling thing by the throat with his left hand.

"Kill it!" Rosie shouted from behind the bar.

Sturgess continued to examine the creature as it writhed in his grip. Its resistance became less and less animated until the oversized head on the thing slumped forward. To his surprise, it did not burst into flames. He dropped it to the floor.

Jud Allen sat silently in his bakery sanctuary. Rhonda was fast asleep on the couch, abandoned by the previous owners. She was dreaming. He wondered about what. His arms were wrapped around his knees, rolling the glass cigar tube between his fingers, trying to summon the memories of the last moments together with his father. Would things have been different if both knew that was to be the very last moment? Streaks of blood and a singular bloody fingerprint were all that was left of any dreams he had of a future with the man that so many people adored, but he struggled to reach.

He was positioned at an angle to both stand watch over Rhonda and observe the madness in the streets below. The commotion died down for the moment. Two tractor trailers pulled out, leaving the blood-soaked streets of the town he called home. The bodies continued burning as the bulldozer pushed human kindling for the bonfire. Smoke filled the air, limiting his view of the killing field at the heart of the fair. Only the edges of Main Street were visible through the headlights of the tractor trailers that delivered death.

Rhonda stirred, seeing him in the moonlight holding vigil. She extended her arms towards him, flexing her fingers to come to her. He wearily complied. Laying down next to her, she placed her head on his shoulder resting on his chest. Closing her eyes once more. Jud stared up at the water-stained ceiling. What would they do next?

An hour passed at Rosie's. Kat swept up the glass and ash from the encounter. Johnny replaced the light bulbs shot out by Colt. The two broken windows bracketing the front door still needed tending. There was plastic sheeting in the storage shed that the family used for a small hot house for tomatoes planted every spring. Ironically, the hothouse was topped by old windowpanes to maximize the sun's potential for the growing process. Currently, they needed the sheeting to replace the panes of the tavern. Aunt Rosie brought out a pot of coffee, sitting it on the table between the four people who had just experienced an unexpected horror together. Michael J. was overdue. They waited.

Rosie leaned forward. With all that just happened, it was time to get answers from the stranger, regardless of his apprehension to talk. His kind demeanor no longer sufficed. It was time for answers.

"So, Mr. Sturgess. You going to explain what the hell just happened?"

Colt took a swig of coffee, setting the cup back down carefully on a cardboard coaster whose brand had long been washed away from the condensation caused by too many bottles. He felt a lot like that.

"Well, ma'am, for that to happen, you're gonna have to suspend belief about what you know about some things."

"I'm suspending," said Rosie.

Kat leaned in as her interest was ignited, as anything she experienced to date paled by comparison. Colt hesitated. If these creatures were this close, he knew time was not on his side. Finding the source was imperative. The longer he delayed, the greater the chance the object of his vision quest would escape.

"Time's kind of pressing, right now, ma'am."

Rosie pulled Michael J.'s service revolver from her apron, cocked back the hammer and aimed for his chest. Kat gasped immediately as she knew of her aunt's fear of guns. She wasn't even sure she knew how to use it. Johnny didn't react at all, simply kept moving Kat's tarot cards around in patterns that only made sense to him.

"Actually, Mr. Sturgess. Right now, we have all the time in the world. I already tried calling the Kinston Police Department, but nobody answered, which is a cause for concern on its own, particularly because my husband is working with them tonight, long overdue, and that's the only way I can get a hold of him. My bar has been pretty banged up by monsters that showed up only after you drifted in. I've got a pinball machine that can't be replaced with a stack of silver dollars, and I don't know a damned thing about you. I ask you this, Mr. Colt, if that is even your real name, what brings you here?"

Johnny broke into the question, standing up abruptly, causing the chair he was sitting in to fall backward on the floor. The gun made him nervous, causing him to react by drawing a familiar memory to light. It was how he coped with stress.

"I like to go fishin'. I went fishin' once with my neighbors. Stepped on a stick in the mud and it flew mud in my eye. It stung. I fixed it though for next time. Got some goggles from my dad's workshop. Still have 'em. I can go get 'em and show you, if you want?" asked Johnny.

Rosie kept the service revolver aimed at Colt. Johnny's sudden interruption didn't distract her purpose.

"Sit back down, John Paul. You can show us later," she said.

Colt leaned forward, tipping his hat back. His posture was almost mocking, inviting her to squeeze the trigger.

"Well, ma'am. You deserve that much. How much of it you believe? That's a different matter."

He poured himself another cup of coffee, took a long draw, setting it back down on the coaster.

"Not that shooting me would have any effect. I've been shot more times than I can count over the years and I'm still walking. May have been easier if I wasn't. Without draggin' it out, my story starts in 1886, a small homestead outside of Carson City, Nevada. My father made a bit of money prospecting during westward expansion by opening trading posts across the west. Eagle Station trading post was his first in the area, that was in…pardon me ma'am, some details are fuzzy. Started a family there. I worked the farm from the time I could hold a pitchfork. Eventually, I marred —"

"Wait, you expect me to believe you are over a hundred years old?"

He took another drink of coffee. "Like I said, ma'am. Suspension of belief. Should I continue, or are you going to squeeze that trigger now?"

Rosie released the hammer, tucking the gun back into her apron. "Hell wasn't even loaded anyhow. I don't know how to do that. Go on ahead, Mr. Sturgess. Interested in seeing where this is going."

"Lizzy. That was her name. She was the first and only woman to sweep me off my feet. Taught the kindergarten at the schoolhouse. I worked on the farm. We talked often about starting a family, but time didn't permit, and fate had other plans. Funny thing about time. Doesn't matter how much stuff you have, can't buy time and it runs in short supply. Now I have more than I need, but nothing to do with it."

He paused. This was difficult for him. It was the first time he spoke about this to anyone, let alone strangers. Perhaps it was the kindness of the barkeeper with the pistol who made him a sandwich. Maybe it was the need to explain why her tavern she invested her life savings in was in disarray. Could it just be the time to unburden himself of the load he carried for over a century? The story continued.

"One spring morning, it was a Saturday, that much I remember. Lizzy was hanging laundry. I had just come in from milking the cows. We had a head of six. A wagon pulled up. Long, lanky fellah with a caravan pulled up, asking for water for his horses. The helping folks we were, we happily obliged. Only proper to help strangers. It was the Christian thing to do. While the horse drank, the fellah opened up the side of his wagon. He was one of those potion sellers that made his way from town to town. Wasn't unfamiliar with them as they came by the trading post to sell their wares, but they were more of a nuisance than anything else. They peddled mostly colored water. Lizzy though, she found the man amusing with the tale he spun about the elixir of life he discovered. With our troubles conceiving, it particularly interested her. She was downright giddy at the possibility. Another quote I've come by in my travels that holds water, 'false hope kills more readily than bitter truth.' Didn't know that then."

Johnny suddenly stopped fidgeting with the cards. He lined up the same three Kat drew all night. "Bingo!" Jumping to his feet, he danced around gleefully holding the three cards.

"Give me those back, brat!" She gave chase until he eventually dropped them. He took up residence on the floor beneath the destroyed pinball machine.

Rosie jumped to her feet to scold the rascal. "John Paul, settle down and now. If you will not listen to the story, go upstairs and watch television."

"But he's done, Aunt Rosie!"

She knew he possessed a strange type of intuition that was unexplainable. Knowing that, she turned to Colt Sturgess, who tipped his cup towards her.

"The boy is right. Don't know what happened next. Mind's a blur. Woke up three days later on a pile of charred wood in my birthday suit. Pardon me, ma'am, don't mean to offend. There was no sign of Lizzy and the house was ransacked. After getting my bearings over the next several days, took my cattle to auction, boarded up the house and set off looking for the caravan. There was no sign of my beloved. The only thing I could go on was what I read on the side of the man's wagon, *Professor Olath's Elixir of Vitae*."

———

The first two tractor trailers from Kinston pulled into the stockyard of Chooch Family Farm and Dairy. Serving the local community with dairy goods and beef products for the past century, Eli Chooch bought it at the turn of the century. He prided himself on staying ahead of the technological advances by putting profits back into the farm. Workers were happy because Eli also ensured they made a living wage, sharing in the benefits the farm offered.

Every autumn, Mr. Chooch opened the farm for day tours, hayrides and one of the most formidable pumpkin patches in the state. It was a three-day affair that ended with a costume contest, fresh baked pies, hot cider, punctuated with games for every age. The farm was a bit off the main highway, but worth a day trip for those looking for a memorable experience. No such celebration would take place this year.

Frick and Frack exited the rigs as soon as they stopped. Blood dripped from beneath the door of the first trailer as Frick swung open the door. He was baptized by a spray of residual blood clinging to the inside. Frack laughed hysterically.

"Shut up, you're —"

"—not going to drive the loader first!"

"I am so! You —"

"—don't even know how!"

After the ramp was lowered, Frick and Frack ascended the blood drenched platform, slipping and sliding as they had outside the corridor to Olath's herringbone parlor. Frick took his seat in the loader, scooping up a wooden pallet securing the bodies that were marked on the initial attack. The flags impaled in the torsos of the victims waved from the movement of the loader backing the vehicle down the ramp. Olath emerged from a Kinston police car that served as the truck's escort.

"Safely, safely, you buffoons! These are the most precious of subjects. They require a delicate hand in transport. Ensure they reach the parlor in a condition most prudent of their importance," said Olath.

Frick shrugged to Frack. Neither understood what the professor was talking about, but they knew where to take the cargo. Walking past the front trailer, Professor Olath heard the screams, sobs, and pounding on the walls from inside the temporary prison of Kinston citizens he captured alive. He pounded back on the side of the external wall.

"No fear, my lovelies. A little longer. Your destinies await a higher purpose. Soon, your fears will be rewarded!"

On the loading dock, a dark figure awaited in the shadows, avoiding the light, both natural and artificial. Olath enthusiastically approached her. He boasted as he walked.

"There is only success to convey. You will be pleased with our selections, and this is only the initial delivery."

Elizabeth stepped forward into the moonlight, her face remained hidden behind the black veil.

"Let's hope so. Time is waning. The sensations in my hands and feet are disappearing by the minute. Do you have one for me?" she asked.

"Of course. She brims with the essence of youth. I chose her to satiate your personal satisfaction," he answered.

"Show me!"

Olath led Elizabeth by her lace gloved hand down the ramp of the loading dock, past the two tractor trailers to the trunk of the police cruiser. The vehicle rocked as whoever or whatever was in the truck was putting up one hell of a fight to get out. A muffled voice rang out. This wasn't a scream of fear like the others. It was a voice of defiance.

"Let me out, you creepy motherfucker. I'll kick your ass all the way back to wherever you came from. I'm gonna rain down a shower of pain on you and all your little clown buddies. LET ME OUT!"

Beneath her veil, Elizabeth smiled. "I like this one."

Olath bowed as he inserted the key in the latch, releasing the trunk lock. Up she popped, blood streaked down her face. She gasped for a fresh breath of night air. Looking up, she saw Professor Olath and the cloaked Elizabeth. Looking down, they saw Emma Adams.

Chapter Six

"Doesn't tell me why you look so good for over a hundred years old or about those things that wrecked my bar." Rosie hadn't finished the interrogation.

Colt stood up. "I can tell you what I know, which ain't much on most of those subjects, but if you don't mind, I'd be much obliged if you could point me to the facilities? Nature's calling after all this coffee."

"So, you can still pee?" Kat asked.

"Yeah, without getting too personal, plumbing works," he answered.

Johnny jumped up from beneath the pinball machine. "I'll show him! I gotta get my fishing goggles, anyway."

Colt disappeared down the hall. Kat scooted her chair closer to Aunt Rosie, who lit up another Kool. The ashtray spilled over, enough room for only one or two more butts. She lowered her voice to a whisper.

"What do you think?"

"Hell, if I know. Never believed in the boogie man until tonight." Rosie reflected. "Something about this stranger in the cowboy hat. He tells you stuff without telling you stuff. You're the tarot card reader! You picking up that vibe?"

"I don't know what I'm picking up. Wouldn't believe any of this if I hadn't seen it for myself."

"Well, whatever he doesn't say will not sit well with your Uncle Mike, and you know how his Russian temper gets!"

Colt re-entered the main room, Johnny in tow. John Paul was wearing a pair of welding goggles that more resembled a scuba diving mask. Somehow, he could breathe through the thing. Instead of sitting down, Colt put one boot up on the chair, leaning forward to address the two women who were his unexpected hosts for most of the evening.

"Times a wastin', so I'll make this long story short. Been hunting this Olath for exactly a hundred years. Followed his trail by the things we killed here tonight. We call them 'ash tokers.'"

"The same Olath with the elixir wagon," Kat said.

Colt nodded.

Rosie picked up on the subtle change of pronouns. "You said 'we.' There are more of you?"

He rubbed the stubble on his chin. How to answer that? "Not exactly. Tracking the 'tokers awhile back, ran into a hunting party outside of Texarkana, a group of Marine vets from Vietnam, call themselves the Smoke Hunters. Caught wind of the things while hunting one weekend. A stray attacked one of their brothers in arms, didn't make it. What started out as a seek and destroy turned into a mission for the group. Damn fools, not sure what makes those guys tick, but they're the best trackers I've come across. But it's not like gathering intel is easy. Can't just walk into a bar like Rosie's and ask if you've seen any unusual creatures or a big, lanky guy named Olath who is easily as old as me or older, selling potions. Just not done anymore."

"Oh, you'd be surprised, Mr. Sturgess. They still pedal potions; they just have medical diplomas now," said Aunt Rosie.

He smiled.

Johnny finally addressed Colt through the thick lenses of the goggles. "You immortal? Can you die? How about Olath? How'd you pay for that motorcycle, not with silver dollars? You steal it?"

Turning to Johnny, Sturgess ran through them one at a time, hoping this would be the volley that would send him on his way. The clock on the wall was working against him. He was fueled with the burning desire to head into Kinston, or at least in that direction. If the last creature he killed by hand, wrapped up in a burlap potato sack by the door, represented how recently it was created, he would guess within the last couple of weeks. He was close this time.

"Not sure if I can die. Been the subjects of attempts, but I heal too damn fast. How? That I don't know. Just as I don't know why that fire I woke up in didn't reduce me to ashes. Olath? Still a mystery, but it's all I got and have carried to find out what happened to Lizzy."

Kat cut in. Her intuition told her otherwise. "You mean revenge. That's your judgement."

He did not acknowledge the observation, merely continued. "As for the Harley, no, I did not steal it. After leaving Eagle Valley, didn't have the heart to sell the farm in the case I found Lizzy. It was our home, after all. Dad took care of it until his passing. In 1918, after the War, young fellah contacted me through the postmaster in Carson City. Was interest in buying all my property to put up housing for returning soldiers. Seemed like a worthy use of the land. I made a tough call but accepted the offer. Carried the cash for a while, then converted it to gold and silver. Never made sense to me, the value of a pile of paper. Was the smart move, especially with what happened in the 1930s."

Sturgess looked around the party of three, wondering if he answered the questions to their satisfaction or was about to see Rosie brandishing the gun once more.

"Think I've done enough talkin' for your lifetime. If I haven't answered everything, I apologize, but I gotta get a move on. You can shoot me now, I reckon. It won't do anything but put a hole in your floor," he said.

Colt stood up, tossing his saddlebags over his shoulder. "Just one more thing. If you're not gonna shoot me, can I use your telephone? Somebody I gotta call."

Rosie sat back; arms crossed. She looked over at Kat, then at Johnny. Some things would have to remain a mystery, and this wasn't about listening to stories. She was holding the man up from whatever his inevitable endgame was.

"Sure, over there behind the bar, but you gotta do me one favor before you speed off on that motorcycle of yours. Help us get the sheeting up on these windows. Won't take more than a few minutes with your help and it might make explaining this all to my husband easier. Still don't know what the hell is keeping him."

Colt agreed. Picking up the receiver on the phone, a rapid screeching busy signal sounded off from the receiver handle. The sound was so loud, even the Babin-Ellis group heard it at the table, where Rosie was crushing out another cigarette.

"Damn, Horace Richards must have fallen asleep drunk at the switching station again. Try the payphone on the wall. It routes through the Charles County terminal," said Rosie.

"What was that you said about 'gossip?'" Kat asked with a broad grin.

"Not polite to question your elders," answered Rosie, lighting up another Kool.

Sturgess did as instructed. He fished out a small pack of survival matches from his boot. Dialing zero for the operator, he placed the long-distance call to the number on a dog tag that had been tucked away inside of the pack. Someone on the other end answered almost immediately. He relayed the alert that he and the Smoke Hunters pre-arranged should any of them track the 'tokers.

"Priority Alpha, repeat, Priority alpha. Targets engaged Shermer, Pennsylvania. En route to suspected drop zone in Kinston. ETA, zero two thirty."

There was a pause as the party on the other end of the receiver took down the information.

"You got all that, Mollie? Transmit that to the group, whatever way you all stay in touch. Thanks, I'm heading in. Sturgess signing out."

He hung up the phone, draping the saddlebags over the bar.

"Where's this plastic sheeting?"

———————

Emma climbed from the trunk of the squad car. She whipped her hair back out of her eyes. After inspecting Olath from head to toe, she turned to face Elizabeth.

"What's your story? Gothic wedding or funeral?"

Olath smiled. It wasn't often he encountered the fearless, particularly in their line of work.

"Courageous as a lion. No appearance of docile submission with this selection. Do you not agree?" he asked.

Elizabeth stepped forward, removing her veil. She was beautiful, yet flawed. Long locks of dark hair framed her face. A noticeable horizontal scar reached around the base of her neck as if it were strangling her beauty. The neckline of her dress plunged downward to her midsection. She stared into Emma's eyes. Olath was correct in his evaluation of this young woman. It seemed a pity to waste as an object of salvage.

"What is your name, child?" asked Elizabeth.

"First off, Morticia. I'm not a child unless you're blind. Second, my name only gets shared with friends. That you are not," she answered.

Emma looked around the farm and all the commotion that was taking place. She noticed Frick and Frack on the loader. Frack surrendered to the fact that he couldn't operate the equipment, but not his need to be next to his twin. They looked ridiculous jammed into the operator seat.

"What's the deal with the Hardy Boys? They Siamese twins or just butt buddies?" Emma crossed her arms in further sarcastic defiance.

Elizabeth once more made eye contact, forcing her influence onto the young girl. Correction, the young woman. Whatever she was attempting, Emma wasn't buying it.

"Either you stop staring at me or I'm going to sock you, then Uncle Fester over there. Not in the mood, especially after the night you all subjected me to."

Elizabeth turned to Olath. "Do you have another one?"

He nodded.

"Get the other ready. This one requires special handling. She's not going to the parlor. I have other plans."

Elizabeth moved in even closer, leaning in to give her a kiss. Emma jumped back.

"Look lady, whatever your gig is, sorry. I'm all about the boys. Nothing wrong with that lifestyle, but not for me."

Olath laughed, which drew Elizabeth's ire. She didn't need to say a word to him. Her expression projected a potential lethality that even he feared. There was a lot about her he feared. Stumbling backwards towards the door of the cruiser, a thought occurred. He straightened up as much as he could, emboldened to face Elizabeth.

"There is another option," he said.

She raised an eyebrow of curiosity.

"The new elixir. Although I would be remiss if I didn't inform you, it has yet to be successfully trialed on a participant."

It was Elizabeth who moved to the back of the cruiser, pulling the door off the hinges, yanking the young woman, who was bound and gagged, out of the back seat. In one motion, she swung her around, depositing her at Olath's feet.

"Test it and now on this one." It was a demand, not a request.

For the first time, Emma felt fear. The sheer strength of the woman was superhuman. Nobody has that kind of strength, nobody. It also occurred to her that at any point, this woman could have killed her with the simple snap of her wrist. Elizabeth turned back towards her. Whatever softness that was in her eyes earlier was gone. It was replaced with a rage that she could feel. The hair on the back of her arms stood up, followed by goosebumps.

"Walk with me," said Elizabeth. This, too, was a demand, not a request.

Emma complied this time.

Johnny led the group of four to the shed behind Rosie's. He was custodian of the keys and spent enough time in there to know where everything was. Having the compulsion to organize, Aunt Rosie and Uncle Mike put his desires to work as often as possible. Rushing to the large, weather-beaten oak door, he opened the lock, quickly disappearing inside, a good minute ahead of the others. He turned on the single bulb with the pull chain, actually a pull string, retrieving the roll of plastic sheeting. Hanging on a nail next to the door was a staple gun.

That would come in handy. Stepping back out under the moonlight, he confidently strode towards the group. Rosie held up her hand for him to stop. Terror washed across Kat's face. Colt shook his head in disappointment. Disappointment in himself for securing his peacemakers back in his saddlebags.

Perched on top of the shed was an ash toker. This one was big. Enormous, in fact. A grin spread out from the middle of its lips to the edge of its cheeks. A viscous slime dripped from its lips, pitter patting on the roof of the shed. John Paul did not know as he peered out at the group in front of him through the fishing goggles that obstructed any peripheral view. The creature just stared at them. It was savoring their fear. Colt entertained the thought of rushing back to retrieve his pistols, or at the very least, the katana sword he affixed to the left side of his 1973 Harley-Davidson FL Electra-Glide. He had abilities not disclosed. The big question was, would this creature follow the bait or stick to the slower targets of opportunity?

Time ran out on his contemplation as the creature leaped forward towards Kat. It had chosen. Instinctively, Rosie pushed her to the ground, jumping in the attacker's way. In a single motion, the thing severed the head off of the barkeeper as it grabbed her body, leaping in one bound up to the roof of the tavern. The blood sprayed across Johnny's goggles. Through the red mist slowly settling on his lenses, he let out a primal scream. A scream that drew the creature's focus on him next. It sprang down from the roof. Colt Sturgess moved to intercept but was too late. The creature brought down both of its hands towards Johnny Ellis, but Johnny reacted a fraction quicker, seizing the thing by the throat, spinning around, and slamming it hard into the ground. It cried out but failed compared to Johnny's wails of anger.

The young man jumped on the creature's chest, never relinquishing the demon's throat. He pounded his free fist into it. Repeatedly, the blows connected. He struck for the woman who had raised him the past ten years, and the other woman who had abandoned him long ago. Frustration rained down with each pummel for every time Gorgar had bested him, every time someone had dismissed his contributions as insignificant and the emotions welling up inside of him he neither understood nor identified, yet felt with the intensity of a raging inferno. This creature was a vessel of purification for a twenty-year-old boy who only connected with three people in the world. One of those laid beheaded three feet away. As the viscous black blood flew, the creature burst into flames. John Paul had killed it. Thoroughly. He continued punching through its burning body. Colt stepped in to get the boy off the smoldering body for his own safety. Kat pushed past him, grabbing Johnny's face between her hands, careful not to burn herself.

"John Paul! Johnny! Listen to me. Focus! It's time. Time to go in. Gorgar's waiting for you."

His head shot up, snarling at her as if a rabid dog was about to turn on its owner. "Gorgar's dead! So is Aunt Rosie!"

The thing beneath him turned to ash. He continued to strike until his fists drew back clumps of earth. Falling forward from exhaustion, his fishing goggle pushed up over his forehead. His focused was blurred. The wet grass beside him, covered with night dew, dispensed the tactile intervention needed to ground him. Closing his eyes, he breathed the night air. Calmness washed over him. Kat was on her knees beside him, her hand rested on his back. She exchanged glances with Colt. Standing up slowly, she reached down for Johnny's hand. He rose in the same manner that she stood as he was guided across the back lot, up the side walkway, and into the tavern. This wasn't the first time that she handled his distress. That was obvious.

Colt followed behind, giving the sister and brother space to recover. Retrieving his saddlebags, he removed one of peacemakers, tucking it into his belt, slinging a speed loader bandoleer around his neck and shoulder. He secured the bags to his Harley, then returned to the rear of the tavern. Having gone through this experience dozens, maybe hundreds of times, it never got easier. Innocent people falling victim to the random attacks of these creatures. Good people. Well-intentioned people. Aunt Rosie was one of those. Here one minute, gone the next.

There was no rhyme or reason to it. It's just what it was. The life he chose to pursuit.

Why he was spared from falling prey to fate was anyone's guess. He certainly didn't have a clue. Too many thoughts stirred up too many emotions. Emotions that wouldn't serve him if his destiny was to be an avenging angel. Colt's regret was he always seemed to be a few seconds too late. One mistake that cost someone else their life. What if he simply kept his gun on him? He could have dropped the thing, which was clearly visible in the moonlight. A million regrets with at least one a day for the past one hundred plus years. Wasn't time for a pity party, though. There was work to do.

He picked up the roll of sheeting, now blood stained, rolling it out on the ground next to Aunt Rosie's body. The head, Colt secured first. If Kat or Johnny came back out, that wasn't something he wanted them to see. In the shed, he found a pile of burlap potato sacks, like the ones they put the non-ignited toker in. That would do. Grabbing a shovel, Sturgess found a small area under a tree that looked like it would serve as a proper memorial. He began digging a simple resting place for a woman who deserved much better.

Upstairs of the tavern, Kat sat on the closed toilet wiping the blood from Johnny with a washcloth from the adjacent sink. He was in no condition to do it himself. When he experienced trauma, there was a shutdown that took place in him. This was by far the worst yet. His mind focused on a solution to a problem until he found one. That was the point when he would return from whatever place he disappeared to within himself. It took him nearly a day to solve the issue with the fishing goggles, the mud, and the stick. Kat feared how this one would work out, as there was no solution to what had just happened.

Maybe Uncle Mike could help whenever he gets home, she thought.

Unfortunately for her, he too met the same plight as his beloved wife, thirty-seven miles away outside of the fair in Kinston. Neither of them would ever come to know the facts of how that all unfolded.

Finishing up with Johnny, she guided him back over to his bed. He laid down on his side as she tucked him in. Outside, she heard Sturgess breaking ground with the shovel. Kat knew what he was doing and didn't want it to draw Johnny any deeper into his quiet place. It was odd that Colt was digging a grave, certainly the police or undertaker should be called to come get the body. How would they explain it though? Kat decided it was best to leave it alone for now and consult Uncle Mike when he got home on what to do about everything. She continued with the tactile therapy, brushing Johnny's hair back with her fingers, also humming to keep his sense of sound occupied away from the burial of their Aunt Rosie.

His eyes fluttered closed, then open, looking up at her. A small smile creeped onto his face.

"Sing me some Ho-ha Napkin, Kitty Kat." That was an immensely positive sign, although Johnny had a unique way of referring to gold record recording artist, Noah Hampton.

She nodded and began with his request. "There's a place that I go to, a place where I roam, a place that's all mine, a place I call home. The sun and the moonlight they tickle my face, my eyes close to get there, it's my special place. Too-night, I won't be alone. Too-night, I'll be on my way home. Because at the end of the day, in my special place, I am enough when I look at your face."

His smile broadened, then flickered with his eyes as he fell fast asleep. Kat exhaled, releasing her own tension. She, too, needed to mourn, but tending to her brother held priority. She delved deeper into her thoughts as she listened to the rhythmic sound of the grave digging. What were they to do now?

━━━◆━━━

"You know, I always wanted a daughter? One with a fierce independence that wasn't reflective of a male-dominated society." Elizabeth strolled down the center of the herringbone parlor, currently unoccupied but about to become very busy.

Go playhouse then, Emma thought, but didn't utter a word after seeing the show of strength of her escort.

"I'm not sure if you're aware of the power I'm offering you. Immortality, my dear. In your case, forever young. Is this something you'd ever thought about?"

Emma stopped to face Elizabeth. "Are you guys vampires?"

Elizabeth roared at the implication. "No, that we are not. But we possess powers that exceed what most people consider natural. You've witnessed this yourself. Each person is different, though. Only a handful of us have realized our true potentials. Once you do, only one thing matters."

"And that is?"

"More…"

They reached the end of the walkway. Elizabeth sat down on the right bench, offering a seat to Emma on the left. Olath entered the parlor accompanied by Frick and Frack, dragging the girl who was in the back of the squad car. Elizabeth nodded to him.

"Down there, I don't want to interrupt our discussion," she said.

Frick and Frack forced the girl down on the bench, strapping her in. The straps were an augmentation that Olath installed, as those who were brought to the parlor were typically less than willing participants of the experiments about to take place.

"I need to replace the elixirs with something new. Keep her occupied," Olath said.

Frick and Frack looked at each other quizzically.

"How are we —"

"—supposed to do that —"

"—without damaging —"

"—the merchandise?"

They chortled, taking a seat to the right and left of the girl.

Emma, watching the entire scene unfold, was getting the jitters. Not like the rest of the evening was anything but a nightmare, but she thought that her bravado may have resulted from adrenaline. For now, she would have to hold her ground. Somehow, it was keeping her alive.

"What's the deal with those two? They always talk like that?" she asked.

"Annoying, isn't it?" Elizabeth answered. "They are compliant and serve a purpose, though. In our line of work, expert help is scarce."

"What exactly is your 'line of work?'"

Elizabeth didn't answer, just stared at Emma. This girl really was devoid of fear. That would make things more difficult. Fear was the catalyst of the elixir. The results were never guaranteed, but those who adapted were always terrified. As for the body part harvesting, that was an entirely different matter, but Emma was not exposed to that faction of the operation. Not yet anyway.

Olath returned from the office of the parlor, currently doubling as his lab. Carrying a jug of dark red liquid, his spidery stride transported him to the receiver bottle on the multilactor unit in front of the struggling girl. He filled it with the liquid. Each unit contained a receiver bottle, designed for doing just that, receiving the milk from the goat the teat cups were connected to. Olath's modifications to the system served an entirely different purpose. Instead of receiving, it was designed as a multi-delivery system. The payload was his elixir vitae. Teat cups were replaced with four syringes that would inject his subjects with the elixir courtesy of the air compressors. With twenty-four stations in this parlor, it was literally a ghoul factory, churning out either successful or unsuccessful test subjects.

His success rate was currently dwindling to around thirteen percent, most of them ash tokers. An additional two percent became functional clown servants, but their life expectancy after the process dropped significantly to five to six months. Even a booster dose no longer worked. Something transpired with human evolution, either through the substantial increase of prescription medications or consumption of processed foods that was resulting in the severe decline in the effectiveness of his elixir. Not that it was ever completely successful. Their need to harvest and replace limbs was evidence of that.

This new elixir was like most of Olath's shots in the dark. Humans weren't meant to live hundreds of years. It's why there is a mortality rate. Eventually, the cells give way, particularly the synaptic connections of the brain. Wiring and rewiring of the connections created a neural path prone to excursions of madness. This band of misfits continued to press for immortality, and their methods for attempting to achieve it over exemplified that fact.

Emma watched as Olath picked up the device once used to milk goats, placing it on the girl's head. Elizabeth was delighted by the process.

"I named it the 'crown of thorns.' Beautiful, isn't it?" she asked.

It was her way to mock accepted forms of religion. They conquered death by their own hand. What need was there for a god? Particularly one created by man.

The girl squirmed under the restraints. Olath pushed the actuator button. In one continuous motion, the air compressor switched on, driving the needles of the four oversized syringes through her skull, pumping the liquid from the receiver bottle into her brain. Her resistance stopped, as did the unit once the bottle emptied. Slumping forward, the girl appeared lifeless as the red liquid dripped from her nose, ears, eventually drooling from her mouth onto the floor in front of her.

Elizabeth watched patiently after Olath turned the unit off. They waited.

"What the fuck?" Emma said, astonished at what she had just witnessed.

She jumped to her feet, but Elizabeth blocked her escape, grasping her arm.

Suddenly, the woman who just received the elixir moved, sucking in a deep breath. She sat still, staring straight ahead. Olath moved quickly to examine her. Clapping his hands once, Frick produced a stethoscope, handing it to him. Frack responded in disgust.

"You always have —"

"—to play the teacher's pet!"

Listening to her heart, he produced a small compact mirror from his pocket, holding it up in front of her mouth. The mirror fogged. The subject was breathing. Olath spun around to Elizabeth, smiling. She closed ranks to his position, dragging a resistant Emma.

Elizabeth touched the girl's face, moving it left to right. Her skin was white, nearly translucent. This was new. And her eyes, her eyes lost all pigment, but the patterns in the iris were all still there. Stepping back, Elizabeth spoke to her.

"What is your name?" she asked.

There was a brief delay. Then the girl looked up at her. "Dawn."

Elizabeth released a laugh of joy. "Dawn. How perfect! Release her."

Olath reacted to the command with apprehension. "But we have yet confirmed the safety factors involved —"

"Don't question me! I said release her!"

Frick and Frack sprang into action, removing the crown of thorns and restraining straps. Elizabeth took Dawn by the hand, helping her to stand. She inspected her hands, then raised the girl's skirt, paying close attention to her feet, then her calves, knees, thighs. Her skin was exquisite, like porcelain, pinching it elicited no pain response. This seemed to delight Elizabeth. This batch of elixir was an overwhelming success as far as she was concerned. Turning to Frick and Frack, she gave new instructions.

"Take her and prep her for the transplant. I will be there momentarily."

"Yes—"

"— My queen."

They both saluted her simultaneously, before leading Dawn outside of the parlor. Olath was confused by the action.

"I thought you sought this one as a companion. The usage of trans-formative limbs was to be reserved for the tagged group?"

"You thought wrong." Elizabeth pushed Emma down on the bench. "This is the companion. Prepare a second trial. Now!"

Emma screamed out, struggling as Elizabeth secured the straps.

"Yes, finally. Fear! That is precisely what we needed."

———————

Colt finished with the burial when Kat reappeared from Rosie's tavern. She joined him graveside as they both stood quietly. Small talk wasn't his thing, nor was lending a shoulder to cry on. His life over the past one hundred years was solitary. He never felt more that way than this moment after burying a woman he could have called "friend" a century ago. He cleared his throat.

"Should we say a prayer or something? Not much of a religious man anymore but would be proper for last rites. You knew her best, anything to say?" he asked.

Kat noticed he wired a makeshift cross from a left-over piece of lattice work they used on the back of the tavern the previous summer. She pulled a dandelion from the grass, placing it on the mound of dirt covering her aunt. Kat knelt. Colt removed his hat, bowing his head.

"God, goddess or whoever's in charge, pretty shitty thing you did tonight. This woman gave of herself to everyone and when it came time for you to protect her, you blew it big time. Anyway, take care of Johnny. He really needs you now. Amen."

Crossing herself quickly, Kat stood back up and ran into the tavern. She held it together until this point, mostly for Johnny. But these last words hit her hard. How the hell was she going to explain any of this to Uncle Mike? Uncle Mike. The thought of him gave her dread. Not because he did anything wrong, but her intuition sounded off alarm bells every time he crossed her mind this evening. Something was wrong. Really wrong. You could set your watch by him. The fact he was out of touch and hours late only meant that something happened. She only hoped he hadn't fallen under the same grim circumstances that they experienced.

Colt sighed, looking up at the moon. *Damned shame,* he thought.

Picking up the shovel, plastic sheeting and staple gun, he rounded the front of Rosie's tavern. There was still a job to do. First there was the matter of the dead toker in the potato sack. He tossed it on the back of his Harley, looping the drawstring around the midsection, dividing the saddlebags. Trusting his message got through to the Smoke Hunters, he knew they'd be interested in seeing this specimen. Especially since it showed cognition. That was unique.

Stapling the sheeting over the windows, he made one last patrol around the tavern to ensure no more monsters were lurking. The things rarely traveled in packs. They were as solitary as him. It was time to leave.

On his final pass, he was met by Kat.

"You just going to leave? Just like that?"

"I'm not exactly good at goodbyes. Besides, figured you'd be happy to be rid of me. Uncle should be home soon anyway, right?"

She shook her head. "Got a feeling he's not coming home. He's never been this late. If these monsters attacked us and we're way out in the middle of nowhere, what happened down in Kinston? Aunt Rosie couldn't get the cops on the phone. Not exactly a thriving metropolis. We know the dispatcher by name."

"Yeah, I kinda thought the same thing, which is why I need to get down there as soon as possible."

"And what do you think you're gonna find? What do you expect to do?"

Colt tipped his hat back, leaning against his motorcycle.

"You don't exactly have a plan, do you? Didn't think so. That sure of yourself you can handle whatever you find? And if you can't?" Kat asked.

"Then I can't, and this all ends here and now."

Kat sighed, looking up at the moon in the same manner he did a moment ago, for the same reason.

"Seems like such a waste, Mr. Sturgess."

He didn't have answers for her, nor had he ever been questioned about the potential of failing at his purpose. Being driven solely by hate and the need for revenge for so long, any other considerations never occurred. Maybe giving the Smoke Hunters a few hours to make their way toward Kinston would be a good idea. He required rest, and his internal clock was winding down. Colt never questioned his mortality, but seeing how precious life was to these three souls stirred something inside of him. Something he hadn't felt since before waking up in that smoldering firepit on his ranch.

"Okay, Kat. I'll pull up for the night in case your uncle shows up. But at daybreak, I'm on the road. We good?"

"We're good. Come on, I'll fix up the spare room for you. It's a little dusty, but I'm sure it's a major improvement over where you're used to sleeping."

"That ma'am, I can guarantee."
The two disappeared through the front door of the tavern.

The dream came to him for the first time in twenty years. He wouldn't be able to realize that until he awoke the next morning, but the images coalesced in his mind, bringing memories to the forefront. Maybe it was the bonding with the Babin family or the memories of his past he shared earlier that night? There was his face. His bald head. The steely grimace. Olath. Peering down at him, while two figures drifted into his periphery. He was being dragged across the ground. The back of his head throbbed with pain with every beat of his heart. Beneath his skin, fire surged through his veins. Something was happening inside of him, a transformation, an evolution. An owl, a tombstone. His own name etched on it. "Colt Sturgess, Born: 1854, Died: 1886." Standing in the graveyard's haze, he spun around to see him again. Olath. This time, ten feet tall, reaching down for him like the unlikely judge of the netherworld.

Colt drew his pistols, but the bullets were ineffective.

"Come and get it now, the elixir of vitae, little lady. Are you interested? Why certainly, it enhances the fertile ground for conception, among other things!" the pallid carny barked.

Flames engulfed Colt. From his viewpoint, a few flickers, then a wave, then an inferno. He was in the middle of it, but the fire within quieted. A rush of cold breathed through him. His body was balancing the external conditions. It was the only thing that made sense. But how?

Sounds of Lizzy screaming. Those screams, unforgivable. He couldn't move. Not a muscle. Night settled in, a moon, an owl, a racoon, smoke. Sitting up, covered in ashes, he rushed into the house naked. After a few steps, he stopped. The grass beneath his feet. He could feel every blade counting each one in mere seconds. There were one hundred three blades under his left foot, eight seven under the right. He heard a crash inside of the house. He hurried to the sound. Was it Lizzy? Was she safe?

Entering the kitchen, he spied the racoon again. Was it an omen or simply hungry, raiding the kitchen? This was only a dream, or was it memory recall? Lizzy, where was Lizzy? Grabbing a pair of trousers from the closet, he returned to the front of the yard. He picked up the scent of the horses to the extent he could taste their perspiration. He focused his vision on the road ahead, searching for any trace of the wagon. The more he concentrated, the further his field of vision increased. His sight extended miles beyond any normal capacity. He stumbled off balance and fell after attempting to refocus back to the farm. What the hell was going on?

"Lizzy!" he called out desperately.

Colt ran back to the house, searching the exterior grounds of the farm. Rounding the orchard, he came face-to-face with the fire pit from where he emerged.

"No, can't be."

The one place he didn't search for her. He trudged to the center of the charred embers and ash. Colt sifted. It took only minutes before he found the first bone. Then a second, eventually a charred skull.

He cried out, "Lizzy!" Dropping to his knees, he cast a plea to the sky, "My god why have your forsaken us?"

Tears seared his cheeks, pain screamed through his flesh. Rising, he stumbled towards the house, into the bathroom. Rinsing his face with water, he slowly raised his head, looking into the mirror.

"My eyes! What in the devil's name? My eyes!"

———◆———

Colt Sturgess awoke to the blinding sun in his eyes. Initially, he was a bit confused transitioning from the dream to an unfamiliar place. After shaking off the cobwebs of sleep, he realized where he was. Getting dressed, he wandered from the back room of Rosie's tavern to the main bar area. He smelled crisp bacon, even in the dream. Johnny was seated at a table devouring a plate of French toast, bacon, and scrambled eggs. Kat appeared from the kitchen, sliding a plate of the same across the bar to Colt.

"About time you woke up," she said.

He rubbed the back of his neck, stretching, then putting his cowboy hat back on.

"You ever take those shades off? Noticed you sleep with them on too," she asked.

He wasn't used to morning conversation. In fact, it annoyed him, at least until his first cup of coffee or two.

"That's a whole different story. You were watching me sleep? Kinda creepy," he answered.

"Actually, Johnny was. I couldn't find him this morning. There he was."

Colt retrieved the plate of food and joined Johnny at the table. Kat brought a pot of coffee around the bar and sat down.

"You're going to have to remove your hat, Mr. Sturgess. Not proper etiquette to eat with your hat on," said Johnny, peering up over his glasses.

Colt shot Kat a curious glance.

"Happens sometimes, after an event. Particularly stressful ones. Johnny gains periods of clarity," she said.

"For the last time, my name is John Paul."

"He can be temperamental, too."

Johnny dropped his fork, turning around until his back faced her. "I don't see the need to refer to me in the third-person when I'm sitting in front of you."

Although Colt adapted to decades of transformations, the change in Johnny was emotionally startling. His own body was another topic for another time. Even that eluded him. It simply was something he accepted. Sturgess began eating. The food was savory to all his senses. Typically, he learned to isolate and control each of them so that he wouldn't experience sensory overload, which shut him down much like a robot receiving too much data. Well, that's how robots worked in the movies. When tapping into memories, however, it acted as a reveille. Plus, the bacon smelled amazing. It was quite some time since he ate fresh, home-cooked bacon.

"Guessing your Uncle Mike still hasn't come home?"

"No, he hasn't," answered John Paul, maintaining his focus on the dwindling stack of French toast.

Kat sipped her coffee, not saying a word. Colt took to eating his breakfast as fast as he could. Indigestion wasn't his current concern. Time was. If the brief respite, although needed, meant losing the trail of Olath and his band of ghouls, it would be another regret in his growing daisy chain of them. Finishing his last bite, he downed one last cup of coffee. It was time to go.

"Thank you both for your kind hospitality. I hate to dine and dash, but if there is any more danger, I'd like to think cutting it off at the source is probably the best way," he said, rising from the table.

Johnny just stared at him over his glasses. Kat nodded in agreement.

"You two going to be safe here?" Colt asked.

"We'll manage, Mr. Sturgess," Kat answered.

They were unusually quiet, although with what they experienced, coupled with the unknown disposition of Uncle Mike, it was understandable. For the last time, Colt Sturgess left Rosie's tavern. He mounted up the Harley, double checked the duffle bag, and tightened the binds on the secured creature. Turning over the engine, he looked back before speeding off toward the rising sun.

Inside the tavern, Johnny looked over at Kat. She smiled.

"Well?" he asked.

"Get your overnight bag. Pack a couple of changes of clothes and clean underwear. We're going to Kinston."

Chapter Seven

Jud Allen stirred. Rhonda laid still on his chest with her arm around him. She was awake but was careful not to disturb him.

"Good morning," she said.

He sat up to greet the aftermath of the night before. Outside, the streets of Kinston quieted down, except for the sound of pouring water.

"Is it raining? Can't be, the sun is shining," he asked, moving towards the window.

Maintaining a modicum of concealment behind the curtain, he looked out towards Main Street, now visible in the sunlight, although the funerary pyre continued to burn. It was now three times larger than when he last checked a few hours ago. The water came from the fire hydrants along the route of the street.

"Whoever they are, they are efficient. Planned everything to the last detail. Washing the blood all away now," he said.

Rhonda rose to join him at the window. She nestled up behind him, wrapping her arm around his waist. It was unexpected, but received with a smile.

"Anything new to report?" she asked.

"Looks like most of the semis have pulled out. Two more still down there. Don't see the creatures, or anybody else. All the hydrants are opened flooding the streets. Think they may have moved to other parts of the town?"

"Don't know. Hadn't really thought about it yet. Not real functional without my morning coffee. I imagine you don't have a coffee pot here?"

"No, just red pop."

"Guess that will have to do."

Rhonda walked over to the nearly full case of their only refreshment. *Had to be a real bitch getting that through the pipe,* she thought.

There were quite a few details he withheld from her, like the pile of charred bodies that continued to smolder. It wasn't something he wanted her to think about. Particularly, that Emma may be one of those.

There were a couple of orders of business they would have to tend to. Foremost, Jud was concerned with the potential remaining members of his family. He reviewed several routes that would navigate them to his house, with the least amount of exposure to whatever may still be lurking. Then, of course, there was food. The snack bags of chips would suffice for now, but Jud worried about the necessity of actual food. They learned about the need to consume water and particular nutrients daily for hydration and cell restoration, among the other hundreds of processes in biology class. Not that he was a worry wort, but it was the thing going through his mind in survival mode. He wanted to be prepared. There would be food at his house, tons of it. Italian families always kept a stocked fridge. Getting there was another issue.

Rhonda beckoned him from across the room. "Come over and sit down. I hate having breakfast alone."

She took up residence on a large area rug on the floor, away from any view of the street below. Jud's tension was making her edgy as well. He sauntered over, sitting down. She handed him a soda. Reaching under the three-legged end table, Jud grabbed two bags of chips, returning the favor by tossing her one.

"Thanks again," she said.

"For what?"

"Saving us last night. It was the first time I felt safe in a long while. Great sleep too," she answered, crunching into a chip.

Her response threw Jud. How could she be so calm? Get a restful sleep and awaken as if the night before never happened? His emotions were a tangle of, well, everything. From the miraculous way the day started to his first make-out session to seeing his father's lifeless body, to the onslaught of the creatures that were something from his late-night movie marathons. He didn't need the recap, but it was surprising she just seemed indifferent to all of it. Shock. That was it. She must be in shock.

"Rhonda, you sure you're, okay? I mean, you're pretty chilled out for all that's happened."

She continued eating the chips without a change of expression. Putting the bag down momentarily, she stretched, then sighed.

"I am worried about Emma. I mean, we ran off, which I feel guilty about not trying to find her, but under the circumstances, there wasn't any other choice. Really sorry about your dad too. That has to suck."

"How about your family? Your mom and sister. Aren't you a little worried about that?"

Rhonda picked the bag back up, crunching the chips.

"Ha. No, not particularly."

Jud was astonished. Neither of them was at the age where they could reflect with adult eyes as to the quality of their upbringing. In his case, he struggled mightily to connect with his father, which he was confident would eventually happen. Perhaps that was a pipedream, but it was the hope of a young man who had yet to make his way in the world and was still reliant on the nuclear family unit. Bills, utilities, rent, college loans, living alone were all ahead of him. His family life was less than perfect, but then again, what teenagers were? Never was he indifferent to the lives of his family, though. Thoughts of losing a parent or sibling were terrifying to him, and one of those was gone. Time would reveal the disposition of the others.

"Seriously? You don't really care what's up with your family?"

She lowered the bag, making direct eye contact with him. "No, now drop it."

It wasn't in his nature to, regardless of the consequences. Particularly with this girl. He fell hard and fast. If there was pain lurking in her, he wanted to help soothe it. Jud obviously had never heard about the road to hell and how it is paved. He stared right back at her, not backing down.

"What's going on? I mean, parents can suck and all, but this isn't exactly a normal situation. Let me help. I rescued us, n'est pas?" His gentle approach failed.

"You wanna help? Don't mention that bitch of a mother of mine again!"

She stood up, walking to the back of the bakery apartment. Jud knew he probably shouldn't have pressed. This was by far the wrong place, certainly the wrong time.

"Stupid, Jud Allen…" he said under his breath.

Rhonda stomped back into the room with a broom in her hand, pointing the bristle head at him. "No, fine! You wanna know why I don't give a shit? Fine. After my father died, she takes up with a total drunk asshole. Then, stands on a pedestal passing judgement on everything I do, especially talking behind the backs of anyone I date, while crowning my sister who has her head so far up her ass, she thinks she's going to live out the American dream on a server salary, while of course, sponging off my mother! So no, I don't care. What I do care about is my best friend, and your best friend Emma, and if she made it out alive. I'd rather go look for her instead of the freaks that call themselves my family, just because we share the same blood. Now move your ass. That carpet needs swept. It's too dusty and killing my eyes."

Jud did as she commanded, watching her as she worked. Of course, he felt stupid for pushing the matter in hindsight. Barely a couple for a day, if that's what they were. He hoped his dumb pressure hadn't changed that. Watching her work, his natural reaction was to help, so he began straightening up the other items in the room. It may have been a great man loft hideaway, but there was a lady present. A lady with deep feelings that he just inadvertently trampled on. He wouldn't make that mistake again.

Colt Sturgess turned down the ramp to Kinston. He made record time. Approaching the town, he immediately noticed the smoke. Pulling the bike off to the side of the road, he dismounted. Colt would have to test the smoke by inhaling it first. He ran into this problem on his first encounter with the 'tokers. They thrived, craving the burn-off from the remains of Olath's test subjects, the unused body parts that rejected his serum. There was something in the serum that when burned, furnished fuel for the creatures that drove them into a frenzy. Unfortunately for them, it also altered their bodies the more they were exposed to it. This smoke also affected Sturgess. Although not with the same results, it immobilized him, crashing him to the ground like a falling timber. The leader of the Smoke Hunters called it "Colt's kryptonite."

The acrid smell from the center of Kinston finally reached him on a gust of wind. Closing his eyes behind his shades, he breathed deeply. Seconds later, he opened them again. This was not the smoke from Olath's twisted left-overs. It was far worse, burning human remains.

"Son of a bitch," Colt muttered as he returned to the seat of his Harley, firing up the machine.

Olath left a trail of bodies wherever he plundered. Over time, his operation grew to where they learned to cover their tracks and covered them well. Small towns were turned into ghost towns where the residents appeared to just up and leave. Fully intact houses, with doors open wide, occasionally broken windows. However, from the outsider's perspective, the houses were nothing more than vandalized or fallen to the habitation of local drug users or indigents. No one cared to investigate and, on the occasions where missing persons cases were filed, they went cold relatively quickly.

It was clusters of missing cases that aided in providing new trails for Sturgess to follow. Newspapers served as his primary source of intelligence, augmented by occasional chatter from locals who loved to spin yarns at dining establishments he stopped at for his own refueling. Colt came to appreciate that not all urban legends were false, particularly those involving lanky bald men accompanied by clowns.

Before meeting the Smoke Hunters, he was limited in information gathering outside of those resources, hoping to find small towns that fit the profile. One of the Smoke Hunters had a brother-in-law who was a Texas Ranger. He was vital in retrieving intelligence on these clusters of missing persons, then reporting them to the hunters. Colt's chance convergence with the group exponentially widened their intel network. Presently, it's what helped him close the gap on Olath's current operation. He hoped that his recent check-in would cause a cavalry call. There was no way to predict what encountering Olath's actual operation would be like.

Continuing down the exit-ramp, Colt slowed his approach to Kinston. One hundred yards to his immediate front, a tractor trailer was parked across the road, preventing access to the town itself. A parking horse sat ten feet in front of it with a radiological sign. From the front of the cab to the back of the tailer, two figures in military grade hazmat suits, complete with gas masks, walked the length of the vehicles. Obviously, a patrol. Knowing the origin of the smoke filling the air, he knew it was a ruse. It was what he couldn't see that concerned him. He proceeded forward with caution. Reaching the parking horse, Colt stopped. The two figures approached.

They made a few critical errors in their deception. The obvious were the smatterings of blood all over them. Getting a closer look at the semi, it certainly wasn't military, carrying the same marks the figures sported: blood stains. Their weapons were shotguns, hardly military issue, obviously stolen from the house of a resident or residents. He was in the right place. For now, he would play along, but he was going to breach this obstacle. Sturgess waved as the two approached with urgency, waving back.

"Howdy," he said with a tip of his cowboy hat.

"Towns closed. Radiological hazard. Clean-up crews are on the scene," a male voice said, muffled by the mask.

Colt pointed up to his ear with his right hand, denoting he couldn't hear them through the masks, which, of course, he could. It was his own form of deception as his left gripped the tsuka of the katana sword attached to the left side of his bike. The deception that he could not hear them only drew them closer.

Perfect, he thought, punctuating his broad smile.

With a singular motion, Colt Sturgess spun off the right side of his bike, unsheathing the sword simultaneously. With a wide arc, he caught both figures with one swing. Their heads dropped over the side of the parking horse; bodies frozen in place. They were both men. Instead of blood, a black sludge oozed from the tops of their necks where their heads were seconds earlier. Colt looked down. Olath's elixir. He was close.

A giddy enthusiasm washed over him in the wake of the gruesome execution. He had never been this close to encounter Olath's henchmen in the flesh, or whatever this was, only the ash tokers. This was also a promising development. They could be killed. Swinging the blade of the sword twice more, he sliced opened the hazmat suits to examine the bodies. Scars ran across each of the men's shoulder joints. One man possessed additional scars above his wrist, right leg, and both wore horizontal scars at the base of their necks that he almost overlooked as his strike was a mere inch above those.

"Rumors are true. The bastard's farming body parts," said Colt.

The rumors came from the Smoke Hunters, the only other group to have encountered any of Olath's abandoned towns. "He always leaves something behind. Thorough, but sloppy," the leader of the group told Sturgess. They recovered a clipboard on one of their ash toker hunts in an abandoned slaughterhouse. The place was recently occupied but cleared out. Nothing of relevance remained except a singular clipboard with several pages of lists of names and numbers. At the top of each page were columns with the headings: Arme, Beine, Kopf. Another member of the Smoke Hunter's father served in World War II as a radio operator and translator. He supplied the definitions: Arms, Legs, Head.

What it meant was speculation. Until now.

Colt returned to his Harley, mounted up and eased slowly onto the end of West Main Street, heading east. Being extremely vigilant for any other presence of Olath's ghouls, he engaged in his unnatural sensory abilities. It was eerily quiet except for the rush of water flowing down the street, draining into the sewer grating. Glancing over into the adjacent creek, the water was rising. There hadn't been a storm in days. This resulted from whatever was the source of the flow. He maneuvered up on to the curb and pressed on.

Reaching the center of town, Colt observed both the sources of the water, spouting from the hydrants and smoke, rising from stacks of bodies in a parking lot of an abandoned carnival. Two tractor trailers sat idling down the street about fifty yards away. There was an absence of human activity. Yielding to caution, he cut the engine, dismounted, rolling his bike towards what appeared to be a government building on approach. He sought concealment for his motorcycle, knowing the noise from the engine would only alert the unseen invaders of this town. Currently, it was being drowned out by the semi engines idling and a torrent of hydrant flow.

To his immediate left, a few yards away, he spied a firehouse with the garage doors open. A pumper and ambulance exited the stalls, but not made it far. Each one appeared to have crashed, the pumper through the front window of a used car dealership, the ambulance straight into a phone pole. Remains of either driver were absent.

Pushing his Harley into the bay of the firehouse, he tossed a couple of rescue blankets from the floor over it after retrieving his saddle bags and katana sword, which he slung over his back. It proved helpful already. Wandering out on to the sidewalk next to the side street, also serving as an aqueduct to the pouring water, he looked for a better vantage point, one from which he could survey the entire town. A church tower a block away screamed out for the purpose. It was his next destination.

The farmhouse was quaint. Too quaint for Elizabeth's liking, a word she used often. Through time, she gained a taste for the exquisite. Her past was of humble origins, long since discarded. It was the immortality she basked in. Like those who came before her, Elizabeth found a particular kinship with Erzsebet Bathory, the blood countess herself who preceded Olath by nearly a century. Elizabeth was drawn to the Bathory legend for reasons known only to her. The unsubstantiated tales of Erzsebet bathing in the blood of virgins to keep her youth either appealed to her growing vanity or satiated her madness. There was the possibility that she believed the practice contributed to her lack of aging. Elizabeth always found time for a special delivery of four drums of blood from Olath's raids to enjoy a bath or two in honor of her Hungarian namesake. Time, after all, was irrelevant.

The basement wine cellar was set for the surgery. Elizabeth laid quietly on a table fashioned from one of the barn doors of Chooch's Farm. Dawn laid prone on an entirely different surgical table, one that was already there, a butcher's block. How fitting.

The rooster crowed three hours earlier, but Olath had to get all the preparations right. He already completed the initial part of the surgery. Elizabeth's arms and legs were expunged. This was a first, as typically the transfers were done in phases: Hands, forearms, upper arms, shoulders, feet, calves, knees, and thighs. She insisted on the entire limbs this time after examining the young woman following the new elixir injection. It was imperative that she have it all and have it now. Elizabeth turned her head to face him as he prepared to remove the four essential limbs from his latest experiment.

"What's taking you so long? This is getting ridiculous, old man!" she snarled.

He looked over at her, merely an animated head and torso presently. Much like the mystery of Elizabeth's fascination with Erzsebet Bathory, Olath's willingness to kowtow to her every demand, welcoming her abuse to a nearly sadistic level was a mystery. After all, he was in control of everything that took place. How easy it would be to drag her out to the hog pen, toss her in and be done with her incessant mistreatment? But no. He carried on as if her demands were routine tasks and he was merely a joyful, compliant servant.

"Of course, my dearest. The finest for you do occasionally require touches of delicacy, ensuring that your beauty and perfection endure."

His flattery overcame her impatience. "Fine, just get on with it."

There was another reason she chose this girl, beyond the potential that Olath's new elixir was the next stage in their evolution. Jealousy. She was beautiful, but it hadn't flourished until the injection took place. Elizabeth wanted to possess it, needed to possess it.

Olath approached the girl on the butcher block. She looked up at him with her dead eyes. A smile melted gently across her lips. She trusted him. He created her. She sensed his intent, closed her eyes, and leaned her head back. For the first time in his long, grisly life, Olath felt a pang of regret. A tear streamed down Dawn's cheek as he made the first incision.

Jud and Rhonda sat on the couch, staring at each other. They finished cleaning their makeshift refuge. One awaited the other to break the ice after their brief argument. Although, to qualify it as an argument, there were typically two participants. Jud felt it was an argument. Having zero experience with women, he wasn't sure what to say next.

"I think I'm going to go out. See if anything's happening from the ground level. Maybe sneak over to McNaulty's and see if they have any of those subs. We're gonna need more than chips," he said.

Whether this was accurate, Jud convinced himself that it was. Water should have been the priority, but he assumed they were getting plenty of that from the red pop.

McNaulty's was a five and dime department store in town owned by the McNaulty family since the town was established. The store was the place everyone went to shop for back-to-school clothes and shoes. Jud also loved their Italian submarine sandwiches with fries. It stayed open past regular operating hours during the fair, as did most of the other downtown businesses, hoping to draw in shoppers during the event. With a little luck, their doors would be open, if they weren't shattered by the fleeing crowd or attacking monsters. There wouldn't be a regular work shift, not this morning. That may prove an issue if the doors were locked.

Jud expected resistance but got the opposite. This girl was a real wild-card, completely unpredictable. He liked that.

"Well, if you're going, I'm not hanging around here. I'm going with!" she said.

"I'd feel a lot safer if you hung out here."

"Not me," she said as she pushed her foot into her sneakers, having them laced up before he could retrieve his rucksack. "All ready, here."

"Okay, but we really must be careful and stay behind me. Not that I'm being bossy, just want to keep you safe."

"Awe, my knight in shining armor!"

He didn't mind the teasing. It made him feel a comfortable part of her world. She didn't mind him taking the lead, although she knew herself capable. It was nice for someone else to place her security first.

They descended the stairs to the panel, turned the lock and quietly crept into the dusty lobby of the defunct bakery. Reaching the door, Jud carefully rotated the inside lock. Stepping into the alley, they were overcome by acrid smoke assaulting their senses with a smell neither ever experienced. Discussion didn't need to take place. Both knew what it was. With caution, Jud and Rhonda moved quickly down the alley, sticking to the shadows.

Colt assumed a position in the church tower. There were feathers and bird droppings everywhere. Neither were any concern of his. He had been in worse locations staking out Olath's minions. Retrieving a set of binoculars from the saddlebags, he scanned the Kinston downtown area. Never having mastered the vertigo that followed using his enhanced vision, these optics were the next best thing. Learning from past mistakes, Sturgess would sit tight, awaiting the Smoke Hunters. An area reconnaissance would be helpful in the planning. It may also shed some light on what happened here from his encounter with the false roadblock. Maybe even Olath himself was lurking nearby. If only he were that lucky.

From his vantage point, Colt observed the fair site was destroyed. He traced the path of destruction to an area at the end of the lot. A demolished vehicle with smoldering remains was the source of the smoke. The pyre was unattended. Two tractor trailers sat to the left of a bank separating the street and the fire pit. There was movement. He patiently continued the surveillance.

Four clowns emerged from the bank, pushing mail bins up the ramps of both trailers. A closer look revealed both bins were overflowing with stacks of currency and coins. Whatever method he was using to breech bank vaults, Olath could make a fortune by sharing that secret. It was always the same with every abandoned town Colt came across. Not only homes looted but also any buildings with a cash storage: banks, stores, gas stations. No sources of funding for his expeditions went untouched.

As he continued examining the town from the church tower, something hit him. This downtown area was larger than the group's typical target. He didn't have time to do any research at this government building on census data, but apparently Olath grew his operation. Colt also wondered how this attack would go unnoticed. The tiny towns, sure, but by the looks of this one, at least a couple of thousand people lived here, enough to have a bank, government building, fire hall and several shops. Olath was growing sloppy or bold, either made him more dangerous.

The clowns finished loading, secured their payloads, and locked up the doors to each tractor trailer. After jumping into the cabs of the trucks, they shifted forward. One truck eased through town,

continuing along Main Street heading east, the other turned down
Central Avenue towards what appeared to be a school. In his periphery,
Sturgess spotted a mass of darkness heading down a hill about a mile
away towards the second semi. Refocusing the lenses of the binoculars,
he saw them.

"Goddamned ash tokers..." he said.

The driver of the truck stopped. The clown on the passenger side
dropped from the cab, hurriedly opening the trailer door, dropping
the ramp. This was a pickup. Suddenly, Colt's focus was pulled back to
the right. It was slight, but he still heard it. Jerking the binoculars in
the disturbance's direction, he saw two people, a young boy and girl,
dashing across Main Street over the wet asphalt. The clowns capped
off the hydrants, but not enough to hide the sound of the splashing
footsteps. Disappearing from his view, he stood to adjust his vantage
point to track them. That's when he heard a second sound, the tingling
of a bell. Slowly resuming his view of the semi, he hoped the sounds
went unnoticed by the stampeded of 'tokers and clowns. The 'tokers
stopped a few yards ahead of the trucks; the clowns turned, looking
back towards downtown Kinston. For a tense moment, it appeared they
would continue on their way. Both groups just stood there, staring at
something that only they knew, attempting to hone in on. Without a
word between the two groups, the ash tokers and clowns rushed back
towards town on foot.

Colt dropped the binoculars to his side, shaking his head. "Shit."

Jud and Rhonda pushed opened McNaulty's, ran through the cash
registered aisle, around the side rail separating the rest of the store from
the café and slid behind the counter. He forgot about the bell above
the door that always jingled whenever someone entered. They took up
immediate cover in case it drew any unwanted visitors that lingered.
After waiting several minutes, Rhonda decided the coast was clear. Jud
followed her lead this time.

Before going any further, the two examined the portion of the store in front of them. The previous night either produced no customers, or everyone escaped safely. It was empty. No bodies, no bonfires, no blood. It felt secure to move forward with their plan.

Disappearing into the kitchen area, it was much smaller than Jud imagined. One fryer, a counter, and a refrigerator that was half the size of the one in the Allen household. The café was never that busy, so expansion was unnecessary. Besides, most people went to the Elks Club or VFW for whatever lunch or dinner specials they were offering for the day. Saturday was tripe day at the Sons of Italy. The best in the state, or so Fred Allen always said.

Opening the fridge, Rhonda produced two of the famous subs. Jud was disappointed to see that they were pre-made. Here, unbeknownst to them, time was of the essence. The two snuck around the front counter, filling up two waxed cups with iced cola to accompany their feast. Jud looked up. An idea struck him. Grabbing Rhonda's hand, he dragged her to the back of the store up the middle aisle through the clothes racks. A door was in the middle of the back wall.

"What an odd place to put a door," she said.

He opened the door, leading her up a flight of stairs to a small area overlooking the entire sales floor.

"I always wanted to come up here. Never even noticed it the first dozen or so times I shopped here. But when they moved the action figures to the back wall, I looked up one day and noticed cranky Mr. Green looking down, making sure I wasn't stealing anything," he said.

Rhonda let out a laugh, biting into the sandwich. He was right; they were good. Despite being in the fridge, even the bread tasted fresh. Jud's confidence waned a tad. Did he just tell her he still purchases action figures? Was that why she laughed? Crap!

"I mean, I wasn't gonna steal anything, and that was a couple of years ago, not like I —"

"Jud Allen, don't you dare lie to me! I know when those figures come out, you're in here the next day. Emma told me the one you didn't have,

'Chopper,' was really hard to find. We went to the toy show at the mall a couple of weeks ago, but they didn't have it either. It's cool you like that stuff. I have the Star Trek ones myself. I've always had a thing for Captain Kirk!"

Smiling, she took a sip from her straw. There was a trace amount of her lipstick left over. *When did she have time to put on makeup and was that all for me?* He thought.

Jud was not only thrilled with the validation of one of his many hobbies, but that Rhonda loved Captain Kirk. This girl was just too perfect. Biting into his sandwich, a rumble from outside stopped their chewing in unison. Fear poured over them both, unintentionally pausing their make-shift lunch date. Peering up over the edge of the store's crow's nest, the front double glass doors of McNaulty's burst open, sending shattered glass everywhere. The two ducked back down, squeezing each other's hand. Maybe this excursion wasn't the best idea after all.

A hoard of ash tokers poured through the doors like an oil spill. Two clowns waltzed in slowly behind them. Looking up at the now empty steel doorframe, a clown with a black hairnet noted the bell hanging from the top of the frame. He crept forward, sniffing the air as he walked. His attention was first drawn towards the kitchen area, then the café itself. The second clown, carrying the oversized mallet from the high striker game Billy Ford worked during the fair, wandered cautiously between the clothing racks, picking up a scent of his own. The 'tokers split off in two groups, following the pair exploring the five and dime store.

Hairnet clown drifted over to the beverage machine where he observed puddles from melting ice. His already over-exaggerated smile widened across his face, revealing multiple rows of teeth and the fact that his mouth stretched the length of his greasepaint. Running his bloody-gloved finger through the water, he tasted it, then let out a screech that was simply indescribable. Mallet clown swung around to face him mid-way across the store. It nodded. The ash tokers moved en masse silently towards the back of the store.

Rhonda and Jud looked at the doorway of the crow's nest. There was only one way in and one way out. Although they didn't dare peek out over the edge again, they could feel the ghouls closing in on their position. Jud closed his eyes, thinking about what to do. Options were limited. He saw the microphone the store used to make announcements, a metal folding chair and a transistor radio.

"C'mon, think Allen, think."

On the sales floor, the mallet clown continued his slow search. Fear was its lure.

"Olly olly oxen free! Treats for you... blood for me!" The clown roared, exciting the ash tokers.

A new sound caused the hairnet clown to stop his search for the origin of the ringing bell. Was it the sound of metal? Steel, perhaps? It turned to face the direction of the unfamiliar noise. There was a flash of light, followed by the screams of a dozen ash tokers. Hairnet clown's head dropped from its shoulders, bouncing across the trail of flickering 'tokers turning to ash. The strike was quick, silent, deadly.

Mallet clown swung around to see a dark figure standing in the aisleway, backlit by the sun's rays from outside.

"Haven't you heard? We're all free now?" Colt Sturgess smiled, shooting the remaining clown between the eyes, before melting into the shadows of the store along the shoe aisle.

Without guidance, the ash tokers went rampant, ripping through the store with reckless abandoned. Not knowing what was going on below, Jud dove for the transistor radio, tossing it over to Rhonda.

"Find a clear channel. Something with music. Preferably loud music!" he said.

Taking a colossal risk, he stood up, thew open the control box on the wall. Searching frantically, he found what he was looking for, a piece of white tape marked "intercom." Jud flicked the switch, grabbing the microphone in his right hand. Rhonda found a local rock station. It was her favorite, WDEV.

Two ash tokers took notice of the movement in the crow's nest, leaping from the floor to the ledge. Colt dropped them with two more shots. They burst into flames, landing in the tropical fish aquariums directly below.

Ironically, AC/DC's Long Way to the Top (If You Wanna Rock 'N Roll) was the song Rhonda found. Jud grabbed the radio, pressing down the transmit button on the microphone. Music blasted throughout the store, giving Colt an additional advantage.

"Music kids are listening to, these days," he said as he sliced through wave after wave of ash tokers.

Curiosity got the best of them and eventually, Rhonda and Jud peaked up over the ridge of the nest. They watched Colt work his way towards the middle of the store, dispatching the skittering little monsters. Even though the fires turned quickly to ash, there were enough synthetic fabrics to catch, igniting a growing fire.

Colt positioned himself between the back of the store and the front entrance, but the fire was closing in from both sides. He yelled up to the couple.

"Get out now, while you can. I'll cover your asses."

Jud and Rhonda flung open the flimsy door, sprinted down the stairs, moving as fast as their feet would carry them to his location. Heat from the growing fire assaulted them as they pushed open the door to their hiding place. From his experience as the family trash incinerator, Jud was fully aware of the safe distance needed to keep from the flickering element. He was always quick to point out when watching a movie how bullshit it was once someone dashed through fire. This one was growing quickly, eliminating safe zones.

Jud yelled to Sturgess as they passed within a foot of him. "You gotta get outta here, mister! Those fires are moving fast!"

"Keep going kid. Me and fire are old friends."

Feet from the door, Jud slipped on the floor, skidding across the glass shards. Rhonda gasped in horror. Not from the fall, but the thing that now stood in the entrance, blocking their escape. The creature was enormous, eight feet tall, maybe even eight and a half feet. The behemoth sneered. Larger than the doorway, it bent over to peer inside. Its face was hideous. A patchwork of stitched skin revealed a collage of flesh puzzle pieces. Mangled hair pulled back in a topknot hung over its shoulder. Reaching forward with a set of hands, then an additional set. The thing had four monstrous arms; biceps shredded as if it worked out at the gym obsessively. If it could fit in one.

Jud scooted backwards, struggling to get to his feet, which were sliding frantically on the glass particles like a Saturday morning cartoon character. The behemoth flexed its mighty arms, pulling the façade off the five and dime, sending the McNaulty's sign crashing to the ground behind him, raining a down a shower of bricks. It roared, knocking Jud, Rhonda, and Colt to the floor of the department store. Colt was the first up, to face off against the monster. Two remaining ash tokers sprung forward behind him, which he dispatched with the katana without turning around.

The lumbering behemoth slammed all four of his fists into the ground, roaring this time for effect. Sturgess stood his ground, sheathing his katana on his back while drawing both of his peacemakers. He took aim, firing shots at the thing, bullets ricocheting off the steel plating on the monster's chest, secured by a set of chains wrapped around its torso. The front plating displayed embossed words with a vault handle: "Kinston Savings and Trust."

"So that's how you boys are knocking over these banks?" Colt asked, tipping his hat forward. "Okay, big boy, let's do this."

He holstered his weapons, reaching back for his katana, but the thing lunged forward too fast. Scooping up Sturgess with his lower arms, it showered him with blows from the upper fists. Jud grabbed Rhonda by the hand, dragging her out into the street. A tan 1972 Oldsmobile delta 88 pulled up like a bat out of hell on to the curb, nearly hitting both. Kat Ellis jumped out of the driver's seat, John Paul from the passenger side. They could see the disturbance inside of McNaulty's. Kat reached into the back seat, retrieving Uncle

Mike's revolver, taking aim at the creature with the death grip on Colt Sturgess.

"Wait! Don't waste your bullets. It's armored up!" Jud shouted before running down the street.

"Jud!" Rhonda called out for him.

Where was he running off to? Was this boy she was falling for a coward?

The behemoth tightened its grip around Colt's chest. Blows from the creature's fists were not achieving their intended result. Sturgess pushed back with all his strength to free himself. His energy was waning, however, as the monster bore down with additional effort to squeeze the life out of the cowboy. It howled with glee, hearing the cracking of bones inside of Colt's chest.

John Paul Ellis stepped forward confidently, lowering his fishing goggles over his eyes.

"Get off him, Gorgar!" Johnny pointed at the behemoth with a purpose before rushing at the creature.

"Johnny, no!" Kat cried out.

Rhonda grabbed her, keeping her from following him into the fray.

———●———

A half block away, Jud reached the front of the Western Auto and Hardware Store. He pushed the door, but no luck. On the corner sat a trashcan. The town placed one on every corner to circumvent the amount of litter from fair attendees. The bottoms were filled with sandbags to keep them from blowing away. This offered an added benefit to Jud, as it would take additional weight to breach the glass entrance to the hardware store. Dragging it over to the door, he hurled it at the glass, his adrenaline pumping overtime. The glass shattered on the first try. Jud ducked under the metal push bar, scrambling back to the tools' section. They had what he sought. He saw it on one of his trips to buy fishing supplies. Where the hell was it, though?

———•———

Johnny Ellis sprung on the behemoth's back, scaling the chains holding the armored plating until he reached the top of it. Too focused on Sturgess, the creature ignored him. Applying his own choke hold around the thing's neck, Johnny reared back, knee in the middle of its back as leverage. The behemoth dropped Colt to the floor in a pile of defeat. Barely conscious, he looked up at the young man in a battle with this unspeakable evil. It spun to the left, then back to the right, trying to shed this new mortal threat. Johnny had situated himself well. Whatever his source was with hand-to-hand tactics, particularly when battling creatures nearly twice his size, it was effective. The behemoth screaming, staggered warily losing consciousness.

———•———

Outside, Jud ran back up the street towards Rhonda and Kat.

"Where the hell did you go?" Rhonda asked with an air of disappointment.

"It's a surprise," he answered, moving towards the hole in the front of the five and dime.

Jud Allen wasn't sure he had the courage to follow through on the hairbrained scheme he dreamed up, not that it would even work. After seeing Colt in a position unable to carry out his task and this strange boy with a death grip on the monster, his time to act was at hand, regardless the outcome. Maybe that would make his dad proud of him. Summoning a draught of bravery, he ran into McNaulty's, bolt cutter in hand. Seeing Jud advance, Colt propped himself up enough to deliver an additional distraction. He, too, seized the strength to summon extended effort, reaching for the peacemaker in his right holster. The pain was excruciating, breathing a chore, but he drew on the thing, firing at it.

Jud jumped over a pile of bricks, aiming the jaws of the cutter at the first chain. Slipping on the debris, he hit shoulder first into the bottom of the armor, dropping the bolt cutters. Reaching down, a hand retrieved them. Rhonda Coulter slid the jaws of the cutter on the first link, clipping it cleanly, then a second. The armored vault door slid to the side, dropping to the floor, falling back towards the two. Jud tackled her, rolling away from the steel plating that hit the ground, teetering once before falling backwards in a loud thud. The thing was now exposed, dropping to one knee from Johnny's continued stranglehold. This was Colt's opportunity for one last burst. Springing forward, he sunk his katana deep into the thing. Pulling downward using gravity and its spine as a guide, he fell backwards atop the vault door, seconds earlier serving as armor.

In agony, the behemoth swung around, catching Colt across the throat with its claws. A last act of defiance for its inevitable end. Blood sprayed out from his neck, contacting the black viscous fluid pouring from the monster. Colt's blood ignited it in a chain of fire that set the behemoth ablaze. The fire from the back of the department store was now fed with an additional source. It was time to get out. Johnny surrendered his hold on the creature. Rhonda and Jud ran out of the building, quickly being engulfed in flames. Kat called for Johnny, but he had yet to appear.

The sprinkler system finally kicked on, dousing the mess, eliminating these intruders from their town. Smoke billowed from the front opening of collapsed bricks, limiting all lines of sight into McNaulty's. Panicking, Kat rushed forward to find her brother. Suddenly, through the dense smoke, he wandered out, dripping wet with Colt Sturgess over his shoulder in a firefighter's carry.

"Leave him go, Johnny! You'll burn up! He's gone!" Kat pleaded.

Johnny continued towards the Oldsmobile, opened the back door, depositing Colt on the seat.

Jud joined Johnny in the back, Rhonda hopped in the front beside Kat.

"Go, go, go!" Rhonda yelled.

"Where?" asked Kat.

"I know where we can go. Just drive." Jud answered, staring at the near-dead cowboy holding a firm grip on a katana sword.

"Where are we going, Jud?" Rhonda asked, turning to face him from the front seat.

"Home."

Chapter Eight

Elizabeth stepped from the hot bath. She considered a blood shower to baptize her new limbs but preferred to get back to the housing she selected: Delaney's Funeral Home. The funeral home was less than three miles from Chooch's Farm. Although the tiny hamlet had less than one-hundred and fifty residents, people still died, people still needed buried. Delaney's was around for over a century and the inside boasted a more opulent time in American history.

Wall-to-wall fabric wallpaper spread the expanse of both floors, only changing pattern by level. Plush carpeting, velvet drapes, heavily lacquered dark walnut railings, trim and accents. The furniture matched the setting, particularly the dining room. A huge drop crystal chandelier suspended over the table set for six, flanked by two wrought iron floor church candelabras and a fireplace, presented a unique dining experience. There was only one viewing room that Elizabeth sealed off. Thoughts of dead spirits wandering into her temporary palace were unthinkable.

Upstairs, the master bedroom presented a large canopied four post bed, complete with a master bath containing a brass four footed tub and the best of all for Elizabeth, a floor to ceiling framed mirror. Above the bed, a domed ceiling with a mosaic of a sun, moon and stars was meticulously crafted from small shards of colored glass, reminiscent of Tiffany glass. *How quaint,* thought Elizabeth. She would have left the design out for a better view of the actual day and nighttime skies, but taste is taste.

There were four other bedrooms that offered similar accommodations, but not the bath or domed ceiling. The walls of the hallways displayed mounted simulated gas light candles, long since converted over by the Delaney family when electricity become the standard. The kitchen was of no concern of hers, as cooking held no interest.

Elizabeth stood naked in front of the mirror. She opened the bathroom door to vent the steam from her bath. She wanted to feel the heat on her new limbs. Hoped to feel the heat on her new limbs. Unfortunately, there were no sensations yet. That took time for all the neural connections to establish. Limb transplantation wasn't an immediate process. Not that any of them even knew how it worked. It was more of a hack and press surgery. Even Olath didn't understand how the new limbs connected on their own. He merely pressed the new ones tightly into the areas where old limbs were removed, dusting with the pre-liquified version of the elixir and the two sections reacted, fusing the muscles, nerve endings, bones, sinews, and tendons. The tissues assumed a life of their own, establishing all the connections for the parts to work.

The potential for great riches was never far from Elizabeth's mind, but Olath strenuously opposed reminding her that their time spent alive would subject them and the twins to lab experiments, dissections. After all, he alone knew the formula. She could still dream, though.

Stretching in the mirror, she admired her new limbs. The luster, the pale perfection. Even her hair took on a sheen that she didn't previously possess. Running her hands up and down her smooth arms and legs, her happiness hit a pinnacle for the first time in what seemed like forever. This was the second time she had thought about that today. Following her literal self-reflections, Elizabeth wandered out into the bedroom. Two large chests of drawers sat in the room. The one with the sit-down vanity was her target. Opening the drawers, she picked up the silky undergarments from the previous owner, slowly savoring the touch of the fabrics. Still no sensations. They were beautiful, however. A black chemise tickled her preference. She held it up to the mirror, admiring the cut of the design. Sliding it over her head, she tied up the laces in the front. It was now hers. Elizabeth searched the next drawer for a bottom. Matching black lace shorts was out of place from the set. Whoever organized these drawers didn't know what they were doing.

Sliding on the panty shorts with the same lace trim as the bottom of the chemise, she admired the fit.

"My new outfit, regardless of if anyone thinks it's proper or not!" she yelled at the mirror. "There is no way I am going to cover these exquisite arms and legs."

Her self-absorption was interrupted by the ringing of a dinner bell. She sent one of Olath's clowns out to retrieve dinner. Part of her was curious about what he brought back. She strode down the Persian carpeted stairs of her new palace like a queen, one deliberate step at a time. Her legs had not yet made the required connections completely yet either, but she would not show that. The clown stood at the bottom of the stairs, gawking as the beautiful half-naked woman descended them. She said nothing, reveling in the perfection of her choices, both manufactured and biological, even if presently the attention was from a reanimated flesh husk, face covered in ridiculously macabre greasepaint.

At the bottom of the steps, she glided past two large bloodstains on the carpet in the house's foyer, presumably the remnants of Mr. and Mrs. Delaney. She entered the dining room like a queen entering a royal court, sitting down at the head of the table. Across from her sat Emma, white eyes blinking at Elizabeth.

"I see you are ready to dine, my sweet?" asked Elizabeth.

Emma snickered. "Nice outfit. You planning a panty raid?"

The reference was lost on her.

"You look absolutely ridiculous! The people who live here don't have any clothes you can wear?" asked Emma.

Elizabeth's temporary moment was being ruined by this child she created. She expected more from her than the reaction of the clown a minute ago.

"I wouldn't dare cover myself up!" she said.

Emma shook her head as she reached for a serving dish at the center of the table, covered with a sterling silver ornate lid. She lifted it, revealing a platter of hamburgers and French fries. She burst into laughter.

"Burger Chef? Are you fucking shitting me? Burger Chef and fries?" Emma couldn't contain her laughter. Elizabeth was not amused.

"It is sustenance, whatever it is called. We need our protein and carbohydrates. They are essential to the restoration process," she growled back.

"Yeah, whatever you say. Since you injected me with this vitae immortality potion, totally against my will, I might add, the least you can do is steak. Baked potato, you know? I can get burgers anywhere."

Elizabeth stood abruptly. "You will have respect for your mother, young lady. Don't make me regret —"

"Regret? Are you kidding me? I'm the one who got kidnapped by Uncle Fester, jacked up with that head harness of death and now I'm supposed to just say 'yes, mommy?' You're not even my mother, that I know of anyway. Thanks to you two, I barely remember anything past last night. Now if you don't mind, Lady Godiva, I'll be in my room."

Emma rose, turned to leave the room, only to spin back around, grabbed a burger, stuffing her mouth full of fries, then scampered up the stairs. Sighing, Elizabeth sat down heavily in her chair.

"This child-rearing may have not been my best idea," she said aloud while downing a glass of wine.

———

The dream played out once more in Colt Sturgess' mind. The wagon, the smoldering ash, the blackened skull of his beloved. He reached back to breach the wall that denied him access to what had happened earlier that day. Even a glimpse of five seconds before the sight of the men dragging him off. Why was that hidden? The face dissolved in every time he tried. His face. Olath with the magic elixir that was going to help them conceive a child. Every single time he saw it, it ignited a fuse. Living that long, being eroded by raw anger and hate left him a cold, shapeless stone. Any potential of planting seeds for growth beyond his vengeance had no chance to take root. His eyes fluttered and opened, revealing the absence of pigment from his iris, much like Emma and Dawn. He looked up to see Kat keeping vigil.

"Hello there, tarot," he said.

She snapped her head in extreme surprise to see him alive, yet alone forming words. It was also the first time seeing his eyes without the dark glasses and blinders. They were striking, if not a little unnerving. He attempted to sit up, but the ribs weren't quite ready for that leap of faith. Slinking back down painfully on the double width love seat, he did not know where he was. At last check, he was plunging a sword into an unspeakable monster.

"You're alive?" she asked with more shock than wonder.

"Yup."

"But how?"

"That, my dear, is one of the great mysteries of time."

"But..."

Kat checked the gauze bandage and wrap that Jud handed her from the medicine cabinet. Colt's blood dried, but when she removed it to check the laceration from the behemoth's last stand, she gasped. There was no trace. Not even a scar. Just the smooth, aged skin of a man in his forties, early fifties, tops. On closer examination, Kat noticed slight movement along his rib line, just beneath his skin. She dropped his blood-stained shirt at once as the movement startled her. It was not anything she saw before, nor wanted to see again. It was as if something were busy at work inside this man repairing the damage he sustained from the four armed monster that nearly ended his life.

"I don't understand," she said.

Colt turned his head towards her, attempting to bear some explanation, without really understanding the healing process himself.

"Seems like I heal faster than a normal man. Not only that, but benefit from a kind of resistance to that sort of damage again. Never had my throat cut before or wouldn't have hurt me. Bones, though, take a little longer."

He grimaced as he rolled on his side to face her. "Still hurts like the dickens, ribs anyway. The lung feels okay though, breathing back to normal."

Kat sat speechless.

"Wonder what your cards have to say about that?" he mused. "What are you doing here anyway, Ms. Ellis?"

She looked over her shoulder at Johnny. "He wanted to look for Uncle Mike."

Colt looked at her suspiciously. "Hm. Why do I get the feelin' that's only a half truth?"

In the next room, John Paul sat in a recliner next to a police scanner. He was focused on the sounds of the bands switching. The only broadcast coming through sporadically was the county fire department, which was quiet on this night. Whatever was going on in Kinston went unnoticed so far.

"John Paul on surveillance, huh?" asked Colt.

"He's back to Johnny after attacking that four-armed thing in the store. Not sure how he pulled that off either," she answered.

"Yeah, I owe him for that one. Another minute, I would have been flat as a pancake. Not sure If I could come back from being crushed like a walnut."

"So, you can die?"

He laughed at the prospect, as he was obviously still there in the flesh. His own flesh.

"No clue, but that's the closest I've come to it."

Colt attempted once again to sit up.

"Where do you think you're going? You're not all healed yet, that I can see," Kat said.

"Wanted to tell, Johnny 'thanks.' Kid got guts."

Kat turned her head, yelling over her shoulder. "Johnny, Mr. Sturgess says, 'thank you for saving him.'"

Johnny looked up over his glasses, nodded, then returned to watching the red diodes scan from left to right on the police scanner.

Colt grunted as he laid back down. "Doesn't talk much, does he?"

"Nope, only when he has something to say."

Sturgess chuckled, sending stabs of pain through his ribs. "We could all learn a lesson from that."

Resuming a supine position, he offered one remaining question before his exhaustion would overtake him, delivering him back to sleep. "What about the other kid and the girl? They make it out okay?"

Kat nodded. "Yeah, in fact, they both got the bank door off, or whatever that was, from that thing you and Johnny were fighting, courtesy of bolt cutters. The boy's name is Jud Allen; this is his house. He's pretty bummed to find it empty. His mom and brother were supposed to be home. His sister is missing, too. Lost his dad last night in the attack. Guess there were tractor trailers full of those ash tokers, like at Aunt Rosie's, but shit tons of them and clowns that pulled up to the fair while it was in full swing."

"Damned shame."

Colt stared up at the ceiling, wondering what they were after in Kinston, other than the obvious. He thought again about the size of the town and how this was not typical of Olath's operation. There was something extra here, unless the mad professor was getting too big for his britches. Whatever the reason, he was somewhere close. If Sturgess was going to continue his quest for vengeance, his body needed to be ready. His eyes fluttered closed, returning to the pit of fire.

◆

Rhonda wandered the upstairs hallway while Jud showered. There were pictures on the wall downstairs in the sitting room where Colt and Kat were. Pictures of a happy family. Many of them posed and taken at Olan Mills' photo studio in the city a half hour away. A lot of families went annually to have a wall of time, documenting the growth of their children. She and Emma once made fun of families that did that as the older one got, the cornier it became. Emma, her mom, dad and brother Eddie had them taken from 1970 forward. Jud's, around the same time frame. Upstairs, though, Rhonda found more candid shots. Photos not posed, not reflective of a tradition that was more of a requirement, but the Allen family simply living in experiences. Those were the photos she envied.

Jud opened the bathroom door, hair still wet, a towel around his waist. The last thing he expected to see was Rhonda outside in the hallway. He left her with Kat downstairs treating to Colt's wounds.

"Oh, sorry," he said.

She laughed. "Why are you sorry? I'm the one wandering around your house?"

"Um, I mean, well. I didn't take a change of clothes in the bathroom, since my room is right next to it. I figured I would just duck in really quick; you know?" He was over-explaining to cover his awkwardness. Rhonda found it adorable.

"Are you done in there? I'd love to clean up myself. If that's okay?" she asked.

"Okay? Oh, yeah, of course. Take your time. Towels are under the sink. Don't use the ones on the back of the door, those are used. Should have put them in the hamper, but didn't expect guests," he blurted out in one continuous sentence with only nervous pauses for punctuation.

Shut up, Jud, you talk too much, he thought.

"Yeah, cool. Won't be long. Just a lot of dust and, of course, my hair smells like smoke," she said.

"I hear that."

Rhonda brushed by him as she entered the Allen bathroom, locking the door behind her. Through all that went on in the past day, she could still send his heart into overdrive, smokey hair or not.

Jud slid on a pair of tidy whiteys and shorts. Sitting down on the edge of his brother's twin bed, he looked at the cork wall in front of him. It's why he chose his brother's bed over his. He wanted to draw the full view of their shared little space. Farrah Fawcett and Cheryl Ladd stared back at him, immortalized on posters. The advantage of the cork wall was swapping posters in and out with ease. Push pins did zero damage to the cork as opposed to nails in conventional plaster. Unfortunately, he wasn't made of cork and the changes taking place within him were constructing more walls.

In the quiet of his room, it was the first time he could let go. He was running on high emotions without a break, doing things he never imagined in even the most intense comic books. This was real life, and he was trapped in the pages. The next panels were yet to be sketched, drawn, inked, or colored, and he wondered precisely what role he would play within the story. The opening of his story was where were the remaining members of his family? Were they safe? What about these new supporting players that entered his life in the past few hours? Finally, her. Rhonda Coulter. His new sidekick, no, much more than that.

She picked up the bolt cutters after he dropped them. They worked together to get those chains cut so that Colt could do his thing. They learned his name from the Kat on the scant four-mile ride to the Allen's residence. Yes, they were partners through the most terrifying yet rewarding experience of their young lives. Whatever happened tomorrow or the next day, that memory was forever etched.

Funny, he thought, *a couple of years ago, didn't really want anything to do with girls.* Now this one who he crushed on from a far and known for just a day was keeping him afloat emotionally.

His bedroom door opened, then closed. Rhonda stepped in from his bathroom in the manner he intended before bumping into her in the hallway. She was drying her hair with one towel wrapped in another. He smiled as the wrapped towel was a beach towel from the previous summer's family trip to Myrtle Beach. Finishing with her hair, she tossed that towel to Jud playfully, then took a seat next to him on the bed.

"You okay?" she asked, stroking his semi-damp hair.

He paused a moment, staring up at Farrah. How on earth could she be playing second fiddle to this girl sitting next to him? *What an odd thought,* he contemplated. He didn't ponder the effect of trauma and how it would affect him. His scrambled thoughts, coupled with his inability to focus, were apparent, just maybe not to him.

"Yeah. Well. I kind of want to say something to you. More of explain something to you."

He scooted to his left, directly facing her. She scooted right to meet him. They took each other's hands, locking fingers.

"I know I pissed you off earlier, about your family and all," he said.

"Oh, that? Nah. I can get pissy fast with family matters, or rather bloodline matters. Takes more than a name to bind people together, whatever it is I'm trying to say."

"I get that. I just want you to know that my family isn't necessarily about white picket fences and a house on the hill, regardless of what you see around here, hung up in McNaulty's frames. Last summer, for example, my parents split..."

"Seriously, Jud. You don't have to go there."

"No, I do. It will help put things in perspective and I need to get it out." She nodded, squeezing his hands tighter.

He continued. "Like I was saying, last summer my parents split. I went with my dad and moved into my grandma's house. It was pretty cool, had my own room finally. Independence, the who magilla, you know? Then the messenger boy thing started. He wanted me to tell things to my mom. She sent messages back. Kind of childish if I think about it now, especially coming from the man who always blamed me when they got in to fights, which was often. See that window over there?"

"Yeah?"

"I actually threatened to throw myself out of it one time during one of their more heated shouting matches, which all of them were, never any physical violence, only verbal. You know, the kind that sticks with you."

Rhonda teared up. She knew all too well the destructive power of words. It showed.

"Sorry, got sidetracked. So anyway, I'm a sixteen-year-old messenger boy, like I'm not dealing with a basketful of my inadequacy issues, trying to patch things up between the two people I love most in the world. Eventually, pay dirt. It worked. Long story short, he moves back in, back to the family in the pictures, right?"

Rhonda smiled. "Congrats, you must have felt good about yourself bringing them back together?"

"If only silver linings existed. Same night we move back in, she starts with her shit again. I step in to calm things down, but dad grabs me by the shirt and throws me across the room. I mean, I was flying. Looking up, there's a monster, more ferocious than the one we saw today, except this one's name was 'dad.' He's got his fists clenched yelling at me and how everything that ever happened in their marriage was my fault. How does somebody live hearing that?"

Jud's emotional sharing pierced her heart, while hardening his. There was much more to this young man than Rhonda Coulter and their best friend Emma talked about, all the time as of late. Perhaps she judged him too harshly when she lost her temper, or they shared more in common that she imagined. She reached over and hugged him; her tears flowed freely. He continued unpacking his emotional luggage.

"Seriously, like how? Worst part is, ever since that incident, I've been trying my best to heal a wound that he created. I need my dad, for some strange fucking reason. Now that's never gonna happen."

He hugged her back, but without the tears. Whatever was going on inside of him, he drove it so deep down inside, it may never come to the light of day. The current disposition of his remaining family members was a concern, but more guided by an intellectual process than an emotional one.

Rhonda looked up into his broken eyes. It may not have been the bond he sought to establish hours ago, but this one being forged with a girl who bought him a shark book from the library was on the anvil.

They drifted together, exchanging a kiss. It was mutual and exclusive. She moved her other leg up on the bed, kneeling in front of him. He mirrored the motion. The beach towel that wrapped memories of the summer trip before the split slipped, dropping to the floor. Neither of them recognized it as a significant chance occurrence. The two slowly laid back on the bed. They were in no rush to explore each other beyond the moment that led to the next, then the next.

Making love for the first time was always an experience that lasted a lifetime. Jud and Rhonda shared their adrenaline, fear, courage, strength, sorrow, and now, their souls. That is what they were exchanging. Staying focused in each other's eyes while their physical union took them to a level of perfection both deserved, their rhythm matched their breathing, fueled by their heartbeats. Nothing mattered for the next few hours except each other. Time and space were meaningless beyond that twin bed facing a cork wall. This was their experience. After the first time was completed, he asked if it was okay if they could do it again; the third time she asked.

———◆———

Downstairs, it remained quiet. Kat fell asleep next to Colt, Johnny in the recliner. Exhaustion distracted him from watching the diodes on the scanner. In the distance, the chaotic screams of wherever the other tractor trailer stopped surrendered to the night air.

———◆———

Miles away, Olath stepped from his work in the herringbone parlor to feel the coolness on his skin after dispatching a semi back to Kinston under the command of Frick and Frack. He hoped that wasn't a mistake. How bad could they screw things up?

———◆———

Three miles away at the funeral home, Elizabeth stared up through the stained glass of her canopy, pondering what to do with Emma next. She was also slightly perturbed the view of the moon was obscured by the mosaic of the moon. Pinching her arm, she felt a slight tingle. This brought her great joy. Perhaps it would come quickly now, or maybe it was merely her imagination.

———◆———

Back at the Allen residence, the scanner lights stopped. A channel crackled with a voice message, not audible at first. The scanner completed two more cycles before fixing on one channel on the low band, unassigned by any official department. A voice fought through the static.

"Priority Alpha received. The eagle has landed. Repeat, the eagle has landed. If message received, report to the armory asap. Repeat, report to the armory as soon as possible. What the hell happened here? Looks like a war zone! Sierra Mike over."

Johnny opened his eyes, attempting to boost the receiver on the scanner.

"How far is this armory?" A voice came from the archway separating the living room from the rest of the house.

Johnny looked up. It was Colt Sturgess, standing in the dark.

"A few miles away, back the way we came. I can show you," Johnny answered, rising from the recliner, readjusting his pants.

Colt approached Kat, who was still sound asleep. He shook her lightly, awaking her from whatever dream she was having.

"Need to get everyone up. We're on the move."

FRED TERLING

Chapter Nine

The Oldsmobile pulled up to the gates of the Army National Guard Armory in Kinston. It stood as the training hub for guardsmen within a two-hundred-mile radius but manned by local Army reserve regulars. Kat hit the horn twice for entry before Colt exited the vehicle.

"Kat, darlin', you lost your mind? You want every 'toker in the area raining down on us? You saw what a little jingle bell brought at the department store." Colt scolded her.

"Sorry, wasn't there for that part."

As he approached the gate, four men dressed in black ops gear sprang up, M-16 rifles aimed at him. He laughed at them.

"Now fellahs, you know those bullets do little good against me."

One man stepped forward, keeping Colt in his sights. He resumed wearing his dark blinder glasses. The man recognized those.

"Damn, Sturgess, don't you ever age? Open her up, gang!" The man shouted to the other members of his ambush team. Colt waved Kat in to park the Oldsmobile.

"Formed you own team, huh?"

"Couldn't wait on you guys draggin' ass," Colt said. "Nah, just some kids that helped with a real ugly that hit us pretty hard in town."

The man patted him on the back. "Looks like they did a real number on the town. A little big for Olath too. He's getting ambitious. That spells trouble."

"My thoughts exactly, Sarge."

"Let's get inside for a debrief. Think you're going to like what we found. A little surprise, so to speak."

The group walked ahead, with Kat, Johnny, Rhonda and Jud pulling up the rear. Entering the guard armory was like walking into a vast hall with nothing in it except the flags representing each of the military branches and multiple United States flags lined along the walls. Even the floor was ultra-sanitized, with nothing but a layer of gray glossy paint. Their footsteps echoed across the hall as the group approached a small circle of men cleaning rifles surrounded by multiple empty folding chairs.

Jud stopped short of the crew, looking over each of them. He was taken aback by the small size of the unit. Colt gave them a down and dirty briefing on who these men were, specifically, the expectation they brought with them.

"This is all you got? Five men and an empty hall?"

Colt turned to him. "You'll come to learn seein' ain't necessarily believin'."

"I saw what that thing did to the side of McNaulty's, single-handedly, well, four handedly. Mr. Sturgess, I appreciate your saving our bacon, but we're going to need an army of Marines or something. I saw how fast those little gremlin things swept through the fair. It was devastating and without Johnny choking that big guy out, you might not be standing here."

Sturgess nodded at Jud. He was right. They needed a plan if they hoped of evening the odds against this overwhelming force.

"He's got a point, you know." Kat echoed her concern.

As far as the Kinston survivors and Shermer crew knew, these commandos were soldiers of fortune. This was their town, and they already endured heavy losses. What was this small group going to accomplish that nearly brought an end to Colt Sturgess?

Jud continued. "My big question is why are we still here? Why not just leave and find help. We're close enough to the highway to get out of town. Hell, I can make it in five minutes on my bike. I don't get it! You all have a death wish or something?"

"First off, who are these fucking kids? You know how I feel about operational security. If you've taken to babysitting Sturgess, they're on your watch," said Sarge walking over to one of the folding chairs, putting his boot up on the seat. "What's the boy talking about? Time for some intel, don't you think?"

The Sarge looked over the rag-tag group of survivors from the town now under Olath's thumb. Each of these people accompanying Colt Sturgess had a piece of the puzzle, or he wouldn't have brought them to the armory. It wasn't the old cowboy's style to pick up strays. It hurt operational efficiency and created additional unknown variables. Such variables could easily lead to catastrophic results. As leader of the Smoke Hunters, he would hear them out for now.

Kat took exception to the characterization. "First off, I'm no kid. I'll have you know, I'm twenty-four years old —"

"Settle down, Kat. Just a figure of speech," Colt said as he walked towards the circle of men. "Jud, hold your horses. There's a reason we're playing this close to the vest."

Before sitting down, Colt handled the introductions. "Citizens of Kinston, meet the Smoke Hunters. You've already met the charmer of the group, The Sarge. From left to right, we have Flower, Brushcut, Flamethrower, Country Boy, and Spectre is the one dragging the spare chairs over. That's with an 're,' not an 'er.'"

They all waved; a couple saluted with three fingers. It was their sign.

"Hunters, meet Johnny, Kat, Rhonda and Jud's the opinionated one. Lost his old man and family to the hoard two nights ago."

"Sorry, man. I feel you. Lost a few brothers myself over time," said Spectre.

Sarge swung his chair around, mounting it from the back facing front. "We got one more, goes by the name of Scout. He's a boot on lookout down there at the base of the entrance ramp; got eyes on the way in and out. Plus, we commandeered the CB radio from an abandoned truck on the table over there. Guessing that was your work, Sturgess by the couple of heads laying under the wheels, unless Olath's using his ghouls as chock blocks these days."

Johnny stood up, walking over to the CB radio. He held a particular interest in the hardware.

"This picking up transmissions to the trucks?" he asked.

"Yes, it does," Sarge answered.

Johnny sprinted out the front of the armory, Kat giving chase.

"What's that all about?" Brushcut asked.

"The kid is good at tinkering with stuff. Real good. Probably has some ideas of what to do with it," Colt answered.

Sarge leaned forward over the back of the chair. "Let's have a SITREP or situation report for you civilians."

Colt recounted the past day since his arrival at Rosie's to crossing paths with the others from the Kinston group, adding details to fill in the gaps between the two locations. Eventually, he reached the portion of their tale where the behemoth made its appearance.

"Eight feet tall with four arms, using vault doors for armor? Had to be one ugly son of a bitch," Flower said.

"I'd like a crack at something like that," Country Boy added with a deep southern drawl.

"Not this thing," Colt assured them, "nearly sent me to an early grave if it weren't for these kids. They saved my ass."

"Kids, huh? You going soft on me, Sturgess?" asked Sarge.

"Like I said before, seein' ain't always believin.' They gave it hell until it dropped," he answered. "Speaking of which, I need to get something from the back of my ride. One toker that attacked the diner. Damnedest thing I ever seen."

"Do tell," said Sarge.

Before Colt could respond, Johnny returned from the outside with Kat. The armory doors banged shut as she followed him over to the table where the CB radio sat.

"Sorry," she said. Noise discipline was not something she was accustomed to practicing.

Under his arm, Johnny carried the police scanner from Jud's house. When asked if he could have it, Jud nodded. His dad would be happy it was being put to good use if he couldn't listen to it any longer. Retrieving a pocket toolkit, Johnny went to work on the back panels of both Fred Allen's emergency services scanner and the radio taken from the tractor trailer. Kat returned to the discussion circle and sat down.

"What's he doing?" Colt asked.

"He said he can fix it so we can hear what's going on when their trucks talk to each other or the home base. Something about dedicated frequencies, but I don't get any of the electronics stuff," Kat answered.

Colt shot a glance over to Sarge, who returned a shoulder shrug. "If the kid knows what he's doing, give him a shot."

Sturgess turned to face his accidental team from Kinston and Shermer. Sarge was right. These four were now his responsibility. *Funny, Lizzy always wanted a family,* he thought. Not quite what he had in mind, but here they were.

"How can I get to the firehouse from here?" he asked.

Rhonda stepped forward, pointing back towards the door of the armory.

"Head back out the door, turn right down the hill. You'll see the fair, or what's left of it, off to the left when you get near the cross street. Hang a left at the intersection. One block up on your right at the end of the street is where it is," she answered.

Kat interjected, "I thought you were worried about making noise? How are you going to get there and back with none of those things that still may be around seeing you? You sure you're all healed to do this?"

The Smoke Hunters snickered in unison.

"Don't suppose you've seen him move, eh, doll?" asked Country Boy.

Colt grinned. "I'll be fine. There and back in a couple of minutes."

Sturgess walked towards the armory door. In a flash, he was gone.

———— ••• ————

Colt Sturgess glanced across the town of Kinston. This was a fresh vantage point from the church tower. Reaching it in a few seconds after departing the armory, he stood at ground zero behind the bank looking at a demolished car, surrounded by three sledgehammers. An odd sight that he would put in his memory bank for a later time, should the need arise.

It took him several months after the incident at his farm a century ago to master moving at the sped-up rate in which he was now accustomed. Counterbalance, so he didn't tumble head over heals with his increased speed, was the primary skill the cowboy needed to master. Stopping was next.

The asphalt glistened with the damp remnants of the fire hydrant purge. Peeking out from the corner of Kinston Savings and Trust, Colt used his other gifts of perception to detect any danger that still may be lurking. The parking lot was a graveyard of chaos. Although the blood may have been washed away, the destruction of the amusement row and the rides lay scattered across the parking lot. Catty-corner from his position, Sturgess spied the firehouse. In a mad dash, he moved past the debris, crossed the street, and arrived at his destination. The safety blankets covering his bike were untouched.

Jud sat quietly with Rhonda, staring at her. She blushed when he held his gaze a little too long. Olath's creatures were the last things on their minds right now. With the rising sun came an afterglow of love's first light. He told her he loved her last night. Did he really mean it, was it something that was said in the heat of passion or a bandage for his soul? Whatever the reason, in that moment, she believed it to be real because she was feeling it for him, and it sure felt real. Real enough to not be concerned with what happened with these monsters that dismantled their town.

The armory door swung open. Immediately, the Smoke Hunters hit the deck, aiming their weapons at who or what was entering. With a sack slung over his shoulder, Colt walked into the armory. Getting back to their feet, the hunters switched their weapons back to safety.

"Christ, Sturgess! Trying to get yourself shot?" Sarge barked.

Colt walked to the center of the room. The entire group reacted to the vile odor of the unseen thing in the burlap sack he carried.

"Left your bike? Didn't hear it," Kat asked.

"I pushed it up from the firehouse instead of riding it. That whole noise thing. Didn't need to take the risk," he answered.

"You covered all that distance, to and from, pushing your motorcycle up that hill in just a couple of minutes?"

Country Boy laughed. "I told you, young blood. The man's quick."

The word "motorcycle" drew Jud's attention from Rhonda momentarily. He thought back on the Electra-Glide he saw pass through town. In all the chaos, he nearly forgot about it. The rider resembled the man standing in the middle of the armory with the stained sack. Until now, he didn't make the connection.

"What the hell's that god-awful smell?" Spectre asked.

"Don't reckon there's a table around here?" Colt asked.

Spectre, hand over his nose and mouth, pointed to a stack of folding tables leaning against a far wall. The group stood their ground, not wanting to get any closer to whatever was in the sack. Sturgess dropped in on the ground, opened one table, retrieved the bag, plopping in down in the center. The Smoke Hunters moved in for a closer look, accompanied by Jud and Rhonda. Kat remained, knowing its contents, while Johnny continued with the radios.

"Show and tell time, gentlemen," Colt said, tipping his hat towards Rhonda, "and ma'am."

Retrieving a bowie knife from the sheath tucked in his right boot, he cut a slit down the middle of the burlap sack, exposing its contents. Each of the group's members gagged as the smell intensified. There was the thing. An ash toker in its infancy, something none ever saw previously. The dark, dry skin had turned gray and moist. The wide-open dead eyes stared up at them from the bald, chubby face. Colt pulled back the remnants of the sack, exposing the elongated arms and legs, tipped with long, sharp black nails. Sarge glanced over at Sturgess.

"This is fresh. Really fresh. Don't think we've run into one of these before," he paused, "which means —"

Colt nodded. "We're close."

Despite the smell, the group couldn't help but to stare at this missing link in whatever twisted evolutionary monstrosities Olath was creating. There was an air of excitement permeating the foul stench. They were always several steps behind the mad professor and his minions. For once, they may be on time. Sarge motioned to Country Boy, who understood, but was less than thrilled with the unspoken command.

"Get that on ice in the cooler below. May need the damned thing, although I'm no biologist, still could serve useful if we hit any snags," he said.

Country Boy scooped up the ash toker, holding the bag like a discarded purse by the slit Colt cut.

"So, what's your surprise?" Sturgess asked.

"Follow me," said Sarge.

———— ◆ ————

Frick and Frack were en route back to Kinston. Olath's faith in them may have been misplaced as they turned off the wrong ramp initially and blew by their exit, missing it by twenty miles on the second attempt. Pulling a U-turn on the following exit was problematic as neither of them had the experience of driving big rigs to maneuver the thing, causing a traffic jam, drawing the attention of the state police, who missed them by a mere eight minutes. Eventually the pair got on the right track, ensuring radio silence, fearing the wrath of Olath. Speeding back towards Kinston, they were seventeen miles away.

———— ◆ ————

Walking around the outside back of the armory, the Kinston group approached something covered by a tarp. Pulling it off like a magician revealing his trick, Sarge stepped back, expecting a round of applause. No one knew what they were looking at, other than a large horizontal black metal drum with eight rubber tubes protruding from valves on the top, capped off on the ends.

"Some kind of new age artsy octopus?" Kat remarked first, finding the thing anything but normal. In fact, it resembled some sort of perverse torture device.

"What am I looking at here, Sarge?" Colt asked.

"Should have inspected the back of that truck after you unceremoniously liberated those clown's heads from their bodies. Discovered a mobile ghoul lab in the back. This here is a tank of Olath's finest. The elixir of vitae, as he called it, on the documents we found outside of that itty-bitty town where we first met."

"You don't say?"

"Oh, I do say. Me and the boys have a plan brewing for how to bring these fuckers down."

Sturgess crossed his arms, examining the apparatus from a distance. He knew of the potential danger of coming in contact with the contents of the drum.

"I'm in, just remember, Olath's mine."

Sarge nodded. "Goes without sayin'. There are three five-ton trucks parked out back, keys locked up somewhere, but that's no big deal. Flamethrower's been hot-wiring cars since he was in diapers. Used to steal MP jeeps for us to take on liberty when we were stationed at Long Binh Post outside of Saigon. My thought is, if we can spread this goo in a centralize location, draw the 'tokers in, then let Flamethrower do his thing, while they're all getting their high off the stuff, we can take them out, or they can start taking each other out. Don't know if the clowns buzz on the stuff, but by the sounds of it, there are only a few of those for every couple of hundred 'tokers?"

"Yeah, that's the way I understand it, from what the kids said and how it went down in that five and dime. Speaking of which, almost forgot about the second semi. May still be there on a road running south off the main street. It stopped there before all hell broke loose. Didn't have time to go back and check it out. It was the cash drop truck, so may be nothin' of value except the money they looted from the bank," said Colt.

"Just money? Sturgess, you are getting soft! Spectre, you and Country Boy, go check it out when we finish."

They nodded as Sarge lit up a cigar before continuing.

"Problem with the plan is not enough firepower. Used the last of our C-4 outside of Morrisville, Kentucky, high ordering a pack of them in full attack. Barely got out of that one."

"Armory here has nothing?"

"Just M-16s. Not even banana clips, so our reload would only be max twenty rounds, although they jam if you put in over 16-18. No, we need demo or something with a hell of a lot of rounds, unless you got ideas. Sounds like we're talking about a serious infestation and if Olath targeted a town ten times what he usually does, he's pretty sure he can pull it off."

Silence fell over the group as they pondered the dilemma.

Jud spoke up. "If we're stuck here on this mission, I think I can help. I know where we can get some heavy-duty weapons."

"How's that kid?" Sarge asked.

"Heavy duty weapons .50 cals at least, maybe even heavier stuff."

"Where's that, Jud?" Colt asked.

"Arnie's surplus out on 51. I get a lot of stuff there, but Top Arnie's told me he has the big stuff tucked away that he 'acquired' when he served as a weapons loader in Vietnam. He served in Korea too."

Sarge considered it momentarily. "You sure the old man's not pulling your leg?"

"He could be, but wouldn't hurt to check it out. Only about twenty miles north, two exits up. We could be there and back in under an hour if he's blowing smoke."

Colt and the Smoke Hunters exchanged glances. There was a lot to consider. Sunrise just broke. There was no telling what was in store for the day. It was the start of a plan, but without additional resources, they were dead in the water, unless they torched the entire town, which was a possibility. Fire was the great equalizer. That wasn't an option as time didn't afford a full, boots on the ground recon of Kinston to search for pockets of survivors like Rhonda and Jud. Somehow, they survived the onslaught. There may be others.

"We can always take a skeleton crew, leave the rest of you behind to back up Scout, should any of Olath's gang return. Where'd you say this place is, kid?" Sarge asked.

"I don't know the exact road names, and there's a turnoff. That's tricky if you don't know it's there. I'd better go with you," Jud answered.

It was a lie, but nobody knew that but Jud. Rhonda smacked his arm, not appreciating his newfound bravado.

The rest of the team gave the three-finger salute after considering the proposition. Sarge relented.

"Alright, let's give this a shot. Brushcut, you and Flower are with me and the kid. The rest of you, buckle down with Sturgess and brainstorm. If this old Master Sergeant is full of shit, we're gonna need a Plan B."

Jud followed the men over to the five-ton, climbing up the step to the passenger side while Brushcut and Flower jumped in the truck's bed. All were armed. As he went to slam the door, Rhonda grabbed it from the outside, sliding in beside him.

"Uh, uh. You're not going anywhere without me, Mr. Allen, and you were gonna leave me without a kiss?"

Flamethrower sparked the wires that turned the engine over. The gas gauge was half full. Easily enough to make a forty-mile round trip.

"Last chance, you two sure you wanna do this?"

"Burnin' daylight, Sarge!" Jud said.

Rhonda rolled her eyes. She hoped Jud's sudden display of hyper-masculinity was temporary. Him standing up to the Smoke Hunters surprised her as was his willingness to lead the away team. This wasn't the awkward boy she and Emma watched rehearsing his greeting next to the demolition car. Something was brewing inside of Mr. Judson Allen.

———◆———

Elizabeth sprang from her bed, startled. Music was blasting from every intercom panel on the walls, an addition the Delaney's made to the home that she didn't notice.

"What is that noise?" She screamed out in agony, cupping her hands over her ears as she raced to the top of the stairs.

The sound grew louder as she vaulted the stairs towards the viewing room that she ordered closed. It was now open, the sliding door removed by force, resting against the far-right wall. She advanced, viewing a closed casket, hopefully a sales model only. Entering the room, Emma was dancing furiously. Seeing Elizabeth enter, she pointed at her, singing even louder. Elizabeth hated contemporary music. It was too noisy and many of the lyrics made no sense to her, particularly in this song. It lacked artistic relevance, although she never took the time to understand it. Perhaps Elizabeth resented the song that referred to a lover being as cold as ice.

"Turn off that horrid sound!" Elizabeth demanded, attempting to speak over the blaring music.

Emma pointed to her ears. "What? Can't hear you!"

"I said, turn it down, you wretched child!"

Walking over to the tape player hooked into the intercom unit, Emma turned the sound down to a conversational tone. That was her definition of compromise. She defiantly kicked a path through the cassette tapes she decided were unworthy of her consideration, discarded all over the floor. Brahms, Bach, some person named Rachmani-something that she couldn't pronounce. Wedding music, Emma thought ill of all of it, although she was living in a funeral home.

"Can you turn it down more, or better yet, off?" Elizabeth implored her, but that would not happen.

"Can I? Yes. Will I? No!"

Emma resumed dancing.

Elizabeth charged at her, reaching for her throat, but Emma deflected the attempt with a grip on her wrist to apply a slow, steady squeeze. She had yet to fully feel sensations, but Elizabeth could hear the cracking of bones.

"Now, now, mommy, that's no way to parent." Emma pushed slightly on her chest, sending her flying backwards across the room, slamming into the wall. In under a second, Emma stood above her.

"Yeah, I'm that strong, and twice as fast. Think before demanding anything unless you want those pretty new little arms and legs of yours crumbled like a cracker. Speaking of which, I'm starving and I want more than burgers."

Elizabeth stood up, looking at the girl she helped to create. In her own twisted way, she did truly think of her as her daughter. Although not by birth, she spared her from the transfer. Her new limbs could very well be Emma's, a thought that she would need to remind her at some point. This was not that time, though.

It was teenage rebellion against the parental figure, Elizabeth thought.

She had no clue, nor experience, just things she read in a magazine she found particularly intriguing called "Cosmopolitan." She read it cover-to-cover for years, particularly the past ten. Taking a deep breath, Elizabeth tried a simpler approach.

"Okay, Emma dear, what would you like for breakfast?"

"Not real fond of the 'dear' tag, but if it floats your boat, have at it. I was thinking a steak. A big ass steak like a T-Bone. Medium well, rare, raw, from the source, I don't care. I'm craving one."

"Where might I find one of those for you at this time of the morning?"

"Um, duh! How about Uncle Fester's farm? It is a farm! Gotta have cows, milk, maybe even a store house of potatoes and ears of corn. It's like a buffet out there!"

Elizabeth considered it. Between the hunts, transformations, and experiments, she stayed away from Olath's work, once her needs were met first, of course. She never had a protégé. Why not? The slaughter of a cow could be amusing. Plus, she never bathed in the blood of an animal. It could be a new experience worth repeating.

"Fine, the farm it is. I will retire to get a pair of shoes. It's dirty out there."

"You better get more than shoes. How about some clothes?" Emma snickered at Elizabeth's obliviousness concerning her present dress.

Elizabeth stopped her progress towards the steps. "What's wrong with this outfit?"

"Are you kidding me? You look like a whore!"

"That is simply not the truth. I've only been with one man."

"Huh, in all these years and body parts, never felt like taking them out for a spin? Too bad for you. Anyway, in that getup, you're going to cause boners or laughter."

"Why would anyone laugh?"

Emma shook her head. "How old are you? Boys laugh when they're embarrassed. Nothing's funny. They still want to ball you, just too awkward to have any other reaction. They're all basically children. We have something all of them want. Flashing it just gives them an excuse for disgusting behavior. You really want that?"

Elizabeth paused, contemplating the girl's comment. It was decades since she entertained any such conversation. Although a beast herself, Emma represented the potential that she always desired. Also, she hadn't mused about herself in any sort of sexual capacity in just as long. Even though a patchwork of other people's flesh, desires did creep in that she typically took care of on her own. Completely liberated from men, it was inspiring to know that perhaps she still projected sex appeal, even if it would not be used for any sort of seduction.

"So, what do you recommend?" asked Elizabeth.

"I don't know, or better phrased, I don't remember, just something that doesn't include nudity," she answered.

Elizabeth ascended the stairs, searching through the wardrobe, then the closet of her commandeered bedroom. Mrs. Delaney had good taste in clothing. Elizabeth recognized many of the labels from Cosmo. She made her first selection, a sheer black dress, exposed shoulders, lace at the wrists. The bottom of the dress carried the same design, but she couldn't see her legs, which was a must. She slid her arms in, searching the dresser for a pair of scissors. Nothing. Returning to the closet, she spied a small sewing basket on the floor to the rear of a row of shoes. Cutting a vertical slice up the middle of the dress it now conformed to her fashion. Looking in the mirror to ensure she made the correct decision; Elizabeth didn't quite match the outfit. Something was missing.

After rummaging through a jewelry box, she made her selections: a pair of pear-shaped drop earrings, a triple string pearl necklace with a diamond brooch, and finally, her veil. The veil became her thing since her creation. It was her steel-blue eyes. The pigment faded, but not as completely as Emma's eyes. The lace covered them enough to buffer her feeling of inadequacy, not that any of them knew why some transformations ended with the pigment loss, but she coveted the look, finding it beautiful in its rarity. It was for her appreciation not to be wasted on the army of ghouls, certainly not on Olath. For that reason, the veil was mandatory. Sliding on a pair of black shoes she randomly selected, she headed back downstairs of the funeral home.

Descending the staircase, Emma applauded from the stained carpet below. "Much, much better."

She turned off the music, replacing the door to a semi-repaired state. Emma also cleaned up a bit, selecting a summer dress from clothes in the basement where the embalming was performed. It was the only one that fit. If it belonged to a client or one of the Delaneys, it really didn't matter.

"How's mine? Not exactly my speed, I'm a jean and tee shirt kind of girl, at least I think I am, but this fits, so…"

"You look beautiful." Elizabeth bowed her head.

Emma was showing signs of civility. That was refreshing. The defiant independence and fearlessness were entertaining, but at some point, they needed to become friends if the two were to move towards any kind of familial bond. This was Elizabeth's newest, fondest desire. Eventually, she just hoped she could abandon thoughts of killing the little monster in her sleep.

"Let's go!" Emma ran for the door.

Elizabeth searched for the keys on the rolltop desk next to the door but couldn't find them.

"Looking for these?" Emma held up the keys, jingling them between her fingers, next to the car.

Elizabeth just shook her head. Progress was going to require patience, more than she currently possessed. Emma jumped into the limousine, starting it up. Surrendering to the thought, Elizabeth circled to the passenger door and entered.

"I wasn't aware you knew how to drive," said Elizabeth.

"I don't."

Emma laughed as she pushed the accelerator to the floor, speeding off in a cloud of trailing dust.

———◆———

Frick and Frack's tractor trailer pulled off the highway, speeding down the exit ramp. Frick hit the brakes, sending the trailer skidding to the right, jackknifing the truck. Frack yelled out, caught by surprise.

"Why did you—"

"—do that for?"

Frick pointed up ahead at the semi they positioned as a roadblock. The bodies of the clowns laid on the ground, headless, the back door of the trailer swung back and forth from the breeze, ramp down.

"We better call—"

"—Professor Olath."

"He's not gonna—"

"—be thrilled!"

Frack grabbed for the CB radio; Frick wrestled it away from him. Frack slapped him on the top of his head. Frick stuck out his tongue.

"We agreed, you drive—"

"—and I get to work the radio."

Frick crossed his arms in bitter defeat.

At the armory, Johnny finished wiring the scanner and CB radio together, shunting the connection to channel eight, giving the transmissions from either, a dedicated channel. He turned the scan mode off, which only required him to monitor one channel without interference from any other.

He patiently sat staring at the blinking diode. Kat sat on the floor beside him, drawing tarot cards, seeking higher guidance for the situation at hand. Would they get through this? What would actions should they consider? She didn't dare wander with her divinations on the matters of life and death. That was predicting the future, which could be altered by any action any of them take from the next moment forward.

The diode held red; Johnny turned up the volume. Initially static, then a voice came across, no, two voices, but weird. It sounded like two people talking, but only one sentence.

"Professor, there seems to—"

"—be a problem in Kinston."

"Is this thing—"

"—even on?"

"I told you I—"

"—should do this—"

"—not you!"

"Professor Olath —"

"—can you hear me?"

Static resumed, as did the flashing red diode, but the name caught the ear of Colt Sturgess from across the room, currently with his feet up, hat pulled down, continuing to rest and recuperate the ribs. He sprung to his feet, toppling the metal folding chair. Reaching the table in less than a second, he leaned in next to Johnny, fully focused. The static broke again.

"What is it you, clods? I knew it was a mistake of grave consequence to task such detours on the evolutionary scale to accomplish an elementary task." It was him, Olath.

Sturgess never heard his voice before outside of his dream. It was firmly rooted behind the wall of his memory. Hearing it for the first time in a century, he reached back desperately to see his face. There was a shape, minor details, but the glaring sun that accompanied the image washed any identifying details he could connect. It was him and he was here. Close by, as was clear by his minions broadcasting over the scanner.

"Why's he talking like that?" asked Kat.

"Some people like to sound a lot more important than they are, sometimes," Colt answered.

"Mission not accomplished, if you ask me. He sounds more like a dork than anything else." Kat's comment meant to amuse, but Sturgess was too focused on the broadcast. This was everything to him.

"Our truck had—"

"—an accident here."

"We stopped because—"

"—the guard truck is —"

"—open and the clowns —"

"—are all dead."

Static ensued momentarily before Olath's voice returned to the scanner. "Fine. You are abundantly aware, however, that my location is substantially removed from yours. It will require a minimal elapse of time to reach you?"

"Aye —"

"—aye, skipper!"

The radio returned to static. He was on his way.

"I don't suppose you can give me a lock on their location, Johnny?" Colt asked.

Johnny shook his head no.

"I can," said Flamethrower from behind him. "Scout has eyes on a TT that jackknifed on the ramp into town. He's holding tight on top of a Foodland, half a click away."

Colt took the walkie talkie from Flamethrower. "Scout, this is Sturgess, situation report."

"Sturgess? Hey, brother. Haven't gotten the pleasure yet, but the boys tell me you're one tough mutha! Glad to have you with us. I've got a semi stopped on the ramp. Drivers are attempting to straighten her out, but don't think they've been around too many rigs. They're in a fix, total clusterfuck. Doubt they're going to get it squared away soon, if at all."

"Hold your position, we're in route. Be careful, Scout, no idea what they're hauling. I've run into a couple of real horrors so far. Any sign of toker activity?"

"None that I observed, but hard to see the little fuckers at night and they bed down during the day, as you know."

"Yeah, I gotcha. That's why you need to be extra cautious. Intel is that these semis are hauling hundreds of them at a clip and the day time thing is out the window. We got clowns too."

"Ain't that a shame? I remember when clowns were fun."

"Welcome to the 1970s, brother. Sturgess over and out."

Colt handed the radio back to Flamethrower, then patted Johnny on the back. "Good job there, John Paul. Keep listening for anything that may be important."

Johnny turned, giving him the three-finger salute of the Smoke Hunters.

"Ready to talk a walk? I'd like to wait for Sarge and company to return, but this may be our only shot. I'd recall the others, start spreading some of Olath's goo." Colt said to Flamethrower.

"Sure, lemme check in with Spectre and Country Boy on their progress with that other semi." He clicked the transmit button on the walkie talkie. "Hey Country Boy, got your ears on buddy? Alpha Romeo recall. Hostiles have landed, target zulu is inbound."

"Hell yeah! We're on our way back. Secondary target was what Colt reported. Hate like hell to leave bins of Franklins and Benjamins behind, but these dead presidents aren't ours. Looks like where your behemoth was hauled in, too. Buckets of meat to feed the thing. If Spectre wasn't so squeamish, I'd drag some back for dinner."

Behind him, Spectre yelled. "Fuck off."

"ETA?"

"Fifteen mikes, lock and load!"

"See you then, over and out."

———————

The limo pulled up to the farm between the slaughterhouse and the parlor. Emma jumped out of the car, followed by Elizabeth. Olath hurriedly approached them.

"I'm sorry if there are no salutations or pleasantries. Our consideration is required immediately in Kinston. There is the appearance of foul play concerning our current operation and —"

He didn't finish his sentence as Elizabeth slapped him across the face.

"I warned you, this was dangerous. Taking on a town of this size. Inevitably, there would be pockets of resistance. Your blitzkrieg of ghouls only created martyrs, which in turned created vengeance. I am completely amazed every law enforcement agency in the state hasn't descended already," she said.

He didn't straighten up after the blow, but assumed the posture of a servant who had been punished. Slumped over, he looked up at her sideways with his long fingers interlocked. His voice lowered to a childish tone, just above a panicked whisper. It disgusted her when he took this physical posture. Nothing but weakness seeped out of him. At least Emma pushed back, nearly breaking her wrist. That earned respect, admiration. This driveling fool offered neither, just continued talking.

"Oh, I assure you, we have the resistance to any such action adequately in place. Our operation is nearing fruition. The last item of relevance was the recovery of currency and coin, which, although overdue, may simply denote a simple inconvenience."

"'A simple inconvenience'? Then why are we needed there? Answer me that?"

"You have a certain way, a gift if I may be so bold, of persuasion that only you possess that creates an environment of pliability should it be required. On our simpler adventures together, your lead opened opportune doors for the rest of us to step in and achieve what we desired to accomplish."

"Exactly! And this time, you had to roll in hard and fast without it. Look what's happened!"

"It was merely a miscalculation on my part in securing trust in those who may have been better suited for other duties."

"Who'd you send?"

"Well, in hindsight —"

"Who did you send, Olath?!"

"Frick and Frack."

Elizabeth brought her fist down hard on the hood of the limo, leaving a dented imprint of her fingers. It hurt. That made her smile. She finally felt pain. Holding out her hand, she shot her gaze at Emma. Whatever boundaries the young woman in the sunflower dressed pushed early, she wouldn't dare to encroach upon now.

Elizabeth possessed an unseen power Olath touched upon. Maybe she was aware of it, maybe not. She exuded a sort of mesmerism, not one of persuasion; it was one of fear. A fear that is not spoken of, even in the darkest recesses of the soul. As her emotions heightened, the object of focus scattered hopelessly into the well of profound despair. Whatever their most calamitous experience was, it paled in comparison. One may even label it as evil, but that was such a simplified, esoteric way to describe it. The only way to remain safe from it was simply avoidance.

Emma handed her the keys to the limo, taking her place in the spacious back of the car. When Olath moved to the passenger door, Elizabeth stopped him.

"Get me a slab of meat, and now. Animal, not human. I'm sure you butchered some for the clowns. We don't move until I get a steak. The faster you tend to that task, the quicker we leave. And bring it on a plate with a potato and silverware!"

Olath bowed, scurrying off to the farmhouse.

Chapter Ten

The National Guard truck screeched to a halt in front of Arnie's Surplus. They knew it was the place by the enormous silver spray pained bomb hanging from a pole that said "Arnie's." An old-timer wearing a Vietnam era field jacket stepped outside of a swinging screen door of the shop, intercepting the group as they disembarked the truck.

"Can I help you, gents?" he asked.

Jud dropped from the five-ton, moving towards Master Sergeant Arnold Phillips, owner of the surplus store. His friends and those who served with the salty veteran simply called him "Top Arnie." Top recognized Jud as he approached.

"Oh hey, Jud, who's your friends?"

Jud paused, thinking about how to answer that question. He didn't truly know any of them, outside of Rhonda, of course. Unbelievable circumstances melted them together. Explaining those circumstances, particularly the creatures behind decimating his hometown, would definitely require a leap of faith. Then there were time considerations. How to answer a simple question, reliably with experience, was a challenge.

"Kind of on a mission, Arnie. Thought maybe you could help," he answered.

Arnie cautiously inspected each of the men from head to toe. "Uh-huh. Not the government, are they? I don't want any trouble with G-men snooping around my operation. I do an honest business here. Cash on the barrelhead. Nothing shady."

Sarge stepped forward. "Definitely not government. We avoid any entanglements with the man as much as we can. Don't exactly plant roots, either."

Arnie tilted his head back, looking at Sarge. "Mercs?"

"Not exactly. We serve our own mission parameters. Rarely reach out for help either, prefer to keep things in house, if you get my drift."

"Uh huh." Arnie wasn't sold.

Rhonda stepped through the line of men, offering her hand for a shake. He took it apprehensively.

She jump-started the stalled conversation. "What these shit kickers are looking for, including my boyfriend, Jud, is some heavy duty, ass kicking weapons. We just came from Kinston where the whole town got run through by these little black gremlins looking mother fuckers. Leveled it. Then there are the clowns —"

"Demonic clowns? Knew those sons-a-bitches were lurking around here somewhere. Saw a semi roll through a couple of days ago with them driving. Thought they were part of the fair. I hate clowns," he said.

Top Arnie looked down at the ground, rubbing his chin, considering what Ms. Coulter just shared.

"Yeah, demonic clowns and you should have seen the monster that busted up McNaulty's," Jud added.

"The five and dime? That's a shame. Get my dress shoes there. Damned fine hoagies too."

Top turned, walking towards the front door while he and Rhonda continued conversing. Sarge and company followed. Brushcut chuckled, whispering to Flower.

"Doesn't matter how old you get; nothing opens doors like a pretty face and nice ass."

Jud glared unapproving of the assessment.

"Settle down bro, it's true!"

The group entered the surplus shop. Arnie assumed his position on a swivel chair behind the wooden counter that was older than him. Service pins, patches, mugs, and various memorabilia covered the counter in display stands. The store stocked rows and rows of everything from rucksacks like Jud's to utility uniforms to ashtrays made from spent cartridge cases from the big guns. All items were military grade, some used, some new.

"So, these clowns and gremlins don't have enough to take care of them yourself?" asked Top Arnie.

Flower joined the conversation. "Negative, Top. A handful of M-16s is all."

"Pussy guns, those are toys. Handgrips made by Mattel. How many of these things we talking?"

"Hundreds, maybe thousands, they attack in waves. My girlfriend and I saw the first attack," Jud answered.

He snugged up to Rhonda finally, now that she broke the ice with Arnie, his friend, by the way. She grimaced at him, not happy with his flip flopping in and out of his soldier of fortune fantasy.

Arnie turned to Sarge. "You all served in country. I can see it in your faces."

"Yeah, all of us did, same unit. Weapons platoon, 199th Infantry."

"Redcatchers, huh? I know about you guys. Defended Long Binh Post against the Cong 275th, gave them hell, you boys did."

"That we did, sir," said Flower.

"Don't call me 'sir.' You know goddamned well I worked for a living being a Master Sergeant, son."

"Understood, Top. I stand corrected."

"How about vampires? Any of those around? You Redcatchers hunted those too. How you got your name, no?"

"Vampires?" Brushcut laughed.

Arnie spun around, pointing his finger in his face. He lit an unintended fire.

"Don't believe in vampires, son? Maybe seems like something for the creature features at the drive-in, but I guarantee the Sarge over there knows what I'm talkin' about, he just can't verify it. Operational security and all that malarky. Didn't matter if it was Cong or US blood, all tasted the same to them. Goddamned savages..."

The group looked at Sarge, who said nothing, just stared ahead, rolling his dog tag along the chain around his neck. Was what Arnie saying the truth or was Sarge playing a poker face because they needed his help and didn't want to poke fun? Hell, half of the group would have never believed the horrors they experienced recently. Flower knew Sarge the longest, next to Country Boy. He, too, shared the million-mile stare.

Arnie faced Rhonda. "See these young kids today? They get confused really easy when talking to their elders. Why I always liked your boy, Jud. Minds his Ps & Qs when he's in here. Tries a little too hard sometimes, so give him slack if he acts like an asshole, but not too much slack. He's young, but he'll learn with age." Top winked at her.

Rhonda grinned. This favoritism was nothing new to her. She exuded a natural charisma and self-confidence that most lacked. Being herself, feeling out every situation and knowing just what to say was second nature to her, particularly with men, regardless of age.

Arnie walked around the counter to the side of the store, pausing. "So, if I have something stashed with a little more kick than those service rifles you all have, what's it worth to you?"

Sarge thought about that. He had a couple of options. Both commodities he currently possessed, placing him in the position to bargain. One not entirely his, but, with all things considered, possession that was nine-tenths of the law.

"We're not looking to buy as much as borrow. If we all come out of this in one piece, we just come back with your stock."

Arnie roared with laughter. "C'mon, Redcatcher. I might have been born at night, but it wasn't last night. Like I said, I do my business with cash on the barrelhead."

Option one was a failure. Sarge tossed out the second.

"Hypothetically, and this I'm just throwing this out there, what if I were to know the location of a certain semi a couple of these clowns ditched before meeting their demise at the hands of these kids here and another hard charger with a personal axe to grind with the leader of these ghouls?"

"You got my attention, Redcatcher. Continue."

"This semi may or may not contain a cargo of commandeered cash looted from the bank in Kinston."

"Sarge!" Jud yelled out in obvious opposition of the implication.

Arnie laughed again, squeezing Jud's shoulder. "Settle down, Jud. Banks have insurance against those kinds of things. FDR signed that into action in 1933. What are they teaching you kids in school? Don't mean to blow up any of your perceptions of old Top Arnie, but what I'm about to show you certainly didn't come through any requisition orders."

Top nodded at Sarge, leading the men to the back wall. He pushed a Marine Corps flag aside, revealing a keypad.

"Semper Fi," Arnie said as he punched in a code.

The door unlocked as he and Sarge entered the small doorway into a larger room. Arnie moved to the center of the room, no bigger than the shed out behind Rosie's tavern.

"This was supposed to be a fallout shelter, constructed during the red scare, but I came up with a better use for it."

He pulled the chain on a ceiling light in the middle of the room. Instead of canned food supplies and the other items one would store in a fallout shelter, various weapons of every imaginable caliber were displayed on the shelves. Beneath a shelf on the right, Sarge spied two Browning M2 .50 caliber heavy machine guns. Sarge reached for one when Arnie grabbed his arm.

"Nah, have something with a little more balls for this mission of ours," Arnie said with a huge grin.

"'Mission of ours?'"

"Yup, supplemental condition. If I'm going to lend you this, need to make sure it comes back safely and of course, you need to take me to that clown truck afterwards or we all walk out of here right now and you go home with your Mattel toys."

This time, Sarge nodded. Arnie pulled a camouflaged covering off the centerpiece of the collection. There it sat on its makeshift tripod, surrounded with at least twenty boxes of ammunition, more ammo covered behind that stack.

"You gotta be shittin' me! You have a —"

"M61 20-millimeter Vulcan Chain Cannon. 'The hand of god,' they called it. All two hundred and forty-eight pounds of her. Six barrels of hate that spit out six thousand rounds per minute. Not a precision instrument, just point and shoot. That enough firepower for you?"

Sarge was speechless, rubbing the top of his head. "The boys are gonna shit when they see what I bring 'em."

"We got a deal on the truck? Those clowns knocked over the bank. That's on them. I happen on the spoils and just leave it there. That's on me. Couldn't forgive myself."

"Hell, I'll do you one better. When this is all over; I'll throw in the five-ton out front, too."

"Damn, Sarge, you trying to make this old man blush?"

He reached down, grabbing one of the .50 caliber machine guns, handing the other to Sarge. "Let's take these as cover fire for when the main course needs a reload. Your boys can handle this heavy beauty."

Sarge turned towards the door after picking up the second .50 cal. "Brushcut, Flower, get in here. Need some muscle."

"Gotta take it around back. I had a special mount built in the back of my Jeep. Never told the welder what it was for. He asked once. I told him none of his fuckin' business. People think I'm a little off as it is, so why ask a second time?" Arnie told Sarge as they exited the room to make space for Brushcut and Flower.

"Holy shit!" Brushcut spit out after entering the room and saw what was awaiting them.

Arnie supervised the effort. Once secured on the mount, the shuttling of ammunition drums began loading the five-ton. This would be a joint effort between the two vehicles. After all was loaded, Arnie drove around the surplus store in the jeep with the payload under the same tarp and rope. He locked up the front of the building. They were ready to go. The Smoke Hunters, Jud, and Rhonda prepared to load up.

Arnie walked over to them, placing a utility cover with his unit insignia on Rhonda's head. "I got the Redcatcher pins, but that's on them to give it to you. Gotta earn that one."

He smacked Jud on the shoulder. "Don't be jealous, Jud Allen. I give you a discount on all the gear you buy!"

Arnie addressed Sarge directly. "I'll take point. Not sure how you got here, but if we cut across the back county service roads, we'll hit Kinston from the north, behind where the action's gonna be. Just keep up. This will cut ten minutes off the trip, but we need to haul ass or it will be longer. Frontal assaults are for the walking dead. I'm gonna need a loader too. Prefer they come with me, in case we run into a hot zone." He pointed to the radio on the dash of the truck. "That thing work?"

"Yup. Just need to get closer to town. Limited range," Sarge answered.

"Well, if you get news that shit hit the fan and were pulling into a firefight, flash your headlights so we know what to expect. If you're all set with the .50 cal assignments, let's move out."

Sarge typically led the group, but with the augmented weapons section and the need for expedience, he felt fairly comfortable with Top Arnie barking the orders. Time was of the essence. There was no need for a pissing contest between the two. The group loaded up with Flower assigned to Top Arnie as his loader. The engine of the five-ton rolled over, Jud handling the hot-wire this time, Sarge pulled behind the jeep as it sped out of the parking lot, spitting gravel.

Colt knelt next to Scout on the roof of the Foodland. He watched as Frick and Frack chaotically attempted to find a solution to the jack-knifed tractor trailer at the bottom of the exit ramp.

"How long they been at it?" Colt asked.

"About a half hour now. At first, they tried to push the cab back, which amazingly they were able too, but it just bent the trailer at a steeper angle," answered Scout.

"Dealing with a couple of real rocket scientists there, huh?"

The radio crackled. Incoming transmission.

"Alpha team alpha. This is alpha team bravo, come in." It was Spectre.

"Alpha team alpha, over," Scout answered.

"We just arrived at temporary HQ, dropped off the payload from recon. Awaiting deployment of Operation: Elixir."

Scout looked at Colt for the response. He was merely his name-sake and not in the position to confirm any orders, particularly ones involving a plan he wasn't aware of. Colt took the walkie talkie.

"This is Sturgess. Any word from the surplus detachment?"

"Not yet, but they should be inbound, by best rough estimate, in communication range at any moment."

Colt hesitated, then gave the command for the first phase of the mission. "Lock and load deploy to pre-designated coordinates, but do not drop the payload yet. Repeat. Hold the cargo."

"Roger that, over and out."

The unit decided after the briefing to continue using call signs and encrypted messaging if some short-wave radio enthusiast happened upon their frequency. If Johnny could jack into channels, the possibility that someone else could too was a possibility they didn't want to confront, particularly with the authorities. Also, if the phone switching terminal was destroyed, per Jud's observation, how long until a service technician showed? This was their mission, their hunt. Much like Olath and Elizabeth, they wanted zero official intervention. Colt and Scout continued their surveillance on the two dimwits who were still attempting to straighten out a seventeen-and-a-half-ton truck by hand, twenty tons if it was loaded.

"Damn," said Scout.

"What is it?"

Pointing up to the top of the on-ramp, a state trooper slowly cruised towards the disabled truck. It pulled up beside it. Frick and Frack turned towards the trooper. He activated his flashers.

"What do we do?" Scout asked.

"Wait. Too much at stake to make a move now."

The trooper exited his vehicle. All Colt and Scout could do was watch. Any interference that close to the ramp could send Olath away to disappear once again. Sturgess hoped for the best but knew that was nothing but a pipe dream. He watched as the two men in the paneled baseball caps talked to the trooper. They lead him to the back of the trailer. After disappearing momentarily, the two men on the roof of the Foodland heard the scream, a horrid sound of crunching, followed by the familiar wave of darkness skittering along the ground.

"Dammit, ash tokers." Colt said, springing to his feet, vaulting the side of the roof and dropping to the ground.

"What the fuck?" Scout murmured, seeing Sturgess' action.

Knowing he didn't possess the same, whatever abilities he just witnessed from the man sitting next to him a second ago, he shouldered his high-powered sniper rifle, taking aim at the gas tank on Frick and Frack's semi.

Scout played out this scenario at least a dozen times while awaiting orders. Loading an incendiary tracer round, he zeroed in and pulled the trigger. The truck exploded, sending a glorious plume of fire into the air, triggering a second ignition of the trooper's vehicle.

He didn't know how many 'tokers made it out of the trailer, but a grin instinctively creased his face as he could hear the chorus of screams echoing within the blaze. Frick's and Frack's bodies were last seen hurling into the air, landing in a field next to the downslope of the ramp. A pack of ash tokers who were lucky enough to escape the explosion rushed towards the town when Scout's second round found its way to the roadblock semi blocking the entrance to Kinston. A new explosion lit up the late morning sky.

Seconds after admiring his accuracy, Scout's attention was suddenly drawn below. He saw Colt step into the middle of the street, presumably awaiting any stragglers that survived the two blasts.

In the center of town, Country Boy, Flamethrower and Spectre were startled by the two unexpected mushroom clouds of fire emanating from the east end of town.

"Think it's time?" Spectre asked.

"I think that's a pretty clear sign. Smoke 'em if you got 'em."

The crew rolled out their five-ton. Flamethrower jumped in the back, grabbing the hose nozzle they affixed to the tank of Olath's elixir. They drove down Main Street, turning up North Central and down Jefferson, eventually turning right on Carver, hosing down the street with a trail of the elixir. Jumping over the curb into the parking lot of the demolished fair, they stopped. Dismounting from the vehicle, they took up their predetermined positions to spring the trap. All they needed was the command of execution, or any sign that the time was now.

<hr/>

The sounds of explosions gave Kat a fright in the armory. She was peeved that she was left on babysitting duty with Johnny, who she was sure wouldn't budge an inch from monitoring the radios. Everyone had something to do but her. She was the one who instigated the trip to Kinston, at least tried to thwart the behemoth's attempt on Colt, and nursed him back to health, although his self-healing powers made her effort on that front obsolete. Yet the cards gave her a simple message that she needed to be here. Was her role to be an ancillary one? A support character who simply provided transportation and unneeded care? She drew one last card before deciding to head up to the roof to check on the explosion. It was the Wheel of Fortune.

Great. shit happens and fate rolls on. *The best I can do is roll with it, trusting my higher self,* she thought.

On her way to the stairs to the roof, she checked in on Johnny. He was still fixated on the radio. Of course. She ran up the stairs until she reached the ladder to the roof. Up she climbed, sliding the latch keep and flipping open the hatch. Striding over to the edge of the rooftop, she could see the burning vehicles on the west side of town. In the center, the abandoned five-ton. Kat saw the trace of the elixir the team spread circling the streets around the parking lot across from the borough building. There was some sort of commotion with small plumes of flames sporadically popping in and out towards the Foodland, but she couldn't quite see what was happening as her view was obstructed by a building with a sign facing the street she couldn't read. Half of the group was hiding around the downtown, but she didn't know where. The other half, with Jud and Rhonda, should arrive at any moment. Kat would have felt a lot better if they were there already.

———◆———

In the armory two stories below her, channel eight on the scanner crackled, then a voice came through for the third time in the past two minutes.

"Frick, Frack. Either of you two or both. Respond. I don't have time for your folderol, respond instantly. We will arrive in a matter of moments. Reply at once."

The message echoed across the empty hall of the National Guard armory. Scanning continued along with the unanswered messages, but the table sat empty, as did the folding chair in front of it. It was abandoned by its monitor.

———◆———

Kat leaned forward, continuing to contemplate her role in this dark adventure. She drew another card, but something pulled her away from it before she could interpret its meaning. Someone was running down Central Avenue towards Main Street. Looking closer, she knew that stride instantly. Only one person ran like that.

"Johnny!!!"

———◆———

Next to the Foodland, Colt engaged the remaining ash tokers. Kitana in one hand, peacemaker in the other, he battled his way through the charging hoard. After igniting the two tractor trailers, Scout joined the fray, choosing a more conventional way to access the ground, the fire escape. He and Colt stood back-to-back, Scout preferring dual wielding a pair of Marine Corps, seven-inch blade KA-BAR Bowie knives.

"How can you move so fast?" he asked.

"Just try to keep up, kid. You're doing just fine," Colt answered.

It was an odd time to converse, but the two were dispatching these creatures with such alacrity, they found it enjoyable in a strange sort of way. In the heat of the battle, neither noticed the limousine that navigated the burning obstacles speeding towards them. By the time they did, it was too late. The vehicle hit both of the slayers, sending them on to the hood of the vehicle, over the roof, depositing them on the pavement.

The car sped forward through the pile of ash and flaming bodies of 'tokers. Responding to the vehicle, the remaining ash tokers shifted their focus, giving chase, leaving the two men laying on the asphalt.

━━━◆━━━

Kat turned the Oldsmobile into the parking lot directly next to the borough building, where she found Johnny sitting on the curb. She rushed towards him, embracing him with both relief and anger.

"John Paul Ellis! What the hell were you thinking?"

He looked up at his sister with tears in his eyes. This she wasn't expecting. Johnny was not readily one to display sorrowful emotions publicly. There was something shiny in his hand. She reached for it, but he wouldn't let it go. Kat pulled him down to sit on the curb. He opened his palm. It was Uncle Michael J. Babin's constable badge.

"I had to warn Colt. There was another message on the scanner. They're almost here. But I found this instead," he said.

A symbol, the ultimate confirmation that their other adoptive parent was gone. It meant more than just a badge. It was their uncle's entire life of service. His selfless dedication to others, even after his retirement. His willingness with Aunt Rosie to open their hearts a little wider to take two unloved teenagers into their lives.

Kat's reflection was interrupted by the sound of a car speeding towards their location. She pulled Johnny up by his hand to move towards safety. That's when she saw it. Stuck on a piece of rusty old staple on the phone pole, gently waving in the air's disturbance from the car that just sped by. She pulled it off from the staple, glancing it over. A smile spread across her face as she hastily folded it up, plunging it into her back pocket.

The two started back towards the Oldsmobile when a figure appeared in front of them. Lost in her thoughts, she failed to notice the long black limousine, now idling to her left on Main Street, stopped and backed up.

"Hello, children." The lanky figure with the pale skin and jagged teeth leaned in towards them with a black umbrella twirling above his head. "Might you inform me as to the whereabouts of mummy and daddy?"

FRED TERLING

Chapter Eleven

The surplus crew was close enough to try the walkie talkie. Sarge picked it up, pressing the transmit button.

"Alpha HQ, alpha HQ, this is alpha charlie, repeat, this is alpha charlie, over."

Nothing but static. No response.

"Alpha HQ, this is alpha charlie, over."

Still no response. Sarge knew there was a problem. Two walkies ran silent, one at HQ in the armory and one with Scout. No response from either. Concern washed over the group in the cab of the five-ton. The other issue was, only Arnie knew this back route and how close they were. Sarge was applying dead reckoning based on the sun's position, but that was merely supposition. He handed the walkie-talkie to Jud.

"Keep broadcasting the same message there, Allen."

Sarge flashed his headlights, which Arnie saw in the rearview of the jeep. He punched the accelerator to the floor. Daylight was burning.

———◆———

Olath's grip on the wrists of both Kat and Johnny was excruciating. Even Johnny's flares of strength that helped dispatch the behemoth couldn't break the hold. Dragging them into the center of Main Street, he released Kat's arm to retrieve his umbrella. She wasn't going anywhere without Johnny. He knew that.

Olath spun around, examining the town, high and low. There were remnants of an obvious ambush when he entered the town. Then there were these two children, as he called them, and of course, the five-ton military truck in the center of a parking lot he cleared a meager two days earlier. The front of the bank was decimated, which meant the withdrawal was made, but the truck with that bounty and his safecracker had yet to report back to Chooch's Farm. Some game was afoot that he wasn't aware of. An opposition force that he meant to address, here and now.

"Come out, come out wherever you are!" he yelled into the air.

His ghoulish voice echoed off the empty storefronts of downtown Kinston. There was no response.

He continued with the taunt. "I have your children here. Certainly, you don't desire for them to perish. Their resiliency is something to admire."

He turned to face the other end of town. The Smoke Hunters watched from their camouflaged positions, eager to charge this asshole to free Johnny and Kat. They did not know who this pale, lanky character was, but by his obvious bravado, it very well may be Professor Olath. If so, they knew he was the property of Sturgess.

The team couldn't abandon the pre-planned strategy as it was sound. Part of the hunt was waiting with the occasional sacrifice. Hopefully, these two young people who fell prey to unwelcomed circumstances would not become further victims of this creepy figure standing in the middle of Main Street next to the idling black limousine. Still, the frustration was unbearable.

"Where the fuck is Sarge?" Flamethrower whispered.

Olath spun around. He, too, possessed ultra-sensitive hearing. Staring directly toward a well concealed Flamethrower, he addressed the hidden hunter.

"There you are! Hiding in the penumbra of chaos. A measure of tactical acumen I can appreciate, but my time and patience have eroded."

His spindly finger reached up toward the pocket in his black leather vest. Before he made his next move, another sound distracted him. The sound of a motorcycle closing in on his location. A 1973 Harley-Davidson FL Electra-Glide to be more specific.

"You're fucked now, asshole!" Kat spouted with glee.

Olath slowly turned towards her, raising his hand.

Colt Sturgess roared up the hill, past the borough building, skidding past Olath. He stopped his bike, deploying the kickstand. Scout laid draped across the back of the motorcycle, gravely wounded from the impact of the limo.

Moving to complete the action of striking Kat, Olath realized his arm laid on the ground beside him in a pool of black viscous fluid. This motorcycle cowboy that should be dead from the car's impact, just severed it clean off with surgical precision. Colt dismounted, walking slowly towards him. Olath increased his grip on Johnny.

"Your current path forward is unrecommended, cowboy. The boy is firmly in my —"

In a blur of motion, Colt moved behind the object of his hate kitana blade across his throat.

"Now, you may survive without an arm or a leg. Hell, maybe even both arms and legs. But without a head. I'm guessin' that's a whole other story." Colt pressed the blade deeper into the flesh of Olath's neck. "This is between you and me. Let the boy go."

With apprehension, he released Johnny's wrist. This cowboy was probably going to take his head. Releasing his only bargaining chip was potentially a mistake, but what choice did he have?

"Kat, you and Johnny get out of here. No reason for bein' out here, anyway. Shoo!"

Kat grabbed Johnny's hand as they ran down Main Street, taking the long way around to get back to the armory. They made enough mistakes, giving away the location of their hideout would not be the next. Besides, Colt was about to kill Olath, and that would be that. Wasn't he?

Colt spun one-armed Olath around to face him. He wanted this man to look him directly in the face, so he knew exactly who it was that finally put an end to his reign of terror. Colt kept the edge of the blade firmly on Olath's throat. Sturgess was disappointed that Olath wasn't begging for his life.

"I'm afraid we haven't yet shared the privilege of acquaintance, sir. I am known as Professor Olath of —"

"I know who you are and I'm afraid we have shared an acquaintance, but it wasn't a privilege. In fact, I'd call it a downright nightmare."

Finally, Olath squirmed. "You have me at a disadvantage, sir. My memory recall is —"

"Enough of this shit. I've waited long enough!"

Colt drew back the sword as the pale, spidery phantasm of his dreams, the man who took everything from him, raised his remaining arm in an irrevocable act of desperate defense. The limb wouldn't block the edge of Colt's sword, even without the added force of a Harley travelling forty-five miles per hour.

"Wait!" a voice shouted out from behind them from the rear of the limousine.

Colt glanced up to see a woman approaching in a black dress with a veil. She was pale like Olath, but a shimmer to her skin. Did the ghoul have a bride? Knowing that he left his wife to perish in a firepit outside of their home, the thought enraged Sturgess. Next to the woman trailed a teenage girl about the same height. Not as old as Kat, more like Rhonda's age. Did they also have a child? It was enough of a distraction to keep Colt from swinging the final blow.

The woman looked straight at him with stark silver-blue eyes he could see from yards away through her veil. His hyper senses easily penetrated the lacy fabric. The girl, no pigment. Like his. What were the implications here? How could this be unless...

"I'd stop right there, lady. If you have something to say to your man, you have about three seconds. You can pass on last rites after that," Colt said.

Elizabeth laughed uncontrollably. "My man? You joking with me, cowboy? I would have disposed of him myself long ago if I didn't need him."

As she drew closer, she couldn't shake a feeling. A feeling that was tucked away, far away in her past. There was something about the cowboy's voice, something familiar. And his face.

Colt broke the gaze of her eyes to get a full look at her. Every detail he knew, a thousand times over, he dreamed of it in earlier times. But the attitude, the bearing, was all wrong. That wasn't the way he remembered her. Was this another of Olath's tricks to keep him from dispensing his final judgement?

Elizabeth, too, was experiencing something that was beyond her understanding, her acceptance, as she drew closer to the cowboy with the sword against the throat of the benefactor of her ongoing life.

The Smoke Hunters watched anxiously, awaiting the death blow so they could put their phase of the operation into motion to smoke out, literally, any remaining 'tokers, clowns and whatever else still inhabited this town. What was the holdup?

"Do I know you, cowboy?" Elizabeth asked.

Emma stepped forward. "Why don't you two kiss already? The attraction is obvious."

Colt froze as his memories burst from the dam of the wall that been holding them back.

"Lizzy?"

The expression dropped from Elizabeth's face, along with any remaining color that laid beneath her porcelain skin. For the first time in centuries, emotions awoke from her as well, other than spite, disappointment and anger. Tilting her head to the side, she removed her veil.

"Colt?"

She was still alive. After a century, she was still alive. Olath didn't kill her, leaving her to burn like he did him. He took her, keeping her alive in the manner that he had the ash tokers, the clowns and the twins. The scars on her shoulders were visible, as the one not covered by the multiple strings of pearls. This wasn't his beloved Lizzy, this was her head on a body crafted by a madman he was about to kill.

Olath sensed Colt's temporary crisis. "Ah, I remember you now. Colt Sturgess. You are also one of my creations, although I am unsure how you have survived the past century without, shall we say, my particular brand of augmentations? So, you are the one behind all of this, foiling my attempt to heighten the prosperity of my operation? I am reminded of the tome by Richard Matheson that speaks of a boogeyman who haunts by day. Are you this legend, or merely another one of us, unable to embrace the truth? I rather liked the ending of that story."

Sturgess looked back at Olath. Could what he said be true? Is he himself one of these ghouls he slaughtered to reach him? His blade dropped to his side. Olath moved back, ever so gently. Elizabeth moved forward to face him. She took off his hat, running her hands over his face, fingers through his hair.

"My god, it is you. How can this be? How can you have lived all of this time? I thought you were dead!" she said, astonished. "And you haven't aged a day, not a minute!"

He lifted his head to face her. Suddenly, it was her. The wall in his memory crumbled, and the missing pieces of his dreams assembled. Colt fell to his knees; his sword hit the ground. His mind was over-whelmed with images he could not control. Perhaps that was why they were held back from him for so long.

<hr>

He saw himself on that fateful day in 1886 as though he were outside of his body watching a grand tragedy. There they stood with Lizzy as Olath approached with the pitch. The elixir that would enable them to conceive a child. Colt was skeptical, as these types of peddlers were a nickel a dozen around the trading post. Lizzy ran into the house to retrieve the bounty. It was up to the men to work out the price. There wasn't much of a negotiation, as this Professor Olath wouldn't budge from five dollars, which was a ludicrous amount of money for what was likely colored water. When Lizzy returned with their safe box, Colt was immediately alarmed that seeing that much money would cause more than an increase in price, but flat-out robbery. His assess-ment was correct. Olath's companions did just that after Lizzy enthusi-astically handed over five silver dollars from the box.

Their assault targeted Colt first, knocking him to the ground, stomping on him as if he were a mere roach. Next came the part that his subconscious hidden from him for a century. The shattered memories that he would have to face, here and now. Olath poured several bottles of the elixir down Colt's throat. The madness took hold at once. He sprung to his feet, swinging wildly at the three men who invaded his property. Running at Lizzy, his sudden transformation terrified her. He saw it in her usually beautiful eyes. One man took a run at him. Colt grabbed the aggressor, snapping his neck and discarding his body across the front of the homestead as if it were a stuffed scarecrow brought in from the field. Lizzy hid behind Olath for protection. The sight of this overwhelmed him. He fell to his knees much like now, dropping to the earth in death, or so it seemed.

Olath's remaining assistant dragged Colt over to a pit where he stored dry wood for the winter. Unceremoniously watching with Lizzy secured firmly underneath his arm, the professor ordered the body set ablaze, along with Sturgess' victim. There it went dark again. Whatever happened next was beyond his memory, but a new one was planted. It was the elixir. That's when it became clear. The lack of aging, the speed, enhanced senses, immunity to fire, unnatural healing ability — they were all the result of Olath's elixir. Yes, he was one of them. It was something that he could not bear.

<hr />

Lizzy called out to him in the present, in the middle of this town named Kinston. Raising his head, he stood slowly.

"My dearest. You are alive!" She tore open his shirt, examining his neck and shoulders for even the faintest traces of scars. There was nothing. "But, I don't understand…"

She reached up for his glasses. "Let me see your eyes, my love!"

He grabbed her hand, stopping her.

"That's not wise. My eyes aren't exactly friendly to your kind," he said with a bitterness that sent a chill through her.

"Oh nonsense, let me see your beautiful eyes. I loved them so."
Elizabeth removed his glasses with blinders. He kept the lids shut
tightly. She prodded.

"Oh, come on darling, I need to see all of you. Look at me. Help
me understand."

Suddenly, he opened his eyes. Unlike in the Allen residence, they
were glowing white. Elizabeth screamed in terror, falling to the
ground. Olath caught her.

"My face, my face, it burns!" Emma and Olath rushed her into the
limousine.

Colt bent down, gathering himself while picking up the katana
sword. He had a job to finish. Especially now.

"I told you, my eyes aren't for your kind," he said bitterly.

Sturgess rushed Olath, but he already made the next move,
blowing the whistle tucked away in his tunic, slamming the door shut
before Colt reached him. Olath punched the accelerator to the floor,
spinning the tires as the car sped off.

A great rumbling started from beneath, over, and above the town.
Something was coming, summoned by Olath's whistle, a lot of things
by the sound of it. The pale professor informed Elizabeth that he had
a plan for attacking a much larger population than they normally do.
Was this the end of what was left of Kinston?

Sturgess helped Scout off the back of the bike, Spectre and
Country Boy rushed in to retrieve him, starting triage. Flamethrower
remained with the mission aim solely on his shoulders now to
execute.

Colt jumped back on his Harley in hot pursuit of Olath and
company. This was his endgame, but this time he wouldn't hesitate.
What he would do with Lizzy and the girl, he hadn't thought through
about yet, but bringing to light that he was merely another of Olath's
experiments gone awry reinforced his resolve. There was no way he
was going to let that limousine escape town.

"Go get the bastard!" Country Boy yelled.

If Kat were still up on the roof overlooking the town, she could have witnessed the flow of ash tokers flooding the streets of Kinston. Lucky for her and Johnny, they were secure in the armory. From every direction on every street, side street and alley way they poured in, paving the damp asphalt of the town with a layer of darkness, a layer of death. They came out of the sewer gratings, popped out of access hole covers, emerging from every nook and cranny in the town. Doors swung open from the now abandoned buildings as parades of clowns led the newly born monstrosities that spawned from Olath's elixirs. Mindless brutal things that only existed to serve their masters, all converging on the location of that single, solitary whistle blast.

Sturgess raced forward, but his movement drew a wave of 'tokers pouring down Carver Street, past the church he originally used as a lookout post. They were created for one purpose and one purpose only, bring death to everything they crossed. Gaining on him, he doubled back up a side street, through a passageway with just barely enough clearance for him. When he cleared it, he looked ahead to see that he was losing ground to the limo.

In the center of town, Country Boy and Spectre scooped up Scout to get out of the path of the converging ghouls. The effort was unsuccessful as the hoard overran them, not even stopping to pick apart the pieces that remained as the flayed men fell to the ground. They never knew what hit them.

Flamethrower witnessed the entire scene, including the utter annihilation of his friends, more than that, his brothers. As a unit, they all experienced more losses than any of them cared to discuss, unless plied with ample amounts of alcohol at a time of their choosing, but this was in a different category.

Beginning the hunt after returning from service, it was more recreational than anything at first, but it became a holy war against the evil that all of them genuinely believed would eventually overwhelm everything that made life worth living. Here in the shadows, with torrents of ash tokers moving with such ferocity, that vision came true. He was the last vestige to harness this evil, hoping Sarge and his team would arrive to finish them. Nervously, he lit the wick on one of the many Molotov cocktails he created for the mission. Flamethrower moved towards his position, maintaining stealth. Rearing his arm back, he threw one with all of his might, then another. It was the third one that drew hoard's attention. He was nothing more than a skeleton after the ash tokers diverted their stream of death towards him.

Sadly, Flamethrower did not live to see that the first one indeed hit its mark, igniting the elixir chain. The fire spread as fast as the creatures were moving, not breaking a link at anywhere along the path, it even caught a sizeable chunk of the skittering things on fire as it completed its path around the block, reaching the source tank in the middle of the parking lot on amusement row. The smoke billowed, heavy and thick, spreading in whichever way the wind blew.

<hr>

Colt's increased speed closed the gap as he neared Foodland, where he and Scout had held off the swarm initially. Behind him, the 'toker reinforcements were catching up. As he passed Foodland with the limo in sight, he was tossed from his Harley, which skidded across the road into the grass next to the railroad tracks. Slowly, he got up from the spill, shaking out the cobwebs.

"What the hell?" he muttered.

A chain hung between two phone poles. From behind each of the poles, out stepped Frick from the left, Frack from the right. Their clothing melted to their skin, hats still smoldering, road-rash on both of their faces. They waved with big smiles to Colt, who stood in the middle of the road watching the rush of darkness heading his way down Main Street. He closed his eyes, drawing his katana once more. The last thing he observed was the limousine speeding up the ramp, disappearing from sight. If this was to be his last stand, he was taking as many of these things with him as he could. Frick and Frack tightened the chain once again, leading the charge forward.

"You know, I'm about fed up with you two boys," Colt said, as he bent down to pick up his hat.

The pair moved around him in a circle, intending to tie him up for the ash tokers, but they made a serious miscalculation. Smoke from the ignited elixir drifted their way. Nothing drove the creatures wild like what their name suggested. Even a slight whiff of the stuff drew them in with a solitary focus. As Frick and Frack began their second pass, they observed the retreating ghouls heading back to the center of town.

"Uh—"

"—Oh."

Colt came down with the full force of his strength on the center of the chain, letting the blade do the rest. Frick and Frack both fell backwards onto the street. Sturgess looked at one, then the other.

"There's an old saying about only the good die young. Not today," he said to the macabre twins.

In one motion, he sheathed the katana, drew his peacemakers, firing a single shot into both of their heads, right between their eyes. They dropped to the ground simultaneously, flopping forward. He checked to ensure they were actually dead this time. No pulses, although that was no guarantee. He dragged one over to the other, securing them with a section of the chain to a phone pole. Tugging on the links, he stood looking towards the haze filling up the town. There was no way he could go back into that; it would render him helpless twenty yards in.

He pulled the Harley out of the grass to assess the damage. It must be my lucky day, he mused, although it was far from that. Mounting up, he sped off in the limo's direction. Maybe his luck would hold out.

Elizabeth continued to scream through the pain from the back seat. Olath rolled up the window of the limo separating the driver's compartment.

Her tantrum continued. "My face! My face! I'm ruined. How could he do that? He's supposed to love me!"

"Settle down, Lizzy. Uncle Fester will fix you! Doesn't he always?" Emma said.

Attempting to calm her down, she couldn't help herself in using the familiar form of Elizabeth's name that Colt uttered moments before. The last thing she wanted to hear was hysterics the entire ride home, but throwing in a jab was too deliciously tempting.

"Don't you understand, Emma. He was to be your father?"

"Really? A shame, actually. I thought he was pretty hot, in a Sam Elliot kind of way, always went for the older guys."

That snapped Elizabeth out of her fit. "Ha! Like you would have a chance. I was his first true and only love. He's been searching for me for over a century. How romantic is that?"

Emma was going to come back with a smart-ass remark but forced herself to bite her tongue. It was quite plain that his sole purpose in traversing the decades was to put an end to Olath. He didn't even know she was still alive. If the fantasy soothed her from the noise, let it be Emma. Besides, it was nice to see this completely vulnerable side of her.

"Why do you think he's still alive when all you need the groovy ghoulie treatment? I mean, it's not like I wasn't watching when you felt up his chest. It was kind of hot," Emma asked.

This was an aspect of the encounter Elizabeth had not thought about, yet considered, as the reunion ended so abruptly. "That, my dear, is an interesting question. You think maybe the elixir actually worked on him?"

"Yeah, but don't get too close. You saw what his x-ray vision did to you."

Elizabeth scooted to the end of the seat, looking into the setting sun. "Interesting," the thought seeped from her lips. "Very interesting."

Chapter Twelve

"What in name of Hades did I pull into?" Arnie shouted as he stopped the jeep after entering the thick fog of the burning elixir.

Sarge slammed on the brakes of the five-ton, not expecting Arnie to stop. He leaned out the window. "Why'd you stop, old timer?"

"Hold your horses, Redcatcher." He walked back to the five-ton. "What in Sam Hill is going on here? And that god awful smell."

"I don't know. Radio silence for the last fifteen mikes. They must have sparked the elixir by the looks of it," said Jud.

"Is this safe to breathe or am I going to have the sudden urge to smear makeup all over my face and start driving funny little cars?" asked Top Arnie.

"I don't know how safe it is. To us, we're good, but it drives the ash tokers bat shit crazy. They're drawn to it like dogs to a bone. Better let me take the lead. I know where we planned on the flame trail," Sarge answered.

"Suits me just fine."

Arnie climbed back into the jeep as Sarge passed him, heading down the hill.

The group looked for landmarks through the haze. Although they were late, time would not stand still. Rhonda saw the outline of the armory, but Kat's Oldsmobile wasn't out front. There was a tractor trailer parked on the street adjacent that wasn't there before.

The ash tokers would enrage after a brief exposure. Much like their previous forms, each response would mimic how they reacted when consuming too much alcohol. There were happy drunks, violent drunks, angry drunks, sleepy drunks, to each their own. Except now, the brains of these foul creatures were reverted to a much more primitive state than a cognitive one. Once they reached their fill of inhaling whatever high they got off of the burning elixir, the frenzy would begin, even turning on each other. Plus, this was an ignition of the actual elixir itself. Typically, the smoke came from the burning of corpses. Human fat burned much more steadily, lasting much longer. Or so they guessed.

Sarge stopped the truck in the middle of the hill, about twenty yards from the edge of the bank on Central and Main. He made the turn and then backed the truck up slowly. This was the best view, giving them the full advantage of holding the high ground. He parked the truck, Brushcut tossed out the chock blocks for the tires and pulled the bed cover off to optimized lines of sight. Sarge walked to the back of the truck, to check in, but Brushcut already thought ahead, locking and loading the .50 cals, lining up ten rows of ammo boxes per gun.

Top Arnie followed Sarge's lead, backing up the jeep. He pulled out his binoculars looking down on the town square.

"Jesus Christ on a cracker." Arnie lowered the binoculars. "I mean, I believed you guys. Well, kind of, but there gotta be tens of thousands of them down there. All huddled around that tanker like it's some kind of unholy statue about to deliver them from evil, but we're the ones about to grant deliverance."

That is precisely what Top Arnie observed. Not only where they huddle around the smoking tanker, but they were stacked on top of each other, writhing in whatever strange ecstasy fueled their chemical nirvana. Clowns marched slowly around the fifty square yard mass of the dark things to some syncopated beat that only they heard. On the other side of them, every clown was accompanied by a newly reanimated fiend, genetically mutated, based on what part of their coding rejected the re-sequencing. Those resembled the one Colt dumped from his burlap sack on the folding table in the armory.

Jud thought about how he always loved Halloween as he looked down at the lot where he started this dark chapter. In fact, it was his favorite holiday. Which was obvious considering his taste in late night creature features. He wasn't so sure if that will hold true if they make it through this night. Fear crept into him as he looked over at Rhonda. When he rushed in on the behemoth, he had nothing to lose. Now he did. Speaking of the behemoth, Jud wondered if there were more of those below and more on point, how far was Colt if they needed him to take care of it? The Sarge approached the two, pulling them aside.

"I gotta ask, although I probably already know the answer. Either of you ever locked and loaded a .50 caliber machine gun before?"

Both shook their heads, "no."

"Nothing to it, really. Jump up here, you two."

Rhonda and Jud climbed up into the back of the five-ton.

"Kinda easy. When we're out, flip up the feed tray cover. We'll call it out. Feed the belt of ammo from the can with the double-loop side first, past the belt-feeder pawls. If the belt doesn't slide out, then you did it right. Slam the cover back down. We'll take care of the bolt action on both sides. All you have to do is keep the ammo chain from crimping, or it will jam the weapon. Do not, and I can emphasize this enough, do not touch the barrel, unless you want to lose your skin. Big thing, just keep cool and listen up. You're fine. Hell, you both fought a monster already."

Top Arnie stepped in front of the hanging tailgate, tossing a pair of gloves to Jud and Rhonda. "Almost forgot those. A little extra protection."

"What time the streetlights go on around here?" he asked.

"Seven-thirty, sharp," Rhonda answered.

Sarge looked at his watch. "We got fourteen minutes. Think they'll hold that long?"

Brushcut shrugged his shoulders. There wasn't anything predictable about any of this.

Sarge retrieved his own binoculars, scanning the battlefield to be. "I wonder where Alpha and Bravo teams are. If they're stealth, they're doing one hell of a job."

Down below, a group of creatures scream out, then another as they began attacking each other.

"We waiting to see if how many of them kill each other off or what?" Arnie asked.

"No. We wait too long, they come out of their high and move too fast for us to target them," Sarge answered.

"Alright, then." Arnie mounted the M61 Vulcan, nodding over to Flower, who nodded back.

"Ready on the left!" Top shouted.

Sarge jumped into the back of the five-ton. He and Brushcut assumed the prone position behind the .50 cals.

"Ready on the right!" Sarge shouted back.

Top Arnie issued the command of execution. "All ready on the firing line. Commence firing when your gremlin targets appear!"

Pulling the charging handle back, seating the bolt, Brushcut looked up at Jud and sang. "Du-na-na-na-na-na."

Jud grinned. He instantly knew the lick and returned the proper response. "Du-na-na-na-na-na."

Rhonda looked back over her shoulder at the two. "Thoroughgood. Nice!"

As the two combined the rift into the accompanying lyrics, the onslaught of bullets reigned down on the mound of ash tokers.

The night was filled with the sounds of non-stop gun fire and the spinning barrels of the Vulcan cannon, volleying with the M2 Browning machine guns. Screams from clowns, their minions and ash tokers joined in a chorus of eminent death delivered at the hands of these six warriors. The sheer quantity of creatures massed together, exploding in an inferno of secondary fires that aided in their efforts.

Colt Sturgess sat on his bike on the hill above Kinston, watching the fireworks. Although his mission remained unresolved, this one was a fitting end for the ones who sacrificed to render these creatures into piles of ash, a proper burial their host bodies deserved.

Kat and Johnny at one point wandered over to the windows but could only see flashes of light from the muzzles through the haze as, after their close call with Olath, they didn't dare wander out to see what the action plan of the Smoke Hunters looked like being implemented. Following a seven-minute blitzkrieg of bullets, designed to penetrate the steel of vehicles, now dark putrid flesh, there was a brief stop in the action to keep the barrels of the weapons from overheating. It was also the opportunity to see if anything still moved in the parking lot that served as hell on earth twice in less than three days' time.

The smoke from the elixir barrel was dissipating into the night air. No movement remained, only piles of ash and bodies of clowns stained with the black substance that transformed their blood. Rhonda and Jud high-fived each other, still riding the high of the moment. Had they really helped put an end to the terror plaguing their town, getting vengeance for their families and friends?

The Sarge picked up his .50 cal, slinging a chain of ammo over his forearm, disembarking the bed of the five-ton. Brushcut followed his lead. Flower and Arnie jumped down from the back of the jeep, tossing their protective headgear in the back. The streetlights flickered on, precisely at seven-thirty, atop the remaining poles not chopped down by stray twenty-millimeter rounds from the Vulcan surrounding the lot once the site of the fire department's' annual fair.

Arnie looked at his watch. "Right on time. Imagine that! A little late for our purpose, but so be it."

Illuminating the killing field gave the team a much better view of their efforts to bring this blight down. Nothing moved, nothing made a sound except the occasional crackling of fires from the clown's bodies.

"On your right," Arnie said, casually lighting a cigar.

Brushcut and Sarge pivoted in that direction, unloading more rounds than was necessary into a surviving clown that shambled toward them. It exploded in a spray of flesh and bone.

Arnie puffed on his cigar, blowing smoke rings. "Ready to go take a look-see?"

Nodding, Sarge issued a departure order. "You kids did great, but I want you to head back to the armory. It's just up the hill. Flower, give them an escort, stand guard, and keep an eye out for any stragglers, as in human stragglers. We'll check for any remaining 'tokers and the rest of our team. Get on the radio up there too and check in every ten mikes, got it?"

"Sure Sarge." Flower grabbed his M-16 from the front of Arnie's jeep and headed off up the hill with Jud and Rhonda.

Arnie, Brushcut and Sarge wandered down the hill, around the front of the bank towards the lot. Sarge could feel Arnie's smile as he passed by the gaping hole in the bank. As the team rounded the corner, Sarge saw the remnant of Country Boy, Scout and Spectre, only identifiable by their commando gear and unit patches. He bent down to examine what was left.

"Fuckin' shame. They deserved better than this."

Reaching over their bodies, he pulled off their dog tags, one at a time, stuffing them in his pockets. Although he was not a religious man, he prayed silently over their bodies. If there was a god, how could he or she permit the creation of such creatures? Brushcut and Arnie also bowed their heads in reverence. At least they completed their part of the mission, for what that was worth.

The gunnery team continued to tour the layers upon layers of ash. How many of these things were there? There was the occasional .50 cal burst into something that wasn't yet dead, although that could have applied to most of the things before the bullet barrage. Still no signs of Flamethrower. Convinced they completed their mission, the three enforcers returned to their vehicles and headed to their temporary home, the armory, Alpha HQ.

On the hillside, Colt waited a little longer for the smoke to clear. It was the opportunity for him to focus his thoughts on what secrets unlocked earlier. He considered a fact he overlooked in his subsequent rush to overtake Olath and Lizzy. Colt had something they wanted. Something Olath himself searched for over however many years he existed. That thing was him. Somehow, he survived the elixir's transformative properties with a few beneficial side effects. As he stared up at the rising moon, he wondered if all these things were a blessing or a curse.

Did Olath realize the same thing? If so, they would be back for him, or at least it was the best he could hope for as he lost them, having no idea where they presently hid. It would have to be somewhere relatively close. Somewhere with a facility for Olath to conduct his gruesome operations, hidden from any immediate access, so as not to draw unwanted attention. Those requirements were in stark contrast to Kinston. Why he chose this town here and now was still a mystery. Perhaps it was a field test of his capabilities. Did the spidery ghoul plan on much bigger targets, expanding his operation to where he could take control of sizeable areas of the country? The consideration was frightening if he could actually execute such a plan.

Sturgess returned to the light of the moon he could feel on his face. Another thought drifted in: why not just let it go? The Smoke Hunters would inevitably track him down, putting a stop to him and his ghoul farming. He could take his immortality and do something meaningful with it. But what? His purpose was so singularly driven any other possibilities were never considered. Maybe it was the fear of getting close, enduring that damage that he couldn't heal.

Aunt Rosie Babin was a sweet woman with two sweet kids for whom she sacrificed, still enjoying a life of her choosing. Yet when he loosened his emotional stranglehold for even a moment, she was beheaded, leaving Kat and Johnny Ellis orphans once again. Now the reappearance of Lizzy, only to watch her swept off by the object of his intense hatred. If this was what love was all about, he'll stick to vengeance.

Looking back down on the town center of Kinston, the streets, buildings, and ash piles were in crystal clear focus. The smoke lifted enough for him to return. Mounting up, he headed to Alpha HQ.

"That's her, huh?" Arnie asked, looking through the gated window at the tractor trailer parked next to the armory on Jefferson Street.

"Yup!" said Brushcut, standing beside him.

"Guess I'll bunk here tonight, check it out in the light of day. Pleasure doing business with you boys." He clanked his bottle of soda with Brushcut's in a mission accomplished toast.

Sarge sat on one of the folding chairs next to Flower, who already stripped one of the M-2s down and began cleaning it. Holding the dog tags in his hand, he squeezed the chains so tightly between his fingers they left a mark on his skin. His weapon sat on the floor, still fully loaded. He was cycling through a myriad of emotions. Losing men was always hardest on the commander. Although they lacked an official chain of command, the Smoke Hunters looked to Sarge for guidance. Title or not, the Sarge felt responsible for this rag-tag group of veterans who he shared blood, sweat and tears with along the fourteenth parallel for two tours. One man was missing in action, but he knew his disposition.

Brushcut shouted over to him. "You know, you don't have to do that. I fired the damned thing."

Flower didn't respond, just kept at it with the oil, punching the bore of the weapon.

"Leave him be, son. I prefer the hardware cleaned before I return it to stock," said Arnie.

Rhonda and Jud disappeared somewhere in the armory. No clue what they were doing, but with their adrenaline pump from the battle, it wasn't hard to guess. Kat sat next to Johnny in front of the table while he continued monitoring the scanner. She would not let him out of her sight again. For the first time, her tarot deck sat unattended to the side.

Anxiously, Kat kept a secondary attention on the door. The cards told her that Colt wouldn't reach his destination. If he did, he may not return. The Ten of Swords was a tricky card to interpret. To the novice, it was an indicator of total disaster, but to the skilled reader, it was one of opportunity to shed old skin and start anew. Whatever the divination, both shared one thing in common: the event that triggered the draw would not be by choice. She inhaled deeply, exhaling a sigh of relief as the sound of an approaching motorcycle increased in volume outside of the armory.

Sarge swung his chair around to face the door, much like when they first met him. Slowly, he pulled the M-2 from the floor, wrapping the ammo chain around his arm. He awaited Sturgess, but with a completely different agenda than Kat's.

Colt entered through the front door. The Sarge stood up, aiming the automatic weapon straight at him.

"Have any luck tracking down your boogeyman?" Sarge asked.

Colt shook his head in defeat. "Boogeyman." He heard the word for the second time today. The first was Olath's description of him. Sarge referring to Olath by the same name was a little more than unsettling to him, but he still had business with Colt.

"Why'd you abandon the team, Sturgess?"

Tipping his hat back, Colt offered no answer.

"Are you crazy? Put that thing down!" Kat yelled, running over to Colt.

"Step away, Kat. Pretty sure the Sarge means business. Don't want you to be part of that."

"I asked you a question, superman? Why'd you leave them to get overrun by those things?"

The rest of the team moved towards the Sarge.

"Ain't worth it, Sarge. Just let it go. You saw how many of them there were. If Sturgess jumped in there, he'd be dead just like the rest of them." Flower said, placing the gun parts on the deck moving to his side.

"Well, I'm waiting. You know what I've been noodling on for the past hour? How we always seem to be a step behind, then we get a primo chance, half the unit gets wiped out and you are nowhere to be found. Why is that? Then I follow that chain of thought." Sarge pulled the weapon up to his waist, locking in the bolt. "You're one of 'em!"

Before he could pull the trigger, Colt was on him in one fluid motion, sending the M-2 in one direction, Sarge in the other. He straddled the Sarge's chest, pressing the attack with a fist reared back at the ready.

"Enough!" Top Arnie yelled, walking over to pick up the machine gun. "If you two boys are finished measuring your dicks, sit down and shut up." He unloaded the weapon, field stripping it, handing the parts to Flower. "Here, you like cleaning them. Have at it."

Top pulled up a chair as the two men got up off the floor. He sat down calmly.

"Now the way I see it, and don't believe we've met, Mr. Sturgess, Arnold Cedrick Martin, Master Sergeant. Served two tours in Korea, three in 'Nam. Friends call me 'Top Arnie,' a pleasure to make your acquaintance. Now both of you, park your asses."

Colt and Sarge sat in the two closest folding chairs like scolded children about to receive their comeuppance. Top Arnie continued.

"Whatever reasons you boys had for undertaking this mission are known only to you. Now we can play the blame game all night long. If only you all would have been better prepared. If only you Redcatchers formulated a plan that didn't rely on old Top Arnie. What if I would have told you all to piss off? But the cowboy here could have single-handedly taken out a mob of monsters that needed forty thousand plus twenty-millimeter armor-piercing rounds and no idea how many boxes of .50 cal ammo you went through? No shit? He can do that? Slap some orange pain on my back and call me a box turtle; I'm impressed! I don't know what the cowboy's involvement is in all this, but I know that we're all alive. Half of your team isn't, and neither is most of this town. Old saying, I like, especially around Christmas time, 'if ifs and buts were candy and nuts, oh what a party we'd have.' Now, take some wisdom from an old timer who's waded in the blood of his teammates, shake hands and be fucking grateful you made it through."

Arnie stood up, walked over to the refrigeration, retrieved another soda, and returned to his view outside of the window of the tractor trailer he would drive off into the sunrise when it broke the horizon.

Sarge still embraced his anger. A few words from an old veteran would not sway his opinion. If anyone understood this in the room, it was the object of that anger, Colt Sturgess. Sarge stood up to address what was left of the Smoke Hunters.

"Brushcut, Flower, pack your trash. We're done here. Deploy at twenty-three hundred hours," he said.

"C'mon, Sarge. We've been at this without a break, on the road for two days now. I need some rest," said Brushcut. "What about Flamethrower?"

He didn't address the missing man. Brushcut was right, Sarge knew it. His anger was clouding his need to find the missing man, regardless of what his gut told him.

"Suit yourself. Two vans, two parties. Leave when you want. I'm out."

Sarge walked across the armory floor, descending the stairwell to the lower level next to the back parking area.

Flower sat back, laughing as he resumed his weapon cleaning. "He always pops his top about something. He'll be back. Just don't expect an apology from him, Mr. Sturgess. Sarge is bullheaded and doesn't like to admit he's wrong. Like ever. But...he needs sleep just like the rest of us."

Brushcut tipped his bottle of soda at Flower. "Got that right!"

Colt rose to check on Kat. He appreciated her wanting to take bullets for him, but the thought absolutely shook him to the core. Maybe he had emotions after all, or at least they weren't as dead and buried as he believed. Sturgess was transforming a little quicker than he was used to, but something was different.

Kat saw him approaching. She moved to intercept.

"Anything further on the scanner, Johnny?" he asked.

"No, sir."

"Can I talk to you, Colt? It's important. At least I think it is," asked Kat.

"Sure, but don't be jumpin' in the way of pissed off mercenaries with big guns, especially for me. He wasn't planning on leaving me in enough pieces to heal, got it?"

"Yep. But I need to talk to you in private."

"Lead the way."

On the roof, Jud and Rhonda sat, huddled together in a wool olive drab army blanket. It was chilly enough to cut the bite of the air and compensate for the drop in body temperate following their first firefight. Although the enemy didn't fight back, more of shooting fish in a barrel, they were experiencing things neither could have possibly imagined when they handed the first sledgehammer to initial fair participant. Something that Colt was deprived of, the underlying theme of his reflections before returning to town.

"So, what do you think's gonna happen next?" Rhonda asked.

"You mean with Kinston or like us?" he answered with a question.

"Either or both."

"I guess at some point, the authorities are going to have to show up, don't ya think? Then I guess some kind of adult supervision, although I don't know how open I'd be to that."

"Me either. Maybe we can just go away? I'm sure there's stuff down in the town we can collect up and sell. Get a couple of tickets to Hawaii or something? I always wanted to go there."

Jud considered the plan. "I don't know about stealing, though."

"Didn't you hear Top Arnie? He said it's not really stealing. You value his opinion, don't you?"

"Of course. I guess I have to think about it." It was then that the full impact of what Rhonda was saying to him showered down like the bricks from the four-armed creature that breached the entrance of McNaulty's.

"Wait, you said 'we can go away?' Like me and you?" he asked with the first sign of untangled enthusiasm since she kissed him for the first time.

She scooted around the blanket to look him square in the eyes. "Yes, silly. JUST me and you. Start over. If it's not totally clear yet, I choose you!"

Jud looked at the rooftop momentarily, then at Rhonda.

"You do? But why me? I mean, with all the other guys —"

"What? You think this is some sort of fling for me in the middle of the apocalypse?"

"No, but, I mean, I'm just a nerdy kid with a bicycle and comic books who has a paper route."

Rhonda took a moment to respond. Where was all this suddenly coming from? Maybe too many doses of adrenaline for young Mr. Allen, peppered with dashes of bravado. Initially, she was offended by 'the other guys' comment, but with a bit of thought, she realized he still lacked solid footing where she was concerned.

"Jud Allen, it's because of all of those things you're different, or didn't you think about that before? As for 'the other guys,' no. I know what they say and whatever you heard before is not true. Boys can be stupid, completely clueless about women. They make shit up about girls they can't have to soothe their own egos. And for the record, last night was my first time too, just so you know. How you couldn't tell with the couple of very obvious signs is beyond me, but yeah."

He leaned forward, arms wrapped around his knees. Jud hated he was so vulnerable around her, but it was something he was going to have to overcome.

"Also, while we're on the subject of us, knock off the over-macho bullshit around the Smoke Hunters. Girls don't like to feel like a trinket when the guys are bonding. Got it?" Rhonda smiled, hoping she hadn't undone all the confidence building she just constructed with her last comment. "Besides, I'm tougher than the lot of you!"

The 'over-macho bullshit' comment was lost on him. Then again, he was a novice with the whole boyfriend thing. He decided to just go with it, shooting her the three finger Smoke Hunter's salute. They both fell backwards giggling. On their backs, looking up at the stars, he noticed the smoke had completely cleared.

"I promise. After stuff returns to normal, I want to look for my family," he said, turning to her, "and Emma. If there's even the slimmest of chances that she's somewhere…"

Rhonda nodded, tears welling up. Those doe eyes again. With everything he witnessed tonight, her beauty overrode the ugliness smoldering below them. He leaned in to kiss her when the hatch to the roof flung open. The pair turned to see Kat emerge from the ladder well, followed by Colt. Rhonda and Jud stood up to greet them.

"Mr. Sturgess, happy to see you in one piece. Was your mission successful?" he asked.

"I'm afraid not, Jud. Came up a little short. Decidin' what's next."

"Sorry to hear that," said Rhonda.

"If you don't mind, we'd be much obliged if we could borrow your rooftop here for a spell?"

"No, of course. Do you need the blanket?"

Kat shook her head "no." Rhonda and Jud crossed the rooftop, disappearing through the hatch. Sturgess followed Kat Ellis over to the ledge of the roof, then sat down. She liked the edge for some reason. It made her comfortable.

"What's on your mind, Kat?" he asked.

"I have something for you, but I kind of wanted to talk to you about something else first," she answered.

"Well, have at it."

"I'm not sure how to say this. I was never great with words, outside of reading cards. It's why I don't have a circle of friends outside of Johnny and the occasional customers at Rosie's who hit on me. Anyway, I guess the words are plain enough…you matter."

You matter. Two words muttered by a stranger who barely knew him. She offered great insight and intuition. He sensed that somehow. Maybe fate hand delivered him to this fly speck on a map called "Kinston." In all his suppositions, meandering and boiling anger, two words from an external source, no, a kind heart, made him a believer. It was a kindness he only felt one other time in the past century. That was three days ago.

"I appreciate that."

"No, I mean it and I need you to understand, more like accept that. You helped, actually saved us twice. Johnny's glued to that scanner down there to help you. Not the macho, bullshit hunters, although I do like Flower. It's why we got into trouble with Olath earlier. Johnny ran out to find you when he heard him arriving on the radio. Luckily, you showed up. Now I started pulling cards, and the Wheel keeps coming up no matter what I ask, so fate is on your side, or against you. Either way, the significance of that card is that fate happens. We don't control most things. But we do on how we react to stuff happening. I know this probably is a lot of malarky to you, but it just doesn't happen like this."

"I understand."

"No, I don't think you do. I found something that can help you, I think. At first, thought about throwing it away, but then there was this crazy idea. If I told you how much you mean to us, everyone downstairs, even the Sarge, although he'd never admit it, maybe, just maybe, it would change your heart. What's going on with you and this Olath character I'll never understand, and you totally may be pissed, but you've spent almost your whole life on something you hate? That I can't understand at all. I mean, I can't even hate that thing for killing Aunt Rosie. I'm really sad, of course, but holding in something that's only going to keep hurting me all the time is nonsense. Think about that for a minute. Your time, energy, all the possibilities you missed starting over. Find something or someone new. Dude, you have like superpowers. Isn't there something useful you can do with them?

"Maybe it's time to kick the training wheels off that sweet bike of yours and start applying a little love. You can start with yourself. Who knows, you may even find something more important than revenge."

Colt sat silently. In his entire life, even pre-Olath, he didn't recall ever having such a conversation, although he didn't contribute to any of it. He was pretty sure he wasn't meant to. Sturgess even admired Johnny for only talking when he had something to say. Presently, Sturgess had nothing to say. Yet, hearing the words out loud gave him pause. It was a long time since anyone gave a damn about Colt Sturgess.

"Kitty Kat, I appreciate your wisdom. I truly do. Sometimes a boot in the ass is what a man needs. Not sure when this journey ends for me, but if the choice presents itself, I promise to look a little deeper before I make it. By the way, hopin' you don't mind the nickname. Seems kinda natural."

"Not at all. It's what Johnny calls me."

She wasn't sure what to expect in having her little rooftop chat. Her intuition drove her with a similar force that his vengeance propelled him. It was twice as strong since the night at Rosie's. Kat said what she wanted to. Now it was up to Colt. Like she said, fate keeps the wheel turning. She simply gave it a spin.

Colt looked over the side of the rooftop. "If you're finished, I'd like to head down and look at the map on the wall downstairs."

Kat leaped to her feet first. Handing him a map, folded to a particular section with a big red circle in the middle.

"What's this?" he asked.

"I think," she paused, "it's Olath's hideout," she answered sheepishly.

Firm with her personal decision to have a talk with him first beat back any doubt that she should have just handed it to him when he entered the armory.

"What makes you think that?" Colt examined the map with a direction from Kinston to the red circle.

"This." Kat reached into her back pocket, removing a folded up, blood-stained piece of paper. "Found it when I went after Johnny. It was stuck to a phone pole across from the fair. Like I said, fate happens."

Examining it, he read aloud, "Bill of Lading. Pickup and delivery. Unspecified cargo was to be received on the far loading dock of Chooch Family Farms and Dairy, Rural Route 8, Germantown, Pennsylvania. Order #29451. Dispatch twelve cabs and trailers to arrive on 8/30/78. Destination, Kinston, Pennsylvania. POC: Professor Ansel Olath."

Slowly, Colt looked up at her, tucking the paper away in his pocket.

"You know I have to see this through."

She nodded her head.

"But I promise. I will think before I act. There may be a couple of people who rely on me, ya' know?" He winked at her as she squeezed him tightly in a goodbye hug.

Uncertain if it would be the last one, Kat held it extra-long. He hurried towards the door that led back to the armory.

"Take care, see you soon, Kitty Kat."

As he disappeared, she wondered if it was for the last time. Sitting back down on the ledge, Kat awaited his departure. She never mentioned the Ten of Swords.

Reaching the first floor, Colt headed to the front door, acknowledging no one. Nothing really needed to be said. Before he reached it, the Sarge called out behind him. He stopped, wondering if he would once more be staring down the barrel of a gun.

"You might need this," Sarge said, tossing him a satchel.

Colt opened it up, revealing a military grade M17 gas mask.

"In case you run into any trouble."

Slinging it over his shoulder, Colt proceeded out of the door.

"Should we give him a tail?" asked Flower, looking up from a pile of disassembled parts.

"Nah, he's on his own," said Sarge. "It was my good deed for the day so I can sleep."

Chapter Thirteen

Elizabeth continued her overdramatized screams of anguish as Emma and Olath escorted her into the farmhouse, across the kitchen and down the stairs to the basement. Olath lifted her up on the butcher block to be seated when she pushed him back.

"I'm not sitting up on this filthy, sticky thing. You still haven't cleaned it up from the transfer surgery!" she screamed at him.

"Of course not. Please tranquilize your emotions until I can prepare adequate accommodations to optimize your comfort," he said.

Emma spied shelving with a variety of table covers in the dim light. Why they were there was anyone's guess. Possibly stored away for the winter or some festival they hosted at the farm. Browsing through them, she found one that she knew would totally offend Elizabeth's stylish sensibilities. Smiling, she chose that one. Slowing her pace to a crawl, Emma returned to the butcher block, shook out the vinyl, red and white checkered stiff cover, ensuring Elizabeth would get a full view of the thing before laying it across the top of the block.

"What is that grotesque thing?" Elizabeth continued with her scream of disapproval. Emma chose well for her torment.

"Just shut up, it's vinyl. It will keep your pretty little ass clean from any of the goo that might soak through. Stop being a baby and get up on the table."

Reluctantly, Elizabeth complied, her hands still clasped over her face. Olath approached hesitantly to examine the damage caused by Colt's gaze. Slowly, she lowered her hands. He gasped. Emma raised her eyebrows in surprise. Lizzy screamed out again in response to their reactions.

"What? Is it that bad? Am I scarred for life?"

Weeping, she covered her face. Emma stepped forward, slowly lowering Elizabeth's hands again.

"Huh, didn't expect that!" said Emma.

"I must confess, this is a complete revelation to me as well," Olath added.

"What?" Elizabeth's tears turned to fury quickly, not knowing why the two were staring at her.

Olath hurried to his worktable, picked up a surgical instrument tray, the contents spilled all over the floor. He rushed back to her side. Holding it up to her face, she gasped.

Emma examined her face even closer than what the reflection revealed. "Not only no trace of the burns that were there before, but you actually look...younger."

Wiping the tears from her cheeks, Elizabeth gazed deeper into her reflection with the attentiveness of Narcissus. Her fingers ran over her face. They were right. She looked down at her hand, then back up to a few remaining lines around her eyes and forehead. Waving her palm over them, tiny tendrils of smoke creeped out from her skin, erasing the age lines. Olath and Emma watched in pure fascination.

"How are you doing that?" asked Emma.

Olath grabbed Elizabeth's hand, examined her palm, sniffing it like an animal. "Perspiration. You touched him!"

A grin spread from the center of his mouth to the edges of his cheeks. His eyes glowed with an unnatural satisfaction.

"You touched him!"

"Touched who?" Elizabeth was not following.

"Sturgess! In the town square. His perspiration is on the palm of your hand. Not only does he not require transformative surgeries, but he also possesses restorative abilities!"

Olath was absolutely giddy. Even his typical flowery, overtly pretentious method of speech surrendered to the discovery. After centuries of work to perfect his elixir, he inadvertently located the patient zero of his success. Or rather, he located them. Elizabeth continued staring at her reflection.

"We must retrieve him at once. I need to begin the extraction of all his precious fluids for examination and isolation immediately. He holds the key to every achievement that has eluded me. There is absolutely no time to waste!" said Olath.

Emma cleared her throat. She was happy to throw a monkey wrench into his revelation. "That is, if your ghouls, clowns, or those two mental midgets haven't already killed him."

He grabbed her by the shoulders, shaking her uncontrollably. Olath let out a primal scream. "No!"

Elizabeth back handed him, which sent him across the room, crashing into a worktable. Those instruments joined the others on the floor.

"Unhand her, you fiend, and don't you ever let me see you lay one of your spindly claws on her again!"

Smiling with the grimace of a thousand demons, Emma waltzed over to him and extended a hand of help. He reluctantly accepted the offer.

Elizabeth stood behind her, a shadow cast across his slumped form. She knew he would revert to this subservient posture after being scolded.

"So, if what you say is true, my beloved has the key to our immortality? If in your rush to judgement, he still lives."

"Yes. It is the universal of truths."

Elizabeth closed her eyes in deep concentration. Olath watched her with a peculiar curiosity. Did she possess some other ability beyond her mesmerism? Was she somehow linked to the cowboy in an undefinable manner? Emma scooted behind her, jumping up on the table. She leaned back, joining in the watch party, swinging her legs.

"Be still child," said Elizabeth.

Olath stopped breathing as if she issued him the command as well.

Moments passed, then she opened her eyes. A smile kissed her lips. "He lives. Better yet, he's on his way."

Olath couldn't contain his enthusiasm. "I shall prepare —"

"No, I will handle this. Go tend to your arm. You look ludicrous with only one."

Elizabeth motioned to Emma, who dropped from the butcher's block. She took her hand.

"Come, Emma. It's time to meet your father."

Colt sped along the dusty back roads that Kat outlined on the map. His mind rushed forward faster than his Harley. There were several options for confronting Lizzy, only one for Olath. Fiercely, he fought back his temper in case Lizzy was first. Then there was the girl. Who was she, and how did she figure in all of this? Decisions would have to be made. Unfortunately, he didn't have the luxury of a consultation of Kat's tarot cards, the counsel of the Smoke Hunters, or any other input from the accidental team of survivors who got him this far along in his journey. The final showdown was at hand, if he wasn't too late.

Slowly, he rolled up the road towards a large farmstead. His Harley pulled off the road. He secured it behind a row of cornstalks closest to a fence line bracketing the property. From a distance, he saw the semis parked next to a large building. Sturgess owned a farm. He knew a slaughterhouse when he saw one, although he kept his stock for milking only. That appeared to be the center of operations.

Speed would be his best ally, that and the cover of darkness. The katana would stay sheathed until reaching the building. He didn't want the moonlight to give him away. With an initial step forward, he traversed the space between him and the slaughterhouse in the matter of seconds. Cautiously, Colt entered the building. It was now time to draw his weapon.

Darkness engulfed him. The rattling sound of chains dripped down from the roof of the structure just ahead of the lairage. He cautiously stepped up the ramp to the stunning room. Another sound found its way to his sensitive hearing, a rhythmic thud, repeatedly. Thud, thud, thud. Not unlike a human heartbeat, but more metallic, as if something were struggling to get free. Thud, thud, thud.

Colt closeted the sound in his mind. It was not his primary focus. Concentration was essential. Pushing through the plastic sheeting, he stepped into the bleeding chamber. The smell of copper assaulted his sense of smell to the point he could taste the blood that collected under the grating beneath his feet. From memory, he knew the slaughter hall was in front of him, the hoisting room to his right. If something were going to attack, this would have been the opportune time. Nothing came, just the continuous thud, thud, thud and rattling of chains that were now directly in front of him. The time for caution passed. Sturgess rushed into the slaughter hall, katana at the ready.

He slid on the floor, struggling to maintain balance. A tangle of tubes held him upright like a marionette. Slashing at them desperately, Colt knelt down after freeing himself to assess his current environment while presenting the lowest targeting point should the attack come from his flanks. An emergency light activated and was now flickering, creating a strobe that was wreaking havoc with his vision. His enhanced speed shot towards where he believed to be the location of the closest wall. Upon crashing into it, something reached for him in the dim light emanating from the slaughter hall from which he just escaped. The limited darkness was temporary hospice from the flashing red light. He looked up at the roof.

Rows upon rows of human limbs hung, grasping at him, kicking at him. Colt swung in a frenzy at the grisly appendages, sending feet and hands scattering across the floor into the room with the suspended tubing. What was left still hung, continued rattling the chains. This was no slaughterhouse; it was a charnel house of horrors. Wiping the fluids from his glasses, Sturgess watched, realized the tubing was infusing the body parts with Olath's special elixir, which he was now covered in from severing the tubes. This was not a good thing. One match and the smoke would put him out of commission, possibly forever. Fire he survived, but the elixir smoke was indeed his kryptonite.

"Damn, left that gasmask on the back of the Harley," he said out loud.

He was now vulnerable. It was too late, though; he had committed. Time to move forward.

The laboratory was directly in front of him. A glass panel stood between him and potentially Olath. Quarters were getting tight. A sword would not be practical, as space was becoming a luxury no longer afforded to him. Once more, he rushed forward, shouldering the panel, hoping his force would be enough to shatter the glass. It did. Across the shards of glass that accompanied his breach, he rolled. Drawing the peacekeepers, Sturgess stayed low, seeking his target. Nothing but thud, thud, thud. It was getting louder.

Colt gave a quick survey of the area to his front and rear. No one responded to his noisy infiltration of the lair. Yet. That became a concern. He certainly was making enough racket, and the flashing red emergency light was adding to the disturbance. Severing the tubes should have set off some type of alarm that Olath's ghastly fusion operation was rapidly losing pressure. Did he infiltrate an abandoned operation? Thud, thud, thud.

Whatever the origin of the sound, it came from the next room. He knelt, trying to remember the layout of the last slaughterhouse he worked in as a teen on his uncle's farm. It was his first and last summer helping there. The experience was something he wished he had never taken part in. After a few days in the stunning pen, he called it quits. Colt just couldn't do it.

He stood looking to his right through the pane that was still intact. It was a slim corridor and if his memory held any water; he was looking at the chilling room. The cold storage would be directly behind that. Which meant, to his immediate front, was the condemned room, where the best cuts of meat were stored. Thud, thud, thud.

Time was wasting. Sturgess knew expedience was paramount. Whatever the sound was, it required investigation.

No stone unturned, he thought.

He rushed around the corner, down the length of the wall, tearing the door from its hinges. An overhead light flickered on in the room. Up one side and down the other, ash tokers in their infancy. This was something he had never seen before, only the finished products. Most were still basic human flesh tone. A handful were in their gray state, revealing their colors only when encountering a clear membrane affixed to the frame. They were packed into the room like some nightmarish womb. Floating in what Colt assumed was more of Olath's elixir, except this fluid was more translucent and not the black color that dripped all over him from the tubes. More like blood.

Sturgess re-holstered his pistols, calling on his katana. He slashed at the membrane repeatedly, but it would not yield. This is the same weapon that cut through a tow chain earlier, like butter. Whatever this was, he would not breach it. Leaning in to see if he even made a nick, one thing pressed its face against the membrane, scratching at it from the inside with berserk fury. It startled Colt as he stepped away. The thing shot back against the wall of the condemned room, thud. Then the right wall, thud. Finally, the left side wall, thud. Each movement sent the other captives floating around aimlessly in the fluid.

"Christ," Sturgess muttered, "it's an incubation chamber."

He experienced enough of this macabre journey into the mind of Olath. It was time to leave. Obviously, the chief ghoul himself was not here. Besides, after all that he just witnessed, a fresh breath of air and a reset was in order. There were limitations to what a man like Colt Sturgess, or any man or woman, could endure. This was one of those thresholds. He sped forward around this room, down the corridor, past cold storage, eventually stepping out onto the loading dock.

Leaning over, he felt as if he were going to be sick for the first time in a century. Dropping off the loading dock, he stripped off his shirt, dropping it to the ground. It was splattered with Olath's elixir, making it a liability, particularly to flame, for as much as a shirt can be one.

"Are you doing that for me, darling?"

Looking up, he didn't notice the limousine sitting there. The passenger door was open, but he only saw a pair of very shapely legs in the moonlight. The engine turned over as the passenger with the legs peered out. It was Elizabeth, or as he knew her, Lizzy.

"Let's take a ride," she said.

"Where's Olath?" he asked.

She waved her hand at him. "He's insignificant right now. Come talk to me first. Then I'll take you to that insufferable creature. Please, Colt. It's been so long."

"How do I know he's not in there with you?"

Emma popped out from the driver's side. "Well, then. You can kill him and it's game over."

"You old enough to drive, kid?" he asked.

"You're worse than her!" Emma slammed the door, gunning the engine.

"Well?" Elizabeth asked with her best seductive look.

Sturgess grimaced. He had yet to decide what to do about the Lizzy situation. For a moment in Kinston, before his memories brought him down, she seemed like his old Lizzy. This woman beckoning him to the car was different. Lizzy was always confident, but shy. It's part of what he loved about her. She glowed with youthful exuberance, saturated with a zest for life, a love of experiences. Looking for rainbows during a thunderstorm with sun peeking through the clouds was the most beautiful thing she ever saw. Until she came across a monarch butterfly fluttering on a milkweed. Life was her pleasure. This woman, however, projected an icy edge, like his katana sword. His sword served one purpose: to kill. Was she Olath's steely edge?

He walked to the car and got in. She threw her arms around him, showering him with kisses as soon as he sat down. Emma shifted to drive, pulling out.

Looking up, Elizabeth saw her own eyes in the rearview mirror. The quarter glass was down.

"Emma, roll that window up, now!" said Elizabeth.

"Are you kidding me? No way. This could get steamier than the Lakeside Drive-in pornos!"

Colt sat back in the seat, pulling his hat down. "Sorry, ma'am, didn't expect such a reception. Caught me off guard."

"Ma'am? Colt, darling. Don't you recognize me? It's Lizzy, your Lizzy!"

"So, you say, yet I don't rightly know yet. Not completely convinced of that."

"Ha!" Emma chortled from the front seat. "And you thought this was going to be easy."

She said it low enough, expecting her passengers would not hear but hadn't counted on the sensitivity of Sturgess. Not that she cared. Emma was just excited to watch this play out.

"Colt, we have so much to talk about, so much to catch up on. It's been so long," said Lizzy.

"Have you been in that slaughterhouse? Any idea what Olath has in there?"

"Oh, I have nothing to do with that old fool's experiments. He could breed a mix of pigs and cows for all I care."

"Not quite what I saw." Sturgess tipped his hat back, casting his full curiosity on her. "If you are my Lizzy, what happened to you? More to a person than just physical appearance, your soul seems amiss."

"Ouch, massive burn," Emma murmured.

Lizzy, Elizabeth, whoever she was, didn't have an answer to the second part of his question. It troubled her, even more so, that it wasn't anything she ever gave any thought to. She looked out the tinted window, fixating on the moon, saying not another word until they arrived at her new home at Delaney's Funeral Home.

The limousine pulled around the back of the establishment, gliding to a stop. Emma did a much better job behind the wheel than her initial attempt. Lizzy exited the vehicle first, leading Colt by the hand around the side of the building, up the carpeted exterior concrete steps and into the foyer. Remaining vigilant, Sturgess continue to sweep the area without looking like he was sweeping the area. He wanted her to feel trusted, as much as she wanted him to feel the same. That faded away when the two stood on the interior carpet of the hall, like the two large blood stains that lingered.

"This your place?" he asked, already knowing the answer.

"Temporary accommodations, for sure," she answered.

"And where might the previous owners be, unless, of course, you've taken up running a funeral parlor?"

She turned around, leering at him. He did not mention the extra effort that she and Emma put into lighting all the candles in the hallway. Sure, they were vigil candles, but they were the only ones available.

"Do you like the place? I love the wood and intricate details in the wallpaper."

He stayed fixated on the stain. There was a disrespect Colt felt in crossing over the threshold of the dead without proper rites of burial. Much like being tossed on a roaring fire with somebody's expectation that all that would remain was bones and ash. Something he experienced firsthand.

"Come on, Colt, darling. Say you love it!"

By then Emma entered, tossing the keys on the dining table, disappearing into the kitchen like any other teen of the era. She returned, taking a seat at the table with a teacup of water and the cold, uneaten cheeseburger from the night before. She would not miss this encounter.

"What happened to you, Liz?" Liz. It was a term he only used when conveying bad news or precursor to the severity of an issue at hand.

"I don't understand. Don't you like it?" The smile finally dropped from her face.

Sturgess exhaled, taking a step forward. She was flitting around the room like a fairy while talking. He grabbed her wrist to focus her attention. Instinctively, Lizzy spun around, striking him across the face with her nails. Scratches appeared on his cheek, disappearing almost immediately as they were made. She gasped at the sight, but more so at the next thing she saw, the back of his hand across her face.

The blow knocked her to the ground. The shock of his action kept her there, yielding actual tears instantly. Lizzy, Elizabeth, Liz, whatever her identity was at this moment in time, all three were stunned by the behavior of this gentle man she loved with all of her heart.

"You never laid a hand on me, Colt. Ever. Never, ever, even raised your voice to me. You ask me what happened to me, what's happened to you? I've done my best to be kind and accommodating, even though you burned my face in that podunk town. I don't seem like the same old Lizzy to you? A hundred years changes a person. And look at you standing there, mister righteous fury. Defending a ghost town after the population is wiped out. From what, Colt? From me? Olath? How about Emma over there? You want to take a swing at her too? Where I'm standing, I'm not the only one who has changed."

She turned around and sprinted up the stairs, slamming her bedroom door. Colt glanced over at Emma.

"Don't look at me. I'm just having a burger."

Colt walked over to the carpeted stairway and sat down slowly. The place was nice, even for a funeral home, and the candles were a pleasant touch. Was his heart so hardened that he already looked past what was in front of him and passed judgement? That judgement was reserved for Olath only. Wasn't it? She was right about one thing, though. He never raised his hand to her, ever. They were the couple that indulged in their differences, learning as they went along. Any problems that arose, they faced them together, that was always one of their strengths.

It was the hate inside him. The uncontrollable, untamable hate. Its origin escaped him. With his restored memories, all he could put his finger on was the moment he first felt the purity of it. Purity was a strange word to apply, but that's what it was. Nothing else mixed with it, influenced it or could quench it. It simply was, and that moment was when the elixir was poured down his throat as he tried to resist. That's when it was born. Whether Olath was the catalyst, it was there somewhere lying dormant, awaiting the opportunity to take control.

Was this the price he paid for his apparent immortality? Wandering through time burdened with something he wished he could carve out of himself with the same precision with which he wielded his blade. Or, as Kat suggested, was there a legitimate choice? Control is an illusion, but if he used his other gifts, maybe, just maybe, he could confine the beast that ran rampant inside of him at its own choosing. Who controlled who? Thud, thud, thud, he thought. Was he a man or merely another incubation chamber constructed by Olath? He could not accept that possibility. It was time for Colt Sturgess to step up. Time to be the man he was never afforded the opportunity to be.

He looked back at Emma before proceeding up the stairs at a normal pace. It was a start.

"Top of the stairs, second room on the left," Emma yelled up to him without leaving the table.

She pulled her knees into her chest on the oversized head of the table chair. Deciding to give them a few minutes to settle things down, she sipped the water slowly. Emma selected that mug for a purpose. It would be the best amplifier to place up against the door to hear what they were saying inside. She smiled at her own ingenuity.

Colt reached the door Emma mentioned. He tapped lightly on it before entering. Lizzy was sprawled out on the bed, face down. This room was also adorned with candles. Was she expecting him, or was this a nightly ritual? He couldn't determine if she was crying or not. He assumed she was. Crying because of him. Colt removed his hat, closed the door, meandering to the dressing table, and sat down on the bench in front of it.

"Go away," she said.

"I'm sorry. Guess I'm a bit off the range here. I've been so driven to find your boss, or whatever he is, and kill him." He paused. "He took everything from us, Liz."

"He's not my boss," she murmured into the pillow. Colt couldn't quite make out what she said.

"Pardon?"

She sat up purposefully. "I said, he's not my boss! I can't tolerate the spindly thing. He makes my skin crawl to look at him, which is why I know nothing he's doing on any day."

"So why do you stay?"

She howled with laughter. "You can't be serious? Haven't figured that one yet, huh? Really?"

He shook his head.

"He keeps me alive, Colt! These parts, these limbs, they're only temporary. They last one, maybe two years tops, then they must be replaced. Only he knows how to do it. He's been doing this for centuries, since the bloody 1700s. Our insides decay at a much slower rate, but eventually those will go too."

He leaned forward, processing what she just said. This was all new information to him. Outside of the ash tokers and clowns' existence, he did not know what they were other than targets, breadcrumbs that he hoped would lead him to Olath. Sturgess never took the time to consider the hows and whys behind the operation. The only clue that it was body farming was that clipboard of notes the Smoke Hunters found in that subsequent clearing of the town Sarge mentioned.

"In that case, I'm guessin' you're not his bride?"

"If that thought wasn't as ridiculous as it sounds, I would have taken my own life a century ago."

"Why didn't you?"

She stood up, walking around the bed, running her hand over the smoothness of the post.

"Funny thing, in the sense of not understanding, no humor, is that I do not know why, but I have the overwhelming sense that he is my protector, my shield. It's deep-seated. There's no explanation for it, but anytime I even contemplated leaving, simply to live out whatever time I have left, the obsession took hold. I'm sure this makes no sense to you, but it is the best way I can explain it in words." Lizzy threw up her hands in frustration. "What's the use? None of this makes sense at all, anyway. Here we are, face to face, talking about him. Even when you first stepped out of that house of horrors of his, your first question was 'where's Olath?'"

Colt looked up at her face. She was moving back into his physical space. In the flickering candlelight, she was the most beautiful woman who ever lived. Even in the light of day, he thought the same thing. Reflecting on what she said, he understood. It was the same as his companion, rage. The last thing he remembered during his flashback, his uncontrollable attack on the group before collapsing on the farmstead. The last sight he saw was her taking refuge behind Olath. Considering his working theory, her need for protection from his reaction to the elixir told him she must have been introduced to the substance shortly thereafter. It made sense. Unless, of course, there was something she wasn't telling him.

"This is going to be harder than she thought…" It's what Emma said under her breath in the limo. Was this some sort of play? If so, what was the finale?

She touched him, which brought him out of his contemplations.

"What are you thinking about?" she asked.

"Just meanderings," he answered.

"Now, come on, Colt Sturgess, I know you a lot better than that!"

She was right; she did. The beautiful half dead creature in front of him also began transforming into the Lizzy he knew. The chilly edge disappeared, replaced by the compassionate understanding that he grew to love.

———————

Emma quietly snuck up the staircase, making her way to the door. She softly pressed the teacup against the wall to eavesdrop on what was taking place on the other side. "Incorrigible little brat," Elizabeth would call her if she got caught. Whatever, she thought.

———————

"What about the girl?" he asked. It was inevitable she would come up. "Emma?"

"Yes. The girl with you driving the limo. Smart mouth, I like her."

Outside in the corridor, she smiled with her ear in the teacup. At least she had one fan.

"She's my daughter…our daughter." Elizabeth hugged him.

"Pardon me?"

Elizabeth raved. Her switching back and forth between personalities was alarming him.

"Isn't it wonderful? I made her for me at first, but then when I discovered you were still alive, I knew it was meant to be. We can finally have the family we always wanted, always deserved!" she said.

"Whoa, Lizzy! You made her?"

"Well, in a manner of speaking. She was a leftover from that dreadful little town on her way to becoming spare parts. I rescued her and now she's ours!"

Outside in the corridor, it took everything in Emma's willpower not to burst into the room shouting "liar!" Although she couldn't remember much before emerging from the trunk of the police cruiser, she did just hear one thing. She was reserved for parts, for Elizabeth's parts! Pressing her ear back to the cup, she harnessed her impulses to see what other half-truths her "mother" was going to serve up.

"The elixir in her veins is experimental. It's the first of its kind to work without turning its host into one of those things that scurry along the rafters." Elizabeth embraced him again.

He pulled away from her. "Lizzy, we gotta talk about this, darlin'. That poor kid downstairs wasn't given any option for what was happening to her. Probably has a family —"

"Whatever family she did have doesn't exist anymore. We're her family now. We can give her all the love and affection she needs."

"Liz, can you hear yourself? This is the same thing that got us into trouble with Olath and his boys in the first place. That overwhelming..."

He stopped. Suddenly, it was crystal clear. Much like the anger and protection aspects the elixir locked into each of them respectively, there was another thing that was overwhelming Lizzy's emotions when the wagon first pulled up on their property: the promise of enhancing fertility. It was more than an overwhelming emotion; it was a mutual desire and the source of most discussions for the previous three months. They wanted to start a family. It was all making sense. The most prevalent thoughts and emotions at the time of the elixir's intrusion into the human body are amplified exponentially. Logical reasoning takes a back seat to the primal needs of the infected. Engaging the mind would require the same effort as battling the four-armed monstrosity in McNaulty's. Explaining it to her may be a little trickier, getting her to accept it might be an impossibility and what to do about the girl downstairs. She was stripped of her future, much like the two of them. Perhaps they were a family, in the most unconventional form ever.

"You were saying, my love?" she asked as he stopped short.

"I was sayin' we had an overwhelming need to start a family."

"And now we have one!"

She straddled him on the bench, showering his face with kisses as he continued to chew on a solution to this dilemma. Plus, Olath was still out there. He took his eye off that prize once, but this was a much more serious issue, actually, several issues. Wading through the possibilities, he pushed to see if there was something in play was that wasn't on the table.

"What now, Liz? I'm kinda at a loss here. There a plan or do I just ride off into the sunset with you needing a refresh every year or two and a daughter who may need the same kinda thing?"

She stood back up, moving towards the bed. Lizzy sat down on it, rolling towards one side, affording him space by her side. He would follow along for now. Sliding in next to her, she took his hand.

"Look up, isn't that the most spectacular thing ever?" She referred to the stained-glass canopy above the bed that she hated on the first night there. "I really disliked this at first, then I considered all the pieces that fit together to make the image. Finally, I realized it was a clock. Follow the shadow from the center of the moon."

She traced the line in the air of the two distinct shadows. Along the rim of the dome, numbers were illuminated by the existing moonlight. "See the numbers? Initially, I didn't even notice them. Amazing what you see when you stare long enough, uninterrupted by the daily chaos of the world. We can have that, you and I and Emma."

While both of them looked up from the bed at the engineering and artistic marvel, Colt's intuition felt this was the moment. The following minutes were going to determine their futures forever. He was right.

Chapter Fourteen

You want me to what?" He couldn't believe he was hearing what she just requested.

Elizabeth pleaded with him. "Before you jump to any conclusions, let me explain how it works."

"I don't care how it works; you're asking me to trust Olath to undo what he put into action a century ago. Want me to put this needle thing on my head —"

"Crown of thorns."

"Crown of whatever, which'll transfer my blood into you, and we can live happily ever after? Is that how it's gonna work, Lizzy?"

She nodded her head, "yes."

It was pure lunacy. Even following the morbid logic chain starting with the restorative powers of his blood ending with the fact he didn't require physical transformations like she did, putting his trust in Olath would not happen. The only thing he planned on putting into him were bullets, as many speed loaders as it took until he was nothing more than a memory, a stain on the pages of time, like the carpet in the foyer of this candle lit asylum. If this was her plan all along, she had to know there was no way he would ever even entertain the mention of it.

"Sorry, Lizzy, but no sale. If we have a year or two left to spend together, then so be it. Olath's not gonna have a hand in anything past that."

Colt sat up on the bed. Lizzy rose, walking around to the other side, sitting down at the dressing table. She said nothing. He was trying like hell to adapt to her changing personalities on the fly, but expecting which was coming next was increasingly difficult. Looking at him through her reflection in the mirror, she blew him a kiss.

"I love you, Colt Sturgess. I wish we had more time," she said.

Picking up the scissors she used to alter the front of the lower part of her dress, Lizzy plunged them deep into her chest. A spray of dark blood tainted by Olath's elixir splattered across the mirror from which she just professed her love. She slumped forward on the vanity.

Colt rushed to the bench, not considering his speed, just using it. He pulled the shears from her chest, more of the vile liquid sprayed except across his face.

"Oh, Lizzy, why'd you go and do that, darlin'? Not now, not again."

Sturgess laid her quietly on the floor in a panic. Emma, sensing something was wrong, beyond her eavesdropping through the teacup, rushed into the room.

"What happened?" she asked. "Did you kill her?"

"God dammit, Lizzy, why?" Emma's question went unanswered.

Emma watched as Colt looked over at the scissors. Picking them up, he slashed the palm of his hand several times until he was able to breach the skin. His blood oozed out. Red blood without the tint of Olath. Pressing his hand on the wound in her chest, there was an immediate reaction. Much like in the farmhouse's basement, smoke poured out from the wound. Not small wisps this time, billowy red smoke poured out from beneath his hand. Lizzy's eyes fluttered, then a deep inhale of air. She revived with a convulsion, then a scream as her feet kicked uncontrollably.

Colt removed his hand from the fatal wound made by the scissors, taking her in his arms, holding her close to his chest. Her lifeless body jerked, then relaxed, jerking again until her arms wrapped around him. Tears streamed down his face. It was the first time he felt emotions of such profound loss, pain and sorrow since the day he picked up the charred skull from the ash pile, believing it was hers. There was no longer any hate, nor anger, nor rage. Only love for a woman he believed lost to him. He squeezed her tighter until he felt her heart beating against his chest, in perfect syncopation with his.

Lizzy looked up at him, touching his face, gently removing his dark glasses. She wanted to see his eyes, even if it meant being scorched again. He shut them tightly for fear of the same effect.

"Trust me," she whispered.

Slowly he opened them, seeing her rich blue eyes staring back at him. The same eyes he once looked into every morning a century earlier. Not only had his blood healed her, but apparently made her immune to his fire, not that his gaze shared that effect on all of Olath's creations. It would have made his task exponentially easier. She smiled at him.

"If it's vengeance you seek, you'll find Olath in the goat milking building next to the slaughterhouse. Finish your business with him. Whatever time I have left with you will be an eternity. I just thought that fate was giving us a second chance. Emma will take you there."

Colt picked her up, placing Lizzy back on the bed. He laid beside her.

Kat's voice kept playing repeatedly in his head. "...fate is on your side, or against you. Either way, the significance of that card is that fate happens. We don't control most things. But we do on how we react to stuff happening."

Colt Sturgess was at the crossroads of vengeance or redemption. The next choice was his and his alone. His journey until now may very well have been the fool's journey, which Kat also explained as the path of the major arc-something he couldn't recall to spiritual enlightenment. He wasn't sure if he believed in any of it, but he had to believe in something, eventually. Maybe this was the time to start.

Emma came out of the bathroom with a partially wet towel and began cleaning the blood from the mirror. He wondered why. Was she another lost soul trapped in this life with nowhere else to go? She had the car keys and obviously knew how to drive. At any point, Emma could have left, but there she was, cleaning blood from the heart of the woman who took everything from her. What was her final emotional chain that kept her shackled to Elizabeth?

"One big happy family," Colt mused.

He returned to staring up through the tiny fragments of stained glass and the illuminated numbers. This time it was more beautiful than before as he saw it with his own eyes, not the filtered lenses of his dark glasses. It was nearing 1:08 in the morning. The exact moment he released the vengeance, surrendering his fate into the hands of the man who controlled both for the better part of his life.

Whether it was a calculated risk or seeing his beloved die in front of him, a calmness washed over him like the water cleansed Lizzy's blood from the temporary mirror moments ago. That was an unexpected response. Very unexpected. Then again, with love, nothing is guaranteed. He wanted more than what may be left of her life. The prospect of immortality together would make up for the lost century.

There was still enough gas in the old man's emotional tank that it kick-started a slight modicum of hope that Olath may very well be able to deliver him unto the same hell he'd been exiled to, of his own choosing. Besides, if there was the slightest motion, one thing out of place, a word that didn't belong, Colt Sturgess would simply kill him.

———

When she awoke from her recovery, forty-five minutes after he informed her of his decision. Lizzy was thrilled with the news that Colt joined her in permitting Olath to perform the transfusion. He lost her once and even if this was to be his last moment, he would spend it with her. There was nothing to lose and everything to gain.

She proposed one last request, a rejoining with their previous life together. Colt showered, cleaning himself off the remnants of the elixir. Lizzy and Emma handpicked one suit in a closet of the Delaney Funeral home. A smart plain black suit, white shirt and bowtie, with matching vest. Sturgess joked about looking like a penguin, but it pleased Elizabeth immensely. It was as if they were suited for a wedding, a renewal of vows with an exchange of mortality from his blood to hers.

Emma said he looked "pretty cool," which he took as a supreme compliment. Although he was of a slightly broader build than the original owner of the suit, it would work for now. Besides, once he returned to his Harley, a fresh denim shirt and a pair of jeans awaited him. His boots were staying on, regardless of the rest of his attire. Even Emma got into the spirit of the thing, selecting a black mini dress from one of the other bedrooms on the second floor. He even shed his protective armor.

Lizzy stuck to her existing wardrobe, finding another dress that was nearly identical to the one she was wearing, without the gaping hole in the front made by the scissors. Tucked away in her personal items that were not the result of looting, a small silk pouch held a treasure she had kept forever: her wedding ring. Sliding it on her ring finger, Lizzy looked up at Colt as tears ran down her cheeks.

Exiting the front of Delaney's, the gruesome patchwork family of three who accepted the outcome of fate, left the way they came, entering the car, speeding off towards destiny a mere two hours before daybreak.

The limousine pulled up outside of the herringbone parlor. Each person stepped from the vehicle. Lizzy led Colt up the steps of the loading dock and into the parlor. Emma remained outside. Her path laid elsewhere, unknown to the two of them. Having witnessed the events of the past couple of hours, she made her own decision. Carry out what Colt abandoned.

The priority was the slaughterhouse. She watched the clowns shuttling gas cans back and forth to keep the generator to the herringbone parlor running. There were a few sitting next to the loading dock. Moving swiftly, without fear of distraction, knowing Olath would be focused on Colt and Elizabeth, she transported them as quickly as possible to the slaughterhouse, unscrewing the lids, tipping them over, spilling the contents of the gasoline cans onto the floor. The nature of the construction of the building aided her in the fuel's dissemination as it ran down the various ramps, designed to keep as much of the blood from the slaughter room floor in that space.

———◆———

Colt followed Lizzy down the narrow walkway of the parlor. He still wore a bandolier of speed loaders, with his peacekeepers strapped to his hips. In his hand, the katana was at the ready. A trust factor concerning Olath was omnipresent and his agreeing to come even this far was conditional on him maintaining possession of his hardware. Elizabeth conceded, although she guaranteed it would not be necessary. Confident she completely controlled the professor, Colt knew better, as his overconfidence nearly costed him dearly.

"The fool will do whatever I demand of him," she reassured him.

He wasn't about to tempt the fate he currently blindly followed.

"Olath! Where are you? We've arrived," she called out.

There was a part of Colt that felt uneasy about the way Lizzy said it. It was as if she planned this and should have been expected. Shaking it off, he searched for even an inkling of vengeance, but it completely disappeared. She took his hand, guiding him to one station. The place was empty, but even without his heightened senses, he smelled the strong copper odor he knew to be blood. He also knew this to be a milking operation for smaller animals, goats perhaps. What Olath was using it for was a mystery to him, beyond what Lizzy explained. Sitting down, he tipped back his hat.

Looking up to the ceiling, Colt observed a chained track of metal, much like the track system of an electric overhead garage door opener. In front of him was a floor control panel of some type he wasn't familiar with.

These newfangled milking machines are pretty fancy, he thought.

They didn't wait long as, from the opposite end of where they entered, a door creaked open and the man himself entered. As Olath approached, he screamed out as smoke jumped from his skin.

"Mr. Sturgess, I must insist you continue to wear your eye protection, as my skin has not yet acclimated to your unique disposition," he said.

Smiling, Colt removed the glasses from his suit jacket, putting them back on. Causing one last jab of pain to the ghoul amused him. Olath noticed Elizabeth sat next to Sturgess but not suffered the same effect that he just experienced. This mystified him. Now he was cautious regarding the original plan. What was she up to?

"I must say, Elizabeth, I would be remiss if I didn't express my perplexing wonder as to why you appear to suddenly be immune to Mr. Sturgess', shall we say, unique abilities with heat projection?"

Elizabeth stood to face him. "You know why, I'm immune, you fool. You were there when I healed from his sweat on my hands!"

He shrunk back into his servile posture, as usual to her reaction.

"Now get on with it. I trust you know what you're doing and what needs to be done?" she asked.

"Yes. I have made modifications to the existing apparatus so a direct fusion line will deliver the desired amount without a portent effect to either the donor or the receiver," he answered.

Colt looked over at Lizzy, unsure what the hell Olath was spouting. For the first time, he looked at the creature, really looked at him. He was a far cry from the specter who haunted his living daydreams and eternal nightmares. No longer was Professor Olath, a peddler of elixirs, his font of fury. There was a strange air of pity that Sturgess felt for him. Why he let this lanky, translucent skinned thing drive his destiny for so long eluded him. Regarding his working theory of seated emotions at the time of transformation lingering, dictating actions from emotions, Colt wondered why Olath put up with the abusive treatment when he was receiving nothing from the relationship with Elizabeth beyond scorn.

Olath moved into position, dropping the crown of thorns down over Lizzy's head, positioning it for the process. Next, he tended to Colt, except for no crown of thorns.

"We will not require the actual head apparatus for you, Mr. Sturgess, as extracting too much of your vital liquid could render you powerless or worse, just a simple stick of the needle into your arm will satisfy the prerequisite for the transference."

"Careful there, Olath. Rendering me 'powerless or worse,' could be hazardous to your health." Sturgess slid the katana from its sheath. "Just my insurance, because I'm not sure I trust you completely, or even like you."

"Understood, and most acceptable. Were I you, my faith would be very nominal."

"That's putting it mildly."

Olath placed the large needle into Colt's arm, fumbling initially as his new limb did not function with the same alacrity as the old, then took his position behind the control panel he used to create Emma.

"We are nearly ready. One moment for the generator to charge the capacitor."

Colt looked over at Lizzy. She smiled, reaching for his hand. Their fingers interlocked, then she kissed the back of his hand.

Outside of the parlor, between the two buildings, Emma finished her task expediently with the aid of her enhanced abilities. All she required now was a spark to ignite the flame. Opening the door to the limo, she pressed the cigar lighter receptacle in. She waited patiently for it to pop back out nice and hot, but it was taking forever.

"C'mon, c'mon," she said.

Finally, it ejected. She stood up on the edge of the door frame, hurling it towards the loading dock of the slaughterhouse. She heard it "tink." Once, twice, a third time, then nothing. Discouraged, Emma walked towards the loading dock when she saw what she wanted, smoke billowing up from the ramp. Light flickered in the doorway from some unknown location within the charnel house. It had begun.

Inside of the parlor, Olath kept a close watch on the three lights in front of him on the control panel. The left red light switched to center yellow. His eyes fixed on the right green, hand hovering over the power switch that would set the entire machinery in motion. The light switch to green. Finally, everything he worked for throughout the centuries was coming to fruition. He slammed his fist into the panel, activating the unit.

Colt's head shot back as the needle generated a series of sporadic electrical currents into his heart, causing immediate cardiac arrhythmia. The compressor then went to work, pumping his blood out faster than his heart could keep up. Instead of transferring into Lizzy, it flowed freely into a large catch container secured to a pole next to him. He forced his head around to see her. Would this be the last time or was this a part of the transference?

The crown of thorns dropped on to her head. Syringes pushed forward with the force from the same compressor. She screamed out in agony. Colt watched her flesh rot and crumble. Whatever Olath injected into her dissolved her very existence before his eyes. Lizzy's hand crumbled in his. Her wedding ring fell to the floor.

Olath gleefully leaped from behind the glass. "Did you think I would leave such a valuable discovery to the chance of two star-crossed lovers? No, I will not be cheated from destiny by a cowboy and his need to be reunited with his past. This moment is for the genius of the ages. If only Conrad could see me now, his vision to consummation through the blood of a common man, a nobody farmer!"

Olath spun around, yelling at the pile of ash that was Elizabeth "Lizzy" Sturgess a mere ten seconds before. The professor continued his rant.

"No longer will I suffer the abuse by your hand. You, my only true love. I tolerated humiliation for something forever to be unrequited. Now, I no longer need your presence to feel complete. No longer do I require your validation to be whole. Now I can set my true plan in motion, the very reason I chose this ambitious undertaking of mine, yes, mine and mine alone."

Colt reached for his sword, but his healing process simply couldn't stay ahead of the rapid exsanguination and the electrical current that forced his heart to perform at a level it was not meant to. His feeble effort sent the weapon to the floor of the parlor. Olath kicked it out of the way, across the floor of the parlor towards the door the two entered. Moving to face Sturgess, he grabbed him by the collar of his suit jacket. This was now his moment to upstage the slayer. One he would revel in.

"Oh, how touching, adornment for your nuptials? Your strength wanes, Mr. Sturgess," Olath mocked, then continued. "This town of yours that you were so diligently in defense of will serve as a convenient conduit. Beneath its streets lies a submerged trolley line, courtesy of the redevelopment flood plan of 1964, connected to a series of abandoned coal mining shafts. Through this connectivity, I shall move a vast army of improved minions, consuming more and more of your precious cities. Your unexpected arrival has provided the blood for my immortality in leading such a force! Providing the next stage in evolution for my experiments. Perhaps after relieving you of the last drop of life essence, I will choose to restore you as one of my slaves?"

The professor threw his hands in the air, cackling madly. That was his purpose all along, although presently, Sturgess could do nothing more that listen to Olath's ravings. In a matter of moments, he would be dead.

Colt's periphery caught sudden movement, glancing to locate the kitana. Smoke was drifting through the doorway. Was this elixir smoke? His tormentor's voice flushed into white noise as he focused final thoughts on Lizzy's face from earlier in the night. The joy she conveyed when he disclosed his decision, their decision. They were to be a happy family once again, but Olath had other plans and it was his final double-cross that took center stage. Colt Sturgess' only comfort was that he would soon join his beloved. His journey ended abruptly. Fate decided, unfortunately, not in the way he imagined. The sounds from the slaughterhouse echoed, but this time within him.

"Thud thud, thud thud, thud…"

Suddenly, Olath spun around to see the smoke's origin, only to be met with the blade of a katana sword. Neither was part of his plan. Emma pulled up on it, then back down. He staggered backwards, inadvertently hitting a button on the control panel. A series of hooks lowered from the ceiling, one impaling him through the middle of his back, pulling him upwards up onto the conveyor guide rail. A special adaptation of his own to move bodies in and out more efficiently without the requirement of unhuman resources. It sputtered then moved his body forward as he cried out, holding his internal organs from spilling out all over the ground.

Emma moved swiftly around to look over the control panel. She saw the power switch for the compressor and switched in to reverse. The catch bottle half full of Colt's blood gurgled before returning the precious fluid back into his arteries, cutting the electrical current from the needle in his arm. Olath's body hit the end of the parlor, resetting the convey track contacts, sending him back towards Emma. She bent over to pick up the katana when another hand retrieved it first.

Colt Sturgess drew back the blade, watching the terror melt across Olath's face. Ten feet, five feet, four feet, three, two, one. A single slice separated the top of the man from the bottom. His innards dragged across the floor as his upper torso continued along the conveyor track to the end contact, triggering the reverse, sending it back down the parlor. This would be a perpetual tour for Olath's corpse until the power was cut. On the floor, Sturgess kicked Olath's lower half out of the way. Picking up Lizzy's wedding ring, he looked over at Emma before he tore the needle from his arm.

He wished his temper could manifest, even for a moment, but it didn't. All he felt was the intense sadness and the deep love for a woman he would never see again. Looking at the seat that she occupied, he thought about her dream of raising a family, with the two of them at the center of it all. That would not happen now, but the anger was gone. Perhaps that was the gift fate yielded. He could finally live again. Lost in his thoughts, he failed to recognize that smoke filled the parlor. Even worse, neither of them knew that in her haste to get the slaughterhouse razed, Emma carelessly left a gasoline trail leading directly to the generator of the parlor.

A sound broke his meditation of the moment. Only heard by him, it was faint. It was the creak of seams from the fuel tank of the generator expanding. It was about to blow.

"Colt, we gotta go, the fire —"

Before Emma could finish the words, Sturgess scooped her up in one motion, engaging his speed with maximum effort to reach the back entrance of the parlor from where Olath entered. Within a foot of the door, the explosion sent them both through the opening of the herringbone parlor and into the cornfield behind Chooch's Farm. Nothing moved except the torrents of fire consuming both buildings.

———•———

Everyone in the armory back in Kinston was fast asleep. Kat opened her eyes. She was having a nightmare. Sitting up in the darkness, she focused on the only available light, an exit sign above the front door and stairs to the bottom level. It had been a while since such a thing happened. Trying to shake off the awful dread that accompanied the initial waking moments of a nightmare, she revisited the images that wandered through her sleep. It was a room, faces peering out through some strange thing that prevented them from spilling out into the world. Her fear was that they just did. Beating on an invisible barrier, the revolting things broke through, navigating another barrier of fire. Screaming out in the darkness. One of them wore the face of Uncle Michael J. Babin. Kat shuddered at the imagery. Laying back down, she struggled to clear her mind to reclaim her sleep. Eventually, she drifted off.

———••———

A scarecrow loomed over him. Ragged pants, flannel shirt, stitched up burlap sack for a head, stuffed haphazardly with straw. One eye remained stitched on with cord, the other missing, obviously pecked off by a crow or some other bird it was supposed to ward off. How fitting.

Colt Sturgess sat up in a daze. Where was he? Using the mounting pole of his new scarecrow companion, he struggled to his feet. Emma sat on the ground a few feet from him, legs crossed, waiting. Obviously, whatever was unique about her particular transformation, she shared similar abilities. More precisely, being able to absorb the shock of an explosion, catapulting them both into the cornfield. Nearly a hundred yards in front of them, the fire rampaged. He looked down at her.

"Your work?" he asked.

"Yup. What you think?" she answered.

"Pretty impressive."

He reached down, helping her up. She put her arm around his waist as they watched the flames reach up to lick the heavens. Occasionally, a smaller secondary explosion would ignite, sending a shower of sparks into the mix.

For a while, Colt thought about walking into the flames himself, but knew it would have no effect. Already experiencing his baptism by fire, this second one he took part as a bystander.

Lizzy, my god, Lizzy, he thought.

He lost her twice, no, make that three times. At least he could bring her back once, only to fall prey to Olath's ultimate betrayal. If only he knew better, not surrendering to the change that he sought at her insistence. The change to be a better man, to be a husband once more, a father for the first time in this most unconventional family. Colt Sturgess released his vengeance. This was the result.

"If ifs and buts…," said Top Arnie. No questioning hindsight.

"You okay? You look a little pale," Emma asked.

He held up the back of his hand, examining it. Even in the moonlight, it was. His balance was a little off too, that he contributed to the impact from the explosion. Maybe it was more than that. He was still a couple of pints shy of blood. Maybe.

"Probably nothing. Just took a good shot to the noggin."

Off in the distance, he heard incoming sirens. Olath apparently hadn't harvested this town, as someone saw the blaze and reported it.

"We need to go, unless you wanna hang around here and talk to the authorities?" he asked with a touch of sarcasm.

"You may not have noticed, but I don't exactly play well with others."

"Yeah, I sort of noticed that. Piggyback ride?"

She smiled, jumping on his back. He tore off around the edge of the farm until they reached his Harley. Upon stopping, the wooziness increased. Getting to some place safe to regenerate became a sudden priority.

"You remember how we get back to that funeral parlor?" he asked.

"Yup. Head down this dirt road, make a left at the end, then a right at the fork, and go straight for about two miles. It's really close by," she answered.

Firing up the motorcycle, the two disappeared into the darkness, heading back to the place that offered so much promise, so much happiness a little over an hour ago.

They just made it before Colt collapsed. Emma tried helping him, but he fought her off. Even in his weakened state, his strength prevailed.

"I got it," he mumbled, struggling to his feet.

His path to the front door was a winding one, appearing to mimic an intoxicated bridegroom on his wedding night. As he cleared the door, gravity took hold.

Emma rushed to the small kitchen, searching through the refrigerator for the best source of protein. She remembered Elizabeth mentioning protein and water. There was plenty of water. It was the protein she needed. With her memories wiped, she struggled to summon any gained learning of the nutrient's source. *Why can't I remember?* Frustration was overtaking her. Not that she forgot every-

thing. It was more of a matter that there were these little bits of information in her brain that simply didn't connect. She lacked whatever
process that produced associations and reference points to relate to the
next, except for bursts of things that survived whatever process she
underwent.

"Burgers. Meat!" She forged a connection.

There was nothing in the refrigerator, but the freezer contained a
solitary package of frozen ground beef. Placing the package in the sink,
she ran hot water over it. It seemed the right thing to do. Emma shifted
to the cupboard doors, frantically searching for something to hold water.
The teacups weren't large enough, but could scoop water out of something bigger. Under the sink, she found a bucket. It would have to do.

The meat in the sink was taking too long to defrost. She pushed it
aside, switching the faucet from hot to cold to fill the bucket. Once
it was full, she reversed the action, sliding the package of meat back
under the scalding water. Rushing to Colt, Emma saw he propped
himself up against the wall in the entryway. His eyes were open, but he
looked like hell.

"Here, drink!"

She began ladling teacups of water to his lips. He drank furiously
until he reached up for the cup, helping himself. Returning to the
kitchen, checking on the raw ground beef, it was still partially frozen,
but would have to do. Again, she dashed to his side, tearing at the
wrapper, freeing the contents. Kneeling beside him, she stuffed a
handful of the uncooked beef into his mouth. He swallowed it whole,
then chuckled.

"You know, Emma, usually have this cooked," he said.

"Shut up and eat. I'm trying to save your life here!"

Sturgess finished the package, rotating between it and cups of water
from the bucket. When he finished, Emma collapsed against the wall
beside him.

"Have to say, don't reckon' I've ever eaten such a fancy meal as this
before," he said.

Somewhere throughout it all, he found a sense of humor to tease her. She leaned up against him as they both succumbed to the events of the night, falling fast asleep. Even dreams didn't have the energy to wander into either of their minds.

⸺ ◆ ⸺

Colored light drifted across the cheeks of Colt Sturgess. Mosaic glass, like the dome above Lizzy's bed upstairs, was inlaid within two panels to the left and right of the front door of Delaney's. His eyes flickered in the morning sunlight behind them. He was still weak, but better. Whatever elixir kept him alive all these years didn't quite have the same restorative magic without the fuel of his blood. Emma's actions the night before may very well have saved his life, but he craved more, which of course meant his body was telling him that if it were to continue its work, he must eat.

He stood up, searching for Emma. She was sitting at the dining table perusing the newspaper Elizabeth cast aside earlier, favoring a fashion magazine instead. The same night she served Burger Chef on a fancy silver platter. Colt walked in, careful not to disturb her, but inadvertently kicked over the bucket.

"Real graceful, Sturgess," she said. "At least I can still read. That's a relief."

Turning a page over in the newspaper, she suddenly stopped, tearing a column from the page. Standing up, she rushed around the table to him.

"You know how to get here? Wait, can you even drive?"

Colt nodded. "I've driven in worse condition."

Looking over the newspaper clipping, it was an advertisement for the Truckstop Café, right off the Interstate.

Emma read the ad that captured her attention. "Home of the Bullfighter's T-bone, twenty-four ounces of pure Texas steak delivered daily. Finish the deluxe, get your name put up on the wall with the other cow-folk who tamed it. Plus, your meal is on the house! $5.99 lunch special includes baked potato or fries and side salad."

He folded up the clipping, putting it in his pocket.

"Got a map that got me here. Should give us a good direction. It's in the saddlebags on the bike," he said.

"Let's get moving then. Time's a wastin' and you're not getting any less fleshy toned."

He pointed down at the bucket, with the spilled water he hadn't drunk. "Can't just leave this here."

"I'll call for maid service. Now let's get moving," said Emma, pushing him towards the door.

Assuming their seats at the Truckstop Café, they noticed only two other patrons sitting at the counter. The trip was short and uneventful, thankfully. Emma didn't have any fear the night before but gripped on to Colt's waist for dear life on the ride there, fearing he would collapse again, sending them both into a guardrail on the interstate only to meet a similar fate as Olath.

The server's reaction to their order was worth the fear factor after ordering not one, not two, but four of the Bullfighter's T-bones as rare as the law allowed. She checked with the chef to ensure they had that many, which Emma mused over making a deliberately snide comment about having less than four shipped in from Texas daily as advertised. Even more surprising, Emma gulped down her first of two, eating the baked potato and salad just so she could get her name up on the wall. At one point, the kitchen staff gathered behind the counter to watch the two of them polish off a grand total of six pounds of steak.

"Seen nothing like that before." Colt overheard the cook say.

When presented the check, Emma pointed out the claim on the add clearly stating that the meal is on the house if the cow-folk tamed it. Since they ate four of them, not only should they be free, but should also get two vouchers for free dinners. Colt stepped in with a crisp fifty-dollar bill, insisting the server keep the change as he felt neither the advertisement nor Emma's insistence should replace a well-made steak.

Compared to his meal of half-frozen raw ground beef and a bucket of water the night before, this was the best he ever tasted.

As they left the restaurant, the staff would spin this yarn into a story of urban legend about the white-eyed married couple on a Harley, possibly vampires, who tamed four steaks, increasing to six eventually eight over the course of the year. The tip was also woven into the tale eventually, as none of them had ever seen a fifty-dollar bill. Ironically, with all Colt and Emma experienced, the thing that cemented their legacy was how many steaks they ate that morning.

In the parking lot, Emma stepped in front of Colt, examining his face. The natural flesh tone was returning.

"So now, what?" she asked.

"I have some friends I need to say 'goodbye' to."

Chapter Fifteen

Rhonda Coulter wearily rose from the bed, stretching. Sliding an oversized spiderman tee shirt over her head, she wandered into the living room of their makeshift hideaway. Jud was standing at the window of the abandoned bakery. The two returned to the place where they first took refuge from the attacking creatures that invaded their hometown. Met with overwhelming resistance by the armory survivors, the young couple left anyway. They wandered away from the protection of the group that would all go their separate ways by morning. Regardless, Jud led Rhonda back with the utmost caution. He learned from his previous mistake. If there were remnants of the creatures or clowns, they could get back to the safety of the armory.

Jud watched the parking lot below where the Smoke Hunters, along with Kat Ellis, were cleaning up the area. Why? He wasn't sure. It was something to do in the aftermath; he supposed. Possibly that it was their town again, and it was their way to reclaim it. There were still missing elements, specifically his family and, of course, Emma. Were they all out there somewhere, hiding like Rhonda and him?

Jud Allen wasn't sure what was next. Eventually, the authorities would have to show up or one of the survivors would inevitably leave, alerting law enforcement of their plight. Although a small town, they certainly weren't invisible, especially with a burnt-out state trooper car on the exit-ramp to their town. Someone would come. The question was, "when?"

Since he and Rhonda were technically minors, they discussed the probability that both would be placed with an existing family out of state, in the event their task of locating any surviving members of their immediate families didn't yield fruit. The potential of them being split up simply would not happen, he decided. Correction, they decided.

As for the search, he set up a map on the wall that Top Arnie gave him from his jeep. Top also taught him a crash course in land navigation and how to conduct a systematic grid search, after explaining what a grid was. There were a few supplies he would need to secure to track their progress, but for now, it was a starting point. A start to a plan of action that would give them something to do, much like what Kat and company were doing below.

He walked over to Rhonda, who was examining the map, then gave her a long, passionate good morning kiss.

"What was that for?" she asked.

"I've decided that I'm gonna greet you every single morning, just like that, for as long as I live."

"Promise?"

"Promise!"

She returned the kiss in the same fashion. As she embraced him, she noticed something beneath his t-shirt, tucked into the waistband of his jeans. She reached down to examine what it was. Pulling up on it, she revealed a stack of crisp one-hundred-dollar bills, bundled with a band that read $10,000. She gasped.

"Where did you get this? Did you rob that truck?"

"Nope, it was a tip from Top Arnie."

He reached into his waistband, pulling out two more stacks.

"Jud! That's thirty thousand dollars!"

"I know, right? Certainly, a good beginning in someplace cool, like Hawaii maybe?"

"But this is stealing!"

"Not really. The clowns stole it. Top got paid for the rental of his guns and he tipped me from that. Like he said, 'that money is all insured, anyway!'"

"But..."

"Just come here and kiss me!"

She did just that. Whatever doubts they had with their personal disposition once the dust settled, this money would give them a new start, wherever that may be. Out front, they heard the familiar sound of a motorcycle approaching. Rhonda went to the window to see if it was indeed him. Jud disappeared to get another surprise. He returned from the kitchen with two coffee cups and a bottle of champagne.

"Looks like Colt's back. Wanna go down and say, 'hi?'" she asked.

"Nah, not right now, let's celebrate!" he said, popping the bottle he also commandeered from the state store on the corner before she awoke.

"Seriously? Like you don't want to see his Harley Electro, whatever you called it? Maybe he'll let you take it for a spin?"

"Nope, I have something more important right here," he answered.

Turning from the window, Rhonda stopped momentarily, looking back down at the street. It was Colt, but he was dressed in a funny-looking wedding suit. The girl with him looked familiar.

"Emma?" she whispered. "Nah, can't be."

Rhonda dismissed her thought as wishful thinking. It was a fresh wound she didn't want to scratch open just yet. Besides, it was part of Jud's plan, and she didn't want to dissuade his effort. She joined him on the couch, picking up a bundle of money fanning it out.

"Hawaii, here we come!"

Colt and Emma pulled up to the town center. The remnants of the warriors who squared off against Olath and his minions were all busy cleaning up Main Street, attempting to return their town to normalcy. Sturgess observed Jud and Rhonda weren't among them. There were also a few additional unfamiliar faces he hadn't seen. Two camouflage vans approached his position as he dismounted with Emma. She was distracted by the thrift store across the street, two doors down from the borough building.

"I'll be right back, have a little shopping to do," she said.

"For what?"

"We gotta get you out of that monkey suit. You look absolutely ridiculous."

"I thought you liked it?"

"I lied."

Colt didn't want to rain on her enthusiasm by telling her he had a fresh change of clothes in his saddlebags. They experienced enough. If an impromptu shopping session was her first order of business, so be it. After all those steaks, maybe his spare jeans wouldn't fit.

She sprinted across the street, reaching the front of the store. The door was locked, but Emma kicked at it until the glass shattered. Ducking under the handle, her shopping spree was about to begin.

"Hey! Why'd you do that? I just cleaned up over there," said one newcomer to the group.

Emma turned, shrugged, then continued into the store.

The lead van stopped, halting the mini caravan. The Sarge rolled down his window to address Sturgess.

"What the hell you wearing? Look like a penguin," he asked.

Colt just smiled, shaking his head. The suit would be his last vestige of Lizzy.

"Well, your mission a success?"

"Yes, and no. Olath is in two pieces, burnt to cinders. He won't be causing any trouble anymore."

"What's the 'no?'"

Colt didn't answer, just held up his hand, dropping his chin. In his rush to leave the farm, there was little time to process Lizzy's demise. Not that he ever would. The circumstances were anything but normal, but how one defines normal is anyone's guess. Olath did unspeakable things to good people. Sturgess couldn't ignore the fact that Lizzy played a major role in that as well. That was an additional consideration it would take time to reconcile.

Time may heal all wounds, but when you're immortal, the wounds may linger a little longer. For now, there was the young woman currently looting the thrift store. He promised Lizzy he would take care of Emma. Colt would keep that promise. Besides, to the best of his knowledge, they were the only two left with Olath's elixir inside of them. Her memories were gone. He almost envied that. How much time she would have before her limbs gave way, he didn't know. Neither did she, it was something they hadn't discussed. For whatever time she had, they would make the best of it. She was his family now.

"Gotcha," said Sarge. "Did a dozen sweeps of the town since day break. Secured as of this moment. Heads throbbing from Top and that damned megaphone calling for survivors. Drew a few out, but no telling if there are strays."

"No sign of Flamethrower?"

Sarge shook his head. "Guess this is goodbye, then. Probably never see you again, and that's good enough for me."

Colt nodded. He understood. Hard feelings remained. It is what it was. Sturgess ended the conversation with a wave.

Sarge and the remaining members of the Smoke Hunters pulled out of Kinston for good. He wondered where the salty master sergeant with the sagely wisdom disappeared to. Top Arnie left with his hardware at the break of dawn after one lap around Kinston with his bullhorn shouting "rise and shine, the gremlins are gone, safe to come out now." It's where the stragglers helping with the clean-up came from.

Colt glanced around the parking lot. There were two people he looked for specifically, one in particular. The two he met at the beginning of this journey. There was a tap on the back of his shoulder. He turned to see Kat Ellis standing behind him. She threw her arms around him, squeezing him for dear life. She was the one in particular.

"Hey, Kitty Kat. Was hopin' you were still around."

"Yeah, Johnny wanted to take a crack at disassembling the Ferris wheel. Gives him something to do, so I'm just keeping busy while he amuses himself with it."

Colt looked over at the collapsed Ferris wheel. He saw Johnny working diligently, with a pile of tools by his side. On top of his head was a cowboy hat, dark shades on his eyes. The augments brought a grin to Sturgess' face.

"Gotta say, I like his style," he said.

"Oh that? Yeah. No clue where he got those. I guess you have a fan," she said. "How did things work out? Was fate on your side?"

"I'm afraid not."

There was a long pause between the two. Each wondering what to say next, following the revelation. Colt broke the silence.

"I reckon you and Johnny will head back to Rosie's now?"

She looked around nervously, crossing her arms. "Yeah, I suppose. Just not sure how I'll manage and all."

Colt reached up to tip his hat back out of habit, but realized it was sitting on the dressing table of Delaney's funeral home. His monument to the past.

"Well, someone pretty wise once told me, 'maybe it's way pastime to kick off the training wheels.' You got this, just trust in yourself." Colt hugged her.

"You know, you can always come with us?"

He sighed. "I can't, but I promise to swing by now and then. Gotta homestead near here, up in the Allegheny's. Not much, but plan on setting down roots. For a while at least."

"Near here?"

"You don't think everything I own is in these saddlebags, do ya?"

"I guess not."

Emma rushed up, with a bag full of goodies from her shopping spree. She dropped the bag on the ground beside him, tugging off his black suit coat.

"First things first. This is a little worn, but that just makes it vintage, which is way cooler than new anyway."

Pulling a bomber jacket from the bag, she slid his arms in one at a time. He didn't recall the last time he hadn't dressed himself. Her enthusiasm for such a simple thing reminded him of Lizzy.

"Here's a pair of jeans, but you'll have to find someplace to dress. Can't have you dropping drawers right here in the middle of town. I know you're attached to those old boots of yours, so I didn't bother. But…"

The last item she pulled from the bag was a cowboy hat. "Ta-da!"

Laughing, he put it on his head. A little tight, but he would not complain. He appreciated the effort and better a little snug than loose. Colt didn't want it blowing away.

Kat reached up, brushing the hair out of his eyes. She had forgotten about the white irises that he hid beneath the dark shades. Looking over at Emma, she noticed the same eyes.

"You guys match. Well, eyes anyway. So cool, so unique."

"Thank ya," Emma said with a bow. "I really dig them too. Two of a kind, don't ya think?" she said, looking up at him winking.

"Settle down there, young one. I'm four times older than you, at least," he said.

"No sweat, grandpa, I've always loved older men and I'll catch up eventually," she blew him a kiss.

He shook his head. "You're gonna be a handful."

"You have no idea!"

Emma walked over to the bike, mounting the pillion. "Ready when you are."

Kat removed Colt's hat. She provided a gift of her own.

"I know it's not much. Most of what I have of any value is back at Rosie's, but I wanted you to have these."

She placed two tarot cards into his hatband. "One from me, one from Johnny. His is the King of Swords, of course, mine is the Ten of Swords, which I struggled with. The message here is although you had a devastating ending to your quest, there is always a new opportunity to start over. The king welcomes such a challenge."

The gesture choked up Sturgess. "Probably one of the most beautiful gifts I've ever gotten. Thank you, Kitty Kat."

He hugged her one last time. "Funny thing about that fate of yours. Sometimes you don't get what you want, but you get what you need."

Kat nodded.

Sturgess mounted his bike, turning on the ignition. Emma giggled behind him.

"What?" he asked.

"Did you just quote the Stones?"

"Who?"

"Ugh, we have some work to do!"

He just smiled as he turned the bike around in the center of town. Passing by the collapsed Ferris wheel, Sturgess saw Johnny standing at attention, rendering the three-finger salute of the Smoke Hunters. Colt returned the gesture.

Emma sang the song she just referenced at the top of her lungs. Mick and the boys would have approved of her rendition.

Epilogue

An image of a female broadcaster on the evening news appeared on a television set.

"Good evening. Top story. A massive fire broke out last night at the location of Chooch Family Farm and Dairy along Route 8 off of Germantown Road. Firefighters spent six hours fighting the blaze, having to deal with multiple explosions from tanks within the compound. Several tractor trailers that were contracted by management were also decimated by the fire. The owners could not be reached for comment. Fire inspectors on the scene made several gruesome discoveries of unidentified human remains. Federal authorities have been called in to investigate. We will have breaking details as we follow-up on that once they arrive. Now to weather…"

<hr />

The fire crews departed. The police cordoned off the areas around the smoldering ash of the slaughterhouse and herringbone parlor, both covered in debris that somehow did not succumb to the heat of the fire. A fresh body laid face down in the mud, blood running from an unseen wound beneath it, creating a pool of crimson in the soaked earth around the property. It was an officer left behind to prevent any curious onlookers from crossing the demarcation line. The police tape was breached to the south of the farm with fresh tire tracks leading to a Foodland Grocery Store delivery truck parked alongside where the parlor stood the day before. The back of the truck was open, awaiting something.

Two figures scoured the rubble, tossing aside aluminum corrugated sheathing that covered the parlor itself. They'd been searching the location for the past half hour. Only they knew what they were looking for in the scorched remnants.

"I found something —"

"—over here!"

The one figure ran over to the other. Together, the two lifted a long metal track lined with a chain. Tugging at the thing hanging from it, they tossed it to the outside of the rubble pile.

"That's half —"

"—where's the rest?"

They continued digging until they came across a container that survived the fire. A quarter of it held a congealed red substance.

"What do you think —"

"—this is?"

"I don't know—"

"—but I want it!"

One of the two figures picked up the container, putting it under his arm. The search continued for another several minutes.

"Here it—"

"—is. Found it!"

They pulled another piece of burnt something from the ground. This one they carried out to the back of the truck, along with the first piece they retrieved and tossed from the pile. Loading both shapeless chunks of burnt detritus into the back of the truck, they slammed the cargo door shut, sealing it.

"Think we can actually —"

"—bring him back?"

"Maybe even twins —"

"—there are two pieces of him!"

They laughed hysterically as they climbed into the cab of the truck. Frick looked over at Frack, pointing up to his forehead. Frack mirrored the motion with the opposite hand, however, as he was still clutching the container he found.

"You have a —"

"—hole in your head!"

Frick grabbed the rearview mirror, looking then touching the wound. Frack followed with the same action. Sitting back, they both looked out the windshield momentarily, anticipating the next cue. Neither spoke for ten minutes, waiting for the other. Frick broke the cycle.

"Where are we —"

"—supposed to go now?"

They looked at each other, speaking as one for the first time.

"Parts unknown!"

Roaring with laughter, the truck started and pulled away from the remnants of what had once been Chooch Family Farm and Dairy.

Colt and the Kinston gang will return in "The Ballad of Colt Sturgess."

FRED TERLING

Author's Notes

I don't quite remember how or why I initially stumbled across the legend of Johann Konrad Dippel. Thankfully, I did. It spawned an entire storyline, characters and a forthcoming series of books based on that brief encounter. Inspiration can come from anywhere.

Speaking of which, the setting for this story was a very personal reach back into time for me. I jumped headfirst into a writing competition at the last moment, which required a bit of short-cutting to ensure I completed the word count in the allotted time. Time travelling back to the 1970s, I tapped into memories of a simpler time in my life where dreams were free to roam, unencumbered by the realities of daily life. This also provided an interesting perspective of looking at experiences through fresh eyes, mixed with memories of nearly sixty years of living with mature eyes.

The result was this story and the subsequent ones to follow. An interesting mix also developed through the storytelling that yielded a roller coaster ride of emotions. It is sweet, funny, morbid, shocking, touching, but most of all, it is a love story. As far as the future of these characters, if you keep reading, I'll keep writing. Deal?

Before closing this brief reflection, I'd like to take a moment and thank my better half, Lori Terling, for supporting my efforts, bringing her years and years of design experience to each project, but most of all, listening to me read my work aloud. Yes, after completing the final edit, I read my work, cover-to-cover, to her. It is essential to help me ensure the writing is rhythmic, there aren't any dangling errors left that snuck by the editor, and explanations of the more complex aspects of the story make sense. She is a power reader that goes through a couple of books a week. Most importantly, she is brutally honest.

www.ingramcontent.com/pod-product-compliance
Lightning Source LLC
Chambersburg PA
CBHW060634260626
47161CB00008B/2888